PARTS PER MILLION

A Novel

by

Mitchell Wido
and K.R. Gordon

This is a work of fiction. Unless otherwise indicated, all the names, characters, businesses, places, events, and incidents in this book are either the product of the authors' imaginations or used in a fictitious manner. Any resemblance to actual persons, living or dead, or actual events is purely coincidental.

This book is dedicated to all of the men, women, and canines of law enforcement.

SHAWANDA

Two years ago

SHAWANDA JACKSON NEVER wanted to be a mother, and Bedford Hills Correctional Facility was certainly no place to raise a family.

A thin rain was falling on the prison, turning the granite walls a tired shade of brown. Built in 1894, its main building could be mistaken for a Victorian dormitory were it not for the chain-link fence and razor wire and guard towers dripping in the rain. The other cell blocks were newer—heavy concrete, narrow windows, cold and unwelcoming. It was the largest women's prison in the state of New York, just thirty miles north of the Bronx, hidden away amid the swanky exurbs of Westchester County.

On any given day it was home to nine hundred and twenty inmates—women who had made bad choices, women who were at the wrong place at the wrong time. Some of them had children they were waiting to get home to. Some had their children taken away and shipped off to foster homes. Some of them were still children themselves. But all of them could agree—Bedford Hills was no place to be a mother.

The rain fell harder as the morning turned to noon. A few women in orange jumpsuits and winter jackets braved the

"Bitch, I *know* you did not just bump into me with your country ass," she spat as she turned to face Desiree Holmes, 6C3785. Didi was a big, middle-aged woman with pasty skin and a confusion of brick-red hair. She was doing fifteen for driving a delivery van into her boss's office and crushing him under a desk.

Didi laughed, showing teeth stained with years of coffee and cigarettes. "So what if I did?" She was tough. She knew she was tough. Latisha knew it too.

This was not the first time the two had jawed like this. It had ended with bloodied lips and bruised ribs before.

Martha was just stuffing Denise's letter back into the envelope when one of the women started shoving. A body flew into Martha as she tried to get out of harm's way. Her little golf pencil rolled on the ground as the shouts started to fill the pod.

In the guard station, one of the officers saw the scrum on the monitor.

"Looks like we got something in six," he said, reaching for his radio. "I'm gonna call it in."

"Give it a minute," his partner said, looking down the hallway. She dropped one of the sliding plexiglass panels in the door to listen to the commotion. "They could just be blowing off some steam."

The first officer shook his head. "That's McGregor and Didi. I don't want the same shit as last time. You remember the paperwork. I—"

He was cut off as a woman in an orange jumpsuit darted past their octagonal station, racing toward Pod 6. The first officer reached for the button to shut it down, not wanting the situation to escalate out of control, but he stopped short.

"Was that Shawanda?"

Shawanda Jackson, 1H2755, five years into a dime for aggravated battery and drug possession, was out of breath by the time her worn-out sneakers skidded across the polished linoleum of Pod 6.

"It's happening!"

The pod went silent. Didi had Latisha's jumpsuit clenched in her fists. Two of Latisha's crew had their fists cocked. Half the pod had squared off for the fight.

But none of that mattered.

A second later, Shawanda was speeding back down the hallway with half a dozen inmates racing after her. Didi dropped Latisha and followed as fast as her bulk would allow. Martha stuffed Denise's letter into her shirt and sprinted after them.

Latisha sucked her teeth, smoothed out the knuckle prints in her jumpsuit, and watched them run.

"Buncha corny ass bitches."

Back in the Eye, the first guard still had his hand over the emergency shut down for Pod 6.

"Wait!" his partner said, holding out her hand. She craned her neck out the door as Shawanda and seven other inmates raced past and down another hallway. "I think it's happening."

Down the hallway, Shawanda dashed for one of the utility closets on the way to Pod 3. She came screeching to a halt, filling the doorway to the closet like a protective shield. The other inmates piled up behind her, desperate to see over her shoulders.

"Is she alright?" Didi asked, choked with worry.

"That's a lot of blood . . ." Martha said, standing on her toes.

Shawanda dropped to her knees. She moved the blankets aside and held her breath.

A beautiful yellow Lab looked up at her, panting and smiling and beaming with pride.

The first puppy had already arrived, wriggling around on the blankets with its blind eyes and its pink mouth and its pink little paws.

The inmates all breathed sighs of relief as Shawanda scooped the little puppy into her hands, no bigger than a tennis ball. The puppy tried to nurse the pad of Shawanda's thumb as she turned around and showed the women. The love on her face was unmistakable.

Shawanda Jackson, a woman who had lived most of her life on the streets, a woman who had seen more and endured more than one person ever should, once again knew what it felt like to be a mother.

BRADFORD

5:27 a.m.
Corner of Eadom and Brill
Philadelphia, PA
July 2019

EVERYONE KNOWS THAT Philly is a shithole in summer. Ever since he was transferred from the Chicago field office, ATF agent Thomas Bradford found himself missing the lakeside cabin where he had spent so many of his best years. Sure, southern Wisconsin was still hot, and the mosquitoes could eat him down to the bone if he forgot to close the screen door on the cabin, but there was something unrelenting about the mid-Atlantic air in July that turned his body into a swamp.

It wasn't even five-thirty in the morning, the sun barely touching the hazy clouds over New Jersey, and he was already sweating through his blue ATF windbreaker. The air smelled like exhaust from the I-95 overpass down the street. God he hated Philly.

"Alright, listen up, let's review the target," the man in charge was saying, standing behind the popped rear hatch of an unmarked black Ford Explorer. Group Supervisor Elliott Glover was a thickset man with an athlete's haircut, stuck at that awkward age that is neither young nor old. He'd been in the agency for six years, transferred over from Homeland

Security, and had risen quickly through the ranks. He'd gone from a probationary agent to a case agent on several multi-defendant RICO investigations. He'd even led a Title III wiretap case—the ones that got your name noticed in HQ. He now was a GS-14 Group Supervisor in Metro Group III, responsible for investigating gun crimes on Philly's north side.

"Jerrald Scott, Caucasian male, thirty-two," Glover continued. "Local PD has him implicated in a mid-level heroin ring. This guy is bringing most of the smack into north Philly."

Bradford watched as GS Glover hauled the battering ram out of the trunk. Straight-up drug dealers weren't usual ATF targets, but the local police had managed to get a solid confidential informant that linked Scott to a shooting a few months back. The detective-in-charge at the Philadelphia PD skipped DEA in favor of ATF and went right to Glover, with whom he'd had a working relationship in the past. ATF prided itself on working alongside the locals, getting down in the shit with them, providing them with cash for criminal informants and buy-money for dope and guns. And when it was all over and the arrests were made, they would take a step back and let the locals stand in the spotlight at the press conference.

Right on cue, the Philly detective stepped forward. He was a tall black man with flecks of white sprinkled in his tight-cropped beard. He addressed the half-dozen ATF agents, two Philly tact officers, and three uniforms as they suited up.

"Scott is a real piece of work," the detective said. "He supplies most of the corners north of Roosevelt Boulevard. He runs his drug business as tight as a duck's asshole, but if we can get him on this gun charge, we'll put him away for good."

Bradford had heard these speeches before. He liked working with local PDs even more than some of his agent peers. Bradford always considered himself a street cop at heart. He started as a beat cop at the tender age of twenty-one in Chicago and did it for five years before going with the feds.

As the detective spoke, Glover tested the heft of the ram. Bradford thought he looked like an aging linebacker still clinging to the glory days, and he must have noticed the expression on Bradford's face.

"Is there a problem, Bradford?"

"None. Not used to seeing the GS ram the door, that's all. Actually, I can't recall a group supervisor being a case agent, either."

Glover's eyes narrowed. Bradford had fifteen years' experience on him, but Bradford was still new in the Philadelphia Field Division, so he had to let the young boss call the shots.

Bradford smiled. "Don't worry, you'll do great. Just be sure to pop it on the first try. Looks bad otherwise."

A few of the other agents tried to swallow their smirks.

"Come on," Glover simmered, peeling away from

Bradford. "Line it up. Outside cover, head out now. We'll hit the door in one minute."

Bradford kept smiling as the half-dozen ATF agents moved out down the street. The uniformed officers pulled away in their marked squads and headed to their positions at the ends of the street, while the ATF agents approached the rowhouse down the middle of the block. Glover took the lead with two agents, one of whom carried a body bunker, a heavy bulletproof shield of laminated Kevlar. Two other agents took up positions on the sidewalks, guns drawn and pointed down. The last two agents kept their eyes on the windows of the two-story rowhouse as the raid team approached the front stairs.

Bradford took up his assigned position, down the alley to cover the back, just as Glover had ordered him during the morning briefing.

That's what happens when you piss off the boss, said a voice in his head, but he didn't listen. He had never been very good at following the rules.

Besides, he'd broken down plenty of doors in his day and had his share of shoot-outs. He didn't need to be on the front porch to know what would happen. Glover would pop the door, then the agent with the body bunker would step into the room, ready to face any threat. Glover would ditch the ram outside and join the third agent, and they would enter behind the bunker agent, then buttonhook left and right, clearing rooms as they went. Usually it happened so fast no one inside would have time to reach for a gun—and even if they did, the shouts of "federal agents" and "police" usually scared sense into anyone stupid enough to try.

Bradford moved slowly down the alley, stepping over broken bottles and discarded syringes, keeping his eye on the back of the rowhouse. Sweat was pooling in his armpits, and despite his focus on the mission at hand, he found himself thinking about his old lake house. He missed fishing in the misty dawns and the cool clear nights. No city lights to dull the stars. He missed duck hunting with his trusty retriever by his side. He had trained Copper from a pup, along with two of his brothers. They were smart dogs, friendly and focused. He had loved them all, but he loved Copper the most. Copper lived longer than the vets expected, but in the end the cancer moved too quickly, and Bradford had to bury his best friend by the lake house one cold autumn afternoon. He'd moved to Philly not long after.

On the main street, Bradford could hear yelling. "Federal agents with a search warrant!" This was followed by the *thud* of the battering ram shattering a deadbolt. Looked like Glover popped it the first time after all.

Bradford drew his gun and waited as he heard the agents' muffled shouts inside. He was sharp, alert, just as he'd been trained, but he hadn't seen a runner in years. Most people knew when the game was up, and he expected the agents inside would give the all clear in a matter of moments.

It was a good thing Bradford was not a betting man, because not a moment after he checked his watch, a pale-

faced man with bad skin erupted from the back door of the
rowhouse, sending the screen door flapping off its hinges. In
one unbroken movement, Jerrald Scott launched himself off
the rickety back porch and tumbled into a pile of weeds and
broken bricks in the cramped back yard. He cursed as the gun
in his hand clattered on the concrete pad near the bottom
porch step.

The lanky heroin dealer was just about to reach for it
when he locked eyes with Bradford.

"Freeze, police!" Bradford shouted, raising his Glock 40
as the years of training automatically took over.

Jerrald Scott hesitated for half-a-second, his eyes on
Bradford. He had a decision to make: fight or flight.

Do it . . . go ahead asshole, I'm ready, Bradford said to
himself. The milliseconds it took for the scene to unfold
seemed like an hour.

Despite the dark circles under his eyes and the Cap'n
Crunch stuck to his t-shirt, Jerrald was smarter than he
looked. In a blink, he left the gun where it had landed, six
inches from his right hand, and sprinted out the other side of
the yard where a gate once stood.

Well I'll be damned, Bradford thought as he holstered his
pistol and took off after him. *We got a runner.*

Jerrald pumped his skinny legs as he wove in and out of
the square back yards, slipping through broken fences and
knocking garbage cans into his path. He expected Bradford to
follow step-for-step, but Bradford kept to the alley, watching

him through each gangway and vacant lot, avoiding the chest-high fences and yard trash altogether. By the time Jerrald leaped the final fence and came out on the busy cross-street, Bradford had closed the gap.

Horns blared as Jerrald dashed into traffic. A gray Honda Civic hit the brakes and laid down a thick line of rubber as Jerrald dashed across the median. Bradford was right on his tail, his blue ATF windbreaker flapping in the hot morning air, exposing the gold federal shield on his belt. Bradford was still fit even though he was on the back end of his forties, and unlike Jerrald, his diet didn't consist of take-out, Mountain Dew, and opioids.

Jerrald sped into the next lane of traffic, nearly getting clipped by a garbage truck, before he stumbled onto the curb in front of a Wawa. Before he could regain his footing, Bradford wrapped two strong arms around his chest and dragged him to the ground.

Bradford cuffed him, and between heavy breaths, informed him of the obvious. He was under arrest.

BRADFORD WAS STILL slick with sweat twenty minutes later as Jerrald Scott sat in the back of the squad car in front of his rowhouse. A dozen agents were going in and out the front door, photographing the scene and collecting evidence in marked bags.

The squad pulled away and Bradford turned to see GS Glover and the tall Philly detective approach him.

"Good work, Agent Bradford," the detective said, shaking his hand. "We got him with that gun and a lot of dope in the house. Looks like we got another killer off the street."

Glover seemed less impressed. It was no secret that he wanted to slap the bracelets on Jerrald himself. He'd only been a Group Supervisor for over a year, and somehow, he always found himself in Bradford's long shadow.

"Bradford," Glover said without warmth, "get debriefed then head back to the field office right away. I got a call this morning about a new assignment."

He wondered what Glover was playing at now. "New assignment?

"We'll talk about it back at the office."

A million thoughts raced through Bradford's mind, but the main one was, *What did I fuck up now?* This reeked of a bullshit management tactic, and Bradford would have none of it.

"Come on, Elliot, don't play that game with me."

For the first time, a hint of satisfaction crept into Glover's voice. "You know that application you put in three years ago? Looks like it finally went through. You're headed down to Virginia."

A sinking feeling took over as Glover began to smile.

"And Bradford, don't forget to pack a leash. You'll need it."

SHAWANDA

Two years ago

SHAWANDA JACKSON HELD the little warm puddle of blond fur in her hand and tried not to cry. The little puppy couldn't even open its eyes as it nibbled on her finger, but somehow, Shawanda held it together. Shedding tears in prison, even tears of joy, meant you were weak. It meant you were soft, that you were a victim, that you could be owned. Shawanda had never been owned in her life. She'd been through far too much to be weak now, so she sucked it up and watched as the helpless little creature wiggled in her palm.

Martha Greene and Didi Holmes crouched next to her, leaning on the plastic playpen fence with their orange jumpsuits rolled past their elbows. Didi's frazzled mass of red hair and huge pale forearms made her look like some kind of redneck warrior woman, while Martha, the former accountant, sat there meekly and quietly, like she always did. Shawanda usually wouldn't give these two inmates five seconds of her time. The white women had their turf and their jobs, the black women had theirs. Nobody crossed paths—especially not with the Latinas, who had their own complex hierarchy of Mexicans, Puerto Ricans, and Dominicans.

But somehow Shawanda ended up with these two, and

none of them seemed to mind as they stared at the beautiful yellow Lab lying on the other side of the playpen fence in the cramped utility closet, smiling and panting as four eager and helpless puppies nursed at her side. Shawanda reluctantly set the puppy down as the vet continued his examination of the dogs.

"This program started right here, in Bedford Hills," the warden was saying proudly. He stood behind the three kneeling inmates, towering in his cheap suit and strong aftershave. A slim woman in her forties stood next to him with a "Visitor" badge pinned to her blouse. Shawanda had never seen her before—she heard she was some reporter from down in the city. Maybe from a newspaper. Or a magazine. Shawanda wouldn't be surprised if it was some tabloid that'd run a headline like "Prison Bitches Raise Bitches in Prison" or some other gotcha bullshit. Everyone loved to get a laugh when you were locked up and dressed like a bottle of orange juice.

"You were saying the program has been picked up by other prisons?" the reporter asked, holding her phone like an old-fashioned notepad.

"That's right," the warden beamed. "We started the program here in '97, but now it's in prisons across the country. And not just women's prisons."

"How'd the program get started? Can you tell me about the idea behind it?"

Shawanda rolled her eyes. Martha giggled. Everyone knew how the warden loved to hear his own voice.

"Well," the warden said, unbuttoning his suit jacket, "it started with the idea to help these women find purpose and meaning while they serve out their sentences. It was all based on the belief that taking care of another living creature would do wonders for our inmates. You see, the warden at the time was a sharp man, and he looked at all these studies by psychologists and sociologists that talked about the benefits of giving inmates a sense of purpose and accountability. But it's not just about helping the inmates take responsibility—it directly gives back to society by providing law enforcement with dogs that save lives."

The reporter looked down at the little puppies and smiled. "So all of these little guys will one day serve in law enforcement?"

"That's right. Our team here"—he motioned to Shawanda and Martha and Didi—"will be responsible for training the dogs over the next twelve months. The puppies will be cared for solely by the inmates. They will be acclimated to people, the environment, and taught basic obedience. Just before their first birthday, representatives from the government will come to the prison and assess the dogs. Those that make the cut head to the academy where they will undergo specialized training. In the case of the puppies raised here, they will be explosives detection canines."

Shawanda grit her teeth. She wasn't sure if it was because she hated the way the warden tried to make himself sound smart, or because she didn't want to think about that day twelve months from now.

Behind her, she heard snickering and the tell-tale sound of gossipy bitches. Sure enough, she looked over her shoulder to see Latisha McGregor, tats up her crossed arms, laughing with the other women in her gang. Latisha gave a twisted little smirk and blew Shawanda a kiss. Shawanda flipped her the bird, low down where the warden wouldn't see.

Next to the warden, the reporter had a concerned look on her face. "And what about the dogs that don't make the cut?"

"Those dogs are reassessed," the warden explained. "Maybe looking for bombs isn't that particular dog's specialty. Other trainers will come out and look at the dog to see if would make a good therapy dog, or a guide dog for the visually impaired. Something that gives back to society in some way."

On the other side of the playpen fence, the vet finished examining one of the pups. Shawanda held out her hand to take it.

"Aww, so cute," the reporter said, bending closer. She asked Shawanda in slow, round words, as if speaking to a child, "What are their names?"

Like you really give a shit, Shawanda wanted to say. She hated it when white people got all condescending, but she knew better than to talk back in front of the warden. "This is Deja."

"What a beautiful name."

"I named her after my niece," Shawanda said, smoothing the soft wrinkle of fur above Deja's closed eyelids.

"Did you get to name all the dogs?"

There was that same condescending tone again. Down the hall, Latisha burst out laughing.

Shawanda drew a deep breath. "Yes, we did. Me and Didi and Martha all got to pick names, but the breeder who brought the mama told us that they all had to start with the same letter. That way they can keep track of all the different litters they have."

"This one is Disney," Didi said excitedly, her red hair bouncing as she pointed. "And that one there is Dunkin."

Martha spoke softly. "And I named Dover and Dolly."

"So precious," the reporter cooed. Shawanda could tell that she wanted to hold one of them but was too scared to ask.

"Here," Shawanda said, reluctantly scooping Deja into the reporter's manicured hand. The little puppy flopped and made a little squeaking sound. She searched for the reporter's thumb pad as if was a nipple.

The reporter instantly melted.

"We're very proud of our women here," the warden said, sounding more genuine than before. "Shawanda here has helped raise two litters already, and all of the dogs have gone on to do great service for this country."

Shawanda's heart ached at the mention of the other litters, and she reached out and took Deja back.

The reporter seemed sad to see the puppy go. She cleared

her throat and stood back up. "Well, Warden Sprat, this is just an incredible story. Our readers are going to love it." She brought out her phone again, but then hesitated as she looked at Shawanda. "I'm sorry, but I have to ask, what are you in here for?" When Shawanda scowled up at her, she backpedaled. "I understand if you don't want to talk about it. I just think our readers would be curious. It would help make it seem, you know, more real for them."

It's been real enough for me already, Shawanda thought to herself, but then simply said, "Battery." She didn't mention the drug conviction, or her sick little brother, or her two younger sisters, or her grandma who had to work two jobs just to make rent on a moldy apartment in a bad part of the Bronx. Nobody gave a shit about the why, they just cared about the what.

"Sorry, warden," the vet said, interrupting the moment. He held one of the puppies in his latex-gloved hand. It was Dunkin. Shawanda and Didi had seen that he was the runt from the very beginning, but the vet looked particularly concerned. "I think this one may have a complication."

Didi put her hands to her lips.

"What kind of complication?" Shawanda asked before anyone could say anything. "He gonna be alright?"

"It's too soon to tell," the vet said, cradling the weak puppy. "His lungs are occluded, and he's having trouble drawing air. We'll have to run some tests." He looked up at the warden for approval.

"Yes, yes, of course," the warden said quickly. "Do whatever you need."

Shawanda watched as the vet stepped over the playpen and took little Dunkin away, carrying a piece of her heart with him.

SHERRY

11:24 p.m.
Near Quemado, TX
July 2019

CUSTOMS AND BORDER PROTECTION Agent Sherry Fry dropped her dusty Ford F-150 Raptor into low gear as she climbed up out of a dry creek bed and onto a deserted fire road. The sharp beams of her headlights illuminated the massive mesquite bushes, lighting them up like ghosts in the darkness. Off in the distance, the black ribbon of the Rio Grande snaked through the dry landscape, drawing a line between two very different worlds.

The blue-green light from the dashboard illuminated her face as she peered out in the darkness. She knew these roads well, but at night they all started to look the same—sandy paths that cut through the scrub brush and dead branches, no signs or fences or buildings to mark the way—and it took her a moment to confirm that she was heading in the right direction after taking a quick glance at the on-board GPS. The rutted road bounced her 5'4" frame and dug the nylon cuff case into the small of her back as she accelerated down the empty dirt track.

"Unit three-six en route to check out the sensors in zone two-alpha-charlie," Sherry said into her shoulder mic, keeping one hand on the sharply-jerking steering wheel.

The tinny voice of the dispatcher down in Eagle Pass responded through her radio. She was glad that it was John on the dispatch tonight.

"Copy that, three-six. We picked up a few more readings on the ground sensors, but so far nothing on the IR. It could just be wildlife."

"10-4. I'll let you know what I find. Over."

Sherry Fry was an eight-year veteran with CBP, and she had seen enough here on the border to know you always checked a sensor whenever it tripped, no matter the time of day or night. Sure, the desert was crawling with critters that always mucked up the ground sensors or triggered the infrared cameras that dotted the desert from here all the way to Yuma, Arizona, but it was her job to go and lay eyes on it.

As her commanding officer always said, "The river is our first line of defense, but nothing beats a pair of eyeballs in binoculars."

It was a shitty saying, but Jimmy Gonzalez was a great CO. He taught her all the tricks a good agent needed when they were out alone in the desert.

The truck bucked and nearly cratered as Sherry throttled over a huge hole in the hardpan, carved out during the last big thunderstorm.

Just then her phone vibrated in the console, the screen lighting up the cabin with white light.

She had a text. It was from Darryl.

its almost midnight. why didnt you call??

She sighed and clicked the button on the side of the phone, darkening the screen. She and Darryl had been married for seven years, and had dated for three years before that. She had given ten years of her life to that man—some would say that they were the best years, but Sherry had never bought into all that BS that said a woman was only worthwhile if she was twenty-four and skinny. Yet best years or not, ten years was a long time, especially when she worked long shifts on the border and Darryl worked all over the country with the Federal Protective Service under the DHS. Their home in San Antonio was empty more often than not, the nursery they had planned to decorate still empty and colorless. When she was being honest with herself, she knew she hated going home. In fact, she felt like doing anything she could to stay away.

When she was in the academy, everyone always warned her not to date law enforcement. Why the hell hadn't she listened?

The Raptor kicked up a spray of dirt as she rounded a corner, weaving through the mesquite and blackbrush. CBP had sensors and cameras and lookouts throughout this stretch of the border, which was one of the most heavily trafficked by drug runners, arms smugglers, and families looking for a new start up north. But even with the seismic sensors and infrared cameras, there was just too much open desert to stop the crossings entirely. It was like trying to hold sand in a colander.

"Thirty-six approaching two-alpha-charlie," she said into her shoulder mic as she drove up a low rise. She took her foot off the accelerator and slowed to a crawl, then reached down and pressed the button that deactivated the brake lights. Out here, stepping on the brakes sent out a red beacon that could be seen from the international space station.

"Copy that, thirty-six. We have backup on standby."

She pulled off the fire road and killed the engine. The bright floodlights bleached the landscape in front of her, but she killed those too, leaving her just with the dim light from the dashboard and the millions of stars in the desert sky.

Sherry grabbed her flashlight and her phone and hopped out of the cab. She looked at the M4 in the rifle rack mounted along the passenger side footwell, and thought about hitting the hidden button just under the dash that released the electronic lock, but talked herself out of taking it. Then she began scanning the dusty ground around the sensor. It was slow going, picking her way around the scrub brush, sweeping the beam of her flashlight over rocks and dead branches. Even though the sun had set hours ago, the desert was still hot, the ground releasing its stored heat.

Her phone buzzed. She took a quick glance.

I'm gettin tired of this Sher will u just call me plz?

She sighed, slipped the phone back into her tactical vest, and went back to her search. To most, it was just the same repetitive landscape, but Sherry had been doing this long enough to know the tell-tale signs. She worked out in large circles, scanning the area, and she hit on something forty feet up the fire road.

Smooth sand.

Sherry ducked down, hitting the smoothed patch of dirt with her flashlight at a low angle. Sure enough, the sharp light revealed little zigzags etched on the surface and shallow divots where rocks and twigs had been rolled or scraped along.

Someone had dragged branches behind them to obscure their tracks.

"Dispatch, thirty-six. I've got possible movement in two-alpha-charlie. Unknown number of individuals heading north-north-east. You can start rolling someone this way."

"Copy that, thirty-six. I'll have seven-one head your way. Unit seven-one?"

"CBP seventy-one is 10-4 on that. Advise ETA is twenty."

Sherry quietly acknowledged Unit 71's transmission as she withdrew her service weapon and followed the smoothed ribbon of sand. She kept her flashlight low, making sure it didn't hit the tops of any of the scrubby brush as she climbed up the low rise. Whoever had pulled the branches behind them was careful, weaving around obstacles and never moving in a straight line.

Eighty feet up the rise, she found her first footprint. It was outside of the swept path, as if someone had stepped too far to the side and it didn't get picked up in the sweep.

She paused and inspected the wide indentation in the sand. It was oblong, with soft edges and a fan of dirt spreading off the base. There were two smooth bands across the middle of the print. She'd seen this pattern before, but not in a long time. They had taped carpet to the bottom of their shoes.

"Clever sonofabitch," Sherry muttered, suddenly regretting not taking the .223 caliber M-4 with its thirty-round magazine. She looked back at the Raptor in the distance, but she had to keep moving forward if she had any chance of catching whoever was out there.

All types of people tried to cross the border. Most of them were harmless families looking for opportunities, but those tracks were easy to spot. There would be dozens of prints from sneakers and sandals, men and women and children's sizes, all clustered together. There might even be tracks from bags or luggage that was being hauled across the ground.

But the only people who cleared their tracks with branches and taped carpet to their feet were professional smugglers. Since they were headed north, it was almost certain that they were bringing heroin or fentanyl across the river.

Sherry broke into a low run up the hill, following the swept track quickly now. She figured that she was rapidly closing the gap on the suspects, and she flipped down the red lens attachment on her flashlight.

When she came to the top of the rise, she clicked off her flashlight and let her eyes adjust to the starry night. She slowed her breathing so she could hear. Crickets. Beetles clacking over rocks. In the distance, something that might have been voices.

She reached down to her utility belt and pulled out her infrared binoculars. In an instant, the desert landscape was revealed to her in a sea of bright green.

Two hundred yards ahead, five men were making their way slowly down the low sloping hill, carrying heavy backpacks and dragging a huge mesquite bush behind them. She was certain that they were heading to a pre-determined meeting place—sure enough, she spotted a van parked alongside the highway a kilometer away. She had to hurry.

Sherry's pocket buzzed again.

"Fuck, not now, Darryl . . ." she cursed under her breath.

She stowed her binos and checked the volume on her radio, speaking low and clear. "Dispatch, I have eyes on five runners, traveling north-north-east. Possible narcotics. Looks like they are heading toward a parked van on Route 277. Mile marker unknown."

"Copy that, thirty-six."

"Seventy-one, I'm eight minutes out."

Sherry turned down the volume on her radio and continued to follow the suspects, closing the ground between them. She knew from her training that her safety—and going home at the end of the shift—was the most important thing. As her CO always said, there will be more coming across the border tomorrow, and the next day. Her career would not be judged by making one routine arrest, but it would be judged if she made a life-threatening mistake.

She had no intention to engage, but she had to keep eyes on them until backup arrived.

The sweat was starting to pour as Sherry made her approach. The grip on her Glock was slick with sweat. Overhead, the dark shapes of bats flitted across the mantle of stars.

The dry ground crunched under her boots as she closed the distance. She was now close enough to hear their voices.

"Rapido. Prisa vamos, Flaco."

"Fuck off, this thing is heavy," Sherry could hear Flaco's reply in hushed Spanish.

Just then her boot came down on a long branch, and it rolled beneath her. The movement snapped a few twigs on a nearby bush.

"Fuck," she muttered, dropping low.

"Hey, you hear that?" one of them asked in Spanish.

The five men stopped in their tracks, scanning the dry, dark desert around them.

"Go check it out," Flaco ordered.

One of the men started to move in her direction, and Sherry knew she had only one option. She stepped out from behind the bush and turned on her flashlight.

"Customs Border Protection, stop where you are! *¡Alto! ¡Al suelo! Policia,* get on the ground, now!"

The five men froze, their eyes unaccustomed to the bright light. For a moment, no one moved. Only their eyes glanced around, looking at one another, questioning.

Sherry's hand tightened on the grip of her Glock.

There was always this moment—this split second when the smugglers decided which way this was going to go. If they played along, they'd be deported and probably dodge justice entirely in the Mexican court system. If they didn't . . .

Sherry's heart was hammering. "*¡Al suelo! ¡Ahora mismo!*"

The men shared a few more glances. Sherry's finger inched down the right side of the Glock's frame toward the trigger.

Then suddenly their hands went up, and all five men lay face down in the dirt beneath their heavy bags.

Sherry let out a sharp breath and immediately sprang to action, cuffing two with metal bracelets and the other three with zip-ties. She worked with one hand the way she practiced at the academy hundreds and hundreds of times, holding the hinged cuffs in her left hand, quickly snapping it over the wrist, the ratchet flipping around the wrist and the teeth engaging. If the suspect complied by bringing his other hand back, the process went quickly. If they didn't, that's when it got dangerous.

Thankfully, these particular drug runners knew the game.

"Don't worry, it's cool," Flaco said in Spanish, his face in the dirt. "We'll be back before you know it."

Sherry knew he was probably right, but she'd rather keep up this cat-and-mouse game than have to take a life—or risk her own.

Three minutes later, she had all five lined up, their bags piled off to the side. A mile away, she could see headlights and flashing blue lights approaching down the highway.

"Dispatch, this is thirty-six. Please have seven-two take a slow-down. I have five in custody, no problem."

The radio cracked an acknowledgment from CBP Unit 72.

Just then, her phone buzzed again.

"Jesus Christ, Darryl," she said. Still keeping her free hand on her now-holstered service weapon, she peeked at her phone.

But it wasn't Darryl. It was Jimmy Gonzalez, her CO.

Hey Fry, R U still at work? just ck'd my email, ur app has been approved! U got the new assignment!! Pack ur bags, ur off to VA!!! Call me wen u can.

SHAWANDA

Two years ago

"Is HE GONNA be alright, doc?"

Shawanda sat nervously in the medical ward of Bedford Hills Correctional Facility, twisting the collar on her bright orange jumpsuit. The number 1H2755 was emblazoned on her chest, but the letters were fading after five years of repeated washings and dryings and wearings.

There were a dozen beds around her, worn out and donated from some hospital back in the '90s. Most were empty, but there were two sick inmates tucked under thin sheets and hooked up to machines. One had cancer. The other had a bad cough, and Shawanda didn't know if it was something she had caught inside the prison.

Usually Shawanda wouldn't set foot in this place. She washed her hands enough as it was, not wanting to catch whatever nasty bugs thrived in an overcrowded prison, but Dunkin was too important to stay away.

"Doc, you hear me?"

She leaned over the clear plastic basin where the puppy lay bundled in blankets. The vet was working with a small syringe, trying to find a place to inject the little guy.

"I'm not going to lie to you," the vet said as he gently

inserted the needle into the thick part of Dunkin's rump. The puppy squealed and tried to open its eyes. "It doesn't look good."

Shawanda reached in and stroked Dunkin's wrinkled forehead. "C'mon, there's gotta be something you can do. What was that shot you just gave him? Ain't that gonna help him get better?"

"It was a dose of ampicillin. It's a broad-spectrum antibiotic, so hopefully it will help knock out whatever infection has taken over his lungs. But . . ."

Shawanda waited for him to finish his sentence. "But what?"

The vet sighed. "But he's too little to run an IV."

"What's he need an IV for?"

"It's the best way to administer antibiotics, and it allows us to control the dose over a long period of time." The vet rubbed Dunkin's tiny, bow-shaped legs. "But this guy's veins are way too small. We usually can't give an IV until they're three or four months old."

Shawanda had heard that tone before. She hated doctors. When she was younger, she had hated sitting in the clinic with her little brother, listening to doctors talk about inflammation and antibiotics and enzyme replacement. All she knew was that her little brother couldn't breathe good, and that he was suffering, and that he needed help. The doctors said it was cystic fibrosis, and he'd have it for the rest of his life. Hospitals and doctors' offices terrified her and made her boil with anger—not because she was afraid of death, but because the smell of sanitizer always made her think: *How the fuck are we gonna pay for all this?*

"There's gotta be something else we can do," she insisted. "I know you got something else in that bag of yours."

The vet placed the syringe in the locked metal sharps container bolted to the clinic wall and shook his head. "We've done all we can. Now we just have to ride it out."

The pain and anger on Shawanda's face must have been plain as day, because the vet—a young Asian guy with almond-colored eyes—softened toward her.

"I'll talk to the warden, see if I can't get you permission to stay with him. He's going to need to be bottle-fed with this antibiotic milk six times a day for a while. I can even show you how to give his next injections, if you'd like."

Shawanda blinked at him. "C'mon, man, we can't have needles up in here. Only the facility nurse can do that, and she'd shit if she saw this dog in here."

"Right, of course, I mean . . ." The vet cleared his throat. "Well, I can at least see if you can get permission to stay with him so you don't have to get a hall pass or whatever you call it."

Dunkin tried to nurse from Shawanda's finger, giving little whimpers.

"Here, feed him as much as he'll take." The vet handed Shawanda a half-dozen bottles of prescription milk and an eyedropper.

"Don't worry," Shawanda said softly. "I'll keep you warm and feed you." She kept thinking about the birth, watching these little puppies emerge from their mama in small translucent sacs. The mother nipped at the sacs with her teeth until they ripped open and the puppy came out, pink and wriggling. First Dover, then Dolly, Deja, and Disney. Dunkin came last, smaller than the rest. Even though she was still in labor, the mama dog would take the time to lick and clean each puppy, carefully nipping at where the umbilical cord attached to their furless stomachs, then guide them towards her teats with her snout. No complaining. No whimpering. Not wanting anything in return. Just pure caring.

The vet watched Shawanda whisper to Dunkin for a moment, then interrupted her. "You know that dogs are born with a happy gene, right?"

Shawanda looked up at him.

"A what?"

"A happy gene. Well, technically, there are three genes on chromosome six that have structural variations that make dogs hyper-social and friendly. Sometimes even people have an abnormality in that genetic region, and they show the same tendencies. It's called Williams-Buren syndrome."

"What the fuck are you talking about, doc?"

"It means that dogs are literally hardwired to love and need love in return." The vet reached out and rubbed Dunkin's soft belly where there was still the dried little stump of the umbilical cord. "Some scientists say that humans and dogs evolved together to such a degree that we wouldn't have survived without them. Imagine a band of hunter-gatherers a hundred thousand years ago. How much safer would they be with a few loyal guard dogs around them at night?"

"You mean people back then had dogs too?"

The vet nodded. "Archaeologists have found evidence of canincs living with humans for as long as we've been around."

"So, what, all those cavemen like tamed some wolves or some shit?"

"Pretty much. All domesticated dogs, from the biggest mastiff down to the tiniest chihuahua, are descended from wolves."

"But I thought wolves didn't like people."

"Well, they don't. Most of them. They're not the killers some people make them out to be, but they don't like too much interaction."

"So how'd they get tamed in the first place?"

"No one really knows. Some scientists suspect that there was genetic variation among wolves that made some less fearful of humans than others. These curious, more social dogs may have followed bands of humans, trying to get scraps of food. Over time, our ancestors may have lured them closer. The rest is history."

"Huh," Shawanda grunted. "True that. Dogs'll do anything for food. We train all our pups with these special treats. Works like a charm."

The vet stood and started packing his travel medicine bag. "Food is a big driver for dogs' behavior. But it's not the only one. It's not even the most important."

Shawanda looked up at him. "Then what is?"

"Love."

In his little blankets, Dunkin started to whimper.

"Love, huh?"

"Yeah, love. They ran a study a few years ago that showed that, given a choice between food or praise, dogs choose praise every time. They love us, and they need love from us in return. We are unlike any other two species on the planet. We need them just as much as they need us."

Dunkin started to nurse on Shawanda's finger again, and she felt more like a mother than ever before.

"You know, doc, I think you might be right."

JASON

2:42 p.m.
Ballroom, Marriott Hotel
Queens, New York, NY
July 2019

"COME ON UP. Don't be shy. What's your name, big fella?"

The heavyset man with tattoos snaking up his neck approached the table slowly. The pretty young woman behind the table smiled at him encouragingly.

"I—uhh . . ." The big man ran his hand through his tangle of thick hair. He wore a faded t-shirt beneath a black leather vest. On the back of his vest was a logo of a tomahawk with two crescent-shaped rockers above and below: the top read "Comanches" and the bottom read "New Jersey." There was a "1%" patch on his left breast pocket, and the smell of motorcycle exhaust and cigarettes clung to him. "Is this the place? You know, for the—" He paused, uncertain. "For the prizes?"

The young woman turned up the wattage on her smile. She was almost certainly a model when she wasn't working the reception table at a big event in a big hotel in the big city.

"Don't worry, you're in the right place," she said as if she were inviting him into a secret.

Her welcoming demeanor seemed to soften him a bit. He ran his hands through his hair again and looked around the room like he could hardly believe it. The three-hundred-person ballroom was decked out with balloons and music and pretty girls and tables stacked with food. In the back there was a stage with colored lights and a banner that read: *Catch Your Dreams Sweepstakes — Welcome Winners!*

"This is fuckin' nuts," the big man muttered into his beard. "I ain't never won nothin' before."

"Well, today's your lucky day," the pretty woman behind the table said with a wink. "Here, let's get you checked in. I just need to make sure your name's on the winners' list. Can I see your driver's license, please?" She grabbed a clipboard and looked up at him.

The big man stiffened for a moment, as if handing over his ID was not something he took lightly.

The woman read his expression perfectly. Without missing a beat, she motioned to the sign behind the reception table.

Winners Must Be Present to Claim Their Prize(s)

She gave a conspiratorial little shrug and said, "Rules, am I right?"

The festive atmosphere must have been getting to him, because a moment later he was reaching for the fat leather wallet on a chain attached to his belt. His eyes were on the midnight blue Chevy Corvette that was sitting in the middle of the room with *Grand Prize* written in big lettering on its windshield.

"Harold Jameson," the woman muttered as she checked his ID against her list. Her smile lit up again. "Here you are. Looks like you've already passed the first round, so you're already a winner. Congrats! Come on inside, grab some food. Your prizes will be announced shortly."

Harold couldn't keep the shit-eating grin off his face as he took back his ID and walked into the crowd. There was music playing from a DJ to the left of the double entrance doors, the food was delicious, and he hardly noticed that there were a few other bikers and rough types mixed in with the crowd.

A dozen more winners trickled in before a handsome middle-aged man took to the stage. The music started to pump and the lights around the stage brightened. All around the room the winners started to whoop and holler, knowing for certain that they'd be the one to drive the shiny new Corvette home tonight—and maybe one of the pretty young models, too.

"Welcome everyone to the Catch Your Dreams grand finale!" the Master of Ceremonies said as he took the mic with a flourish. Jason Hernandez was a man of average height and average build, but he made up for it with movie-star charm and dark wavy hair that rarely had a strand out of place. More than one jealous admirer had accused him of dying it, but he had no problem admitting that God had blessed him with two remarkable gifts: a tireless sex drive and a great head of hair.

"Alright ladies and gentlemen, we've kept you waiting long enough," he said as the bright lights shone in his eyes. He'd been doing this job for a long time, and now that he'd finally gotten his big promotion, his boss finally let him organize this whole event. It cost the agency a pretty penny, and not all of the top-brass liked the idea, but this had been Jason's dream for years. He could hardly believe the big day had finally come.

He could feel the excitement bubbling in the crowd. He could see the outlaw bikers and the deadbeat dads and the bail jumpers and the crooked attorneys and the hit-and-run drivers and the insurance scammers. He could see them all smiling, eating, drinking—each without the slightest clue.

"And now to announce the first big prize of the night," he said, flashing his Hollywood teeth, "let me be the first to tell you that you're all under arrest."

For a moment, the room stood still. A few of the winners near the stage started laughing at the supposed joke. The music was still going, the lights were still flashing, but most of the others were not sure that they heard what they thought they heard.

Then United States Marshal Jason Hernandez flipped the badge out of the breast pocket of his crimson jacket. The music cut out, the overhead lights kicked on, and in an instant, three dozen marshals and New York City police officers were storming in from every door, guns drawn. A few of the models pulled service weapons and handcuffs from their garters under their skimpy sequined cocktail dresses.

Some of the "winners" continued to laugh, while others stood there pie-eyed in shock. Some swore and spat. Some bolted for the doors, only to be tackled by uniformed officers. But in no more than thirty seconds, every last one of them was face down and cuffed.

Marshall Jason Hernandez watched it all from the stage with a wonderful sense of satisfaction.

"I CAN'T BELIEVE that actually worked," Marshal Bill Simmons said as he ate the last crab cake. "I mean, seriously? Out of the sixty-three fugitives with known addresses or current Facebook accounts, we got forty-one to show up here tonight. *Forty-one*. You're a genius, Jase. A real freaking genius."

Jason soaked in the praise. He took another sip of coke and watched as the last of the fugitives were logged and hauled out to the fleet of squad cars outside. They'd all be processed here in Queens, and then shipped to whatever jurisdiction had a warrant out for their arrest. In the end, it all went better than he could have hoped. Bottom line, nobody got hurt and everyone was going home with the same amount of holes in 'em as when they got here.

"Well, I do deserve the credit," Jason said matter-of-factly, "but not all of it. A few years back I was working with this guy from Houston—you know Jack Rogers, right?—anyway, Jack told me that they used to do this thing with a raffle at an old church, where they'd get maybe five, six guys at a time. That got me thinking. Then a few months ago I did a Google search, and wouldn't you know, the office down in Nashville did something like this and had it all up on the local news. They got like twelve fugitives on that sting. They didn't have the food and the car and the girls, though. That was my idea. I figured go big or go home."

Simmons dusted the crumbs from his shirt. "That was one hell of a gamble. I thought the section chief was gonna have a stroke when he saw the numbers for this."

"Come on, it wasn't so bad. I got a guy down at the dealership who lent me the car for the day, and we got the ballroom at a discount. The drinks and the food and the models, well, that was a little costly. But it was worth it, yeah?"

"I'd say. *Forty-one . . .*" Simmons looked up from his plate of food and watched as one of the non-marshal models stopped to tighten the strap on her high heels as she walked out. Simmons clearly appreciated the view. "I can't believe you want to give all this up for a pack of dogs."

"Just one dog," Jason corrected. K-9 units in the Marshal's Service were rare. There were only about twenty-five nation-wide, and he'd waited years for a spot in the elite training program to open up. Most other marshals would probably see it as a lateral move, but for Jason, it was the next challenge to conquer. He'd brought home over two hundred fugitives in his career, not counting tonight, but he always wanted to make a bigger impact. When he got the call that he'd made the program in Virginia, he knew he had his chance.

"But you're just gonna be spending your time in courthouses all day hanging out by the magnetometers," Simmons protested, as if the idea made the crab cake turn over in his stomach.

Jason laughed and slapped his old partner on the back. They'd been together for six years, and it was the one sad note in an otherwise happy day. "I'll miss you too, buddy. And besides, it's not just bomb detail at federal buildings. Think about what happened in Austin. There are a ton of wackos out there making bombs—and now that I'm a handler, the next time someone tries to place one, I'm the guy with the dog that's gonna find it!"

SHAWANDA

Eighteen months ago

SHAWANDA JACKSON STOOD in front of the industrial dryer and watched her world spin round and round. Sometimes it felt like everything was falling apart—like she herself could fall apart—but she always held tight. There were too many people counting on her. People back home. People in here. For her entire life, she had been the leader of the pack. She was the one who took care of her sisters and her brother; she was the one in charge of the Puppies Behind Bars program. She was the mom to all these beautiful puppies. She had it together.

That was why it had broken her heart when little Dunkin had died in her hands.

The vet had called it "wasting puppy syndrome." It sounded like a bunch of bullshit to her, like something someone says when they don't know what the fuck is going on.

All she knew was that little Dunkin had held on for dear life, working his weak little lungs for as long as he could. She had spent day and night with him for six long weeks, trying to nurse him back to health, trying to get some weight on those skinny little bones of his.

But no matter what she did, Dunkin kept slipping away from her. And then, one day, he was just gone. Gone like so many things she'd lost in her life.

The buzzer on the dryer buzzed, and Shawanda popped the door. The orange jumpsuits were hot on her hands as she pulled them out, but it felt good to feel something. Anything.

In the weeks after Dunkin's death, she had tried to focus on her work. She needed something to do, something to keep her occupied. She took on extra shifts whenever she could, trading work for stamps or food from the commissary. Anything to keep her busy.

And of course, she still had the other pups to look after. Didi and Martha had stepped up big, but Shawanda was still the one in charge, and she had to keep those two crazy ladies in line. They didn't know the first thing about training dogs, and Shawanda had to show them how to get a dog to sit, how to heel, how to stay.

But when she wasn't with the puppies, working in laundry was Shawanda's favorite type of work. She hated working in the electrical shop or in the cafeteria. Too much chatter, too many people. Down here, she could just focus.

She had always been the one to do the laundry for her siblings, but the smell of detergent and warm polyester always reminded her of her mother. Nina Jackson spent all day cleaning office buildings, but somehow she always managed to keep her own home spotless. Her father was a custodian at Yankee stadium, so there was no dirt or grime to be found in the Jackson household. They were good, hardworking people. Honest and loving. Then one evening, on their way home from work—carpooling like they always did in the family's run-down Acura—a drunk driver swerved into their lane while they waited to make a left-hand turn. He hit their car so hard that they were pinned into the back seats, and the fire department had to take half-an-hour to cut their bodies loose.

Thankfully none of the children were in the car, but in an instant, Shawanda became the mother for her little siblings. Far too soon.

Just then the door to the laundry swung open, and a few women walked in. It must have been getting close to shift change.

"Yo, what up Shawanda," one of them said to her.

"Sup," she replied with a curt nod.

She wasn't tight with these women, but they respected each other well enough. They stayed out of each other's way. Just the way she liked.

But then Latisha McGregor strolled in, her sleeves rolled up her arms. It had been a while since Latisha had pulled laundry duty. It was usually reserved for inmates who were on good behavior. Shawanda wondered who Latisha had had to screw to get off bathroom detail.

"Well, well, if it isn't the dog lady herself," Latisha said as she leaned against one of the washing machines. "Where your bitches at? You got 'em in a box here or somethin'?"

Shawanda didn't respond. She just folded her laundry. No use getting into a fight and losing her privileges. Latisha was a piece of shit, and shit was gonna smell no matter what you do.

The silent treatment seemed to work. Latisha gave a mocking laugh and started the next round of laundry.

It never ceased to amaze Shawanda that women could go through so many clothes and bedsheets, even in prison.

The women in the laundry room started to chat, gossiping about the latest prison yard drama, but Shawanda kept her head down and focused on her work.

It was a few minutes later when she realized that Latisha had come up to her folding table. She leaned across the table and spoke directly into Shawanda's face.

"So whatchu think. You gonna get me a job working with them dogs too?"

"You wouldn't like it," Shawanda replied. She suddenly wished she had a knife. Something to defend herself in case Latisha made a move.

The other women in the room had gone quiet, watching them without making it look like they were watching.

"And why's that? You don't think I can't give a dog some kibbles?"

"There's more to it than that," Shawanda replied, focusing on the clothes and not Latisha's hot breath in her face.

"Like what? Teaching the dog to sit, roll over, beg, all that shit? Man, that's easy. I had my mamma's dog doin' all that back home." Latisha clicked her tongue. "So what makes you so special, huh? Why you get all this special treatment?"

"What you talking about, special treatment?" Shawanda said, her temper rising. She looked up and met Latisha in her eyes. "Ain't no one treating me special."

Latisha gave another mocking laugh. "So, what, you think the warden goes around and shows off the rest of us to fancy-ass white ladies with that visitor badge? Ha!" She made a crude impression of the reporter. "*Oh, I just love your dogs. Can I have one too? You're just so special.*"

Shawanda clenched her fists around the jumpsuit she was folding. She worked hard. She did what she had to do. But she was not special. There was nothing special about spending five years behind bars while her family grew up without her. Special was for people who had never struggled in their lives. Special was not for people who fucked up.

Latisha must have sensed that she hit a nerve. She leaned in close.

"Ain't that right, princess?"

Shawanda slammed down the jumpsuit and went nose-to-nose with Latisha.

"The fuck your problem!" she shouted, drawing *ohhs* from the other women in the laundry room. Everyone was openly watching now.

Latisha squared off and didn't back down.

"My problem is you tryin' to be something you ain't. None of these folks give a shit about you. You know what these dogs are once they leave here? Cops. Police. And you helping them." She sneered at Shawanda as if she were trash. "You just an Uncle Tom training their bitches."

Shawanda was about to crack her on the jaw when a guard stepped into the room. He must have heard the shouting.

A few of the other women snickered into their hands.

"Jackson," the guard said. "Take a walk."

Shawanda's cheeks were burning as she stormed out.

"That's right," Latisha taunted, bouncing on her toes. "The police love they bitches!"

Shawanda raced down the hallway, passing dozens of other inmates, but she did not go back to her cell. Instead, she went straight to the workroom where the puppies lived and trained. She needed to be with her family.

She didn't care what Latisha said. These dogs were the only thing she had to keep her going. One day soon, she'd be able to get back to her life, to her sisters and brother—but until then, these dogs were her entire life. And they were what kept her alive.

CAMERON

3:54 p.m.
Forward Operating Base (FOB) Davidson
Nangarhar Province, Afghanistan
July 2019

THE SUN WAS relentless as it split the noonday sky. To the south, the jagged spine of the Spīn Ghar Range and Mount Sikaram still held their snow, forming a frozen border with Pakistan, but down in the dry wide valleys there was no relief from the burning glare.

CIA Security Specialist Cameron McNeil pulled a crumpled pack of Marlboro Reds from his tac vest and tapped out a smoke. He was tall, early thirties, with a thick shadow of stubble on his hard cheeks.

He lit his cigarette slowly, the flash of the flame momentarily overtaking his eyesight. He'd been smart enough to bring a few cartons with him when he shipped out six months ago. No PX at this outpost. It was whatever you brought with you or whatever you could barter from someone else. On his first deployment, he'd only brought a few packs, thinking that tobacco was tobacco everywhere you went. Wrong. He knew America had its share of fucked-up problems, but one thing it did right was cigarettes. When he was feeling particularly philosophical, he'd stop and ponder what that meant in the grand scheme of things.

But today, Cameron McNeil was not feeling philosophical. All of his focus was on the cloud of dust rising beyond the chain-link fence to the east. He could hear the old diesel engine rumbling closer. He was in charge of perimeter security—responsible for everything that came in and went out of the base.

He quickly scanned the compound with seasoned eyes hidden behind his Oakleys. His men were getting into position. Two CIA contractors in gray polos and tac vests and desert camo trousers were taking up positions on either side of the gate. Two more crouched behind the concrete blast shield, their M4A1 automatic rifles at the ready. To his left, an Army corporal behind a semi-circle of sandbags was checking the belt of the .308 caliber ammunition on the mounted M240B machine gun.

FOB Davidson was, in theory, one of the most secure locations this side of Jalalabad. It was a CIA facility with a full Army detail, a sprawling cluster of dusty pre-fab buildings and Con-X containers surrounded by perimeters of chain-link fence and concrete T-walls. Most access points and sensitive installations were reinforced with a line of Hesco barriers, those huge wire-framed sacks that served as oversized sandbags, thick enough to smother most blasts. There had been a number of attacks in years past, but no one had ever breached the perimeter. No one stationed here had ever been killed inside the base.

But none of that made Cameron McNeil feel secure as the old diesel truck rumbled up the hill and came into view. This was a routine delivery, planned days ago, but McNeil knew all too well that nothing was routine on the front lines against a faceless adversary. He took a long drag on his cigarette, the sun searing his neck where it emerged above his vest.

The truck lumbered closer, bringing a wall of dust with it. It trundled towards the main gate of the compound. McNeil could see that it was a canvas-covered Nissan Atlas truck.

His stomach filled with fire.

His ears started to ring.

He had to blink away the hot white spots that suddenly filled his vision.

Why did it have to be a Nissan Atlas?

Chill out, man, he ordered himself, drawing down hard on his smoke. He rubbed his face and chased away the ghosts that stalked him. *Chill the fuck out.*

The truck belched and rumbled up the unpaved road, and in moments it had reached the barriers set up in a serpentine fashion that forced vehicles to slow to a crawl. Afghanistan's version of speed bumps. The brakes squealed as it came to a full stop at the vehicle search pad just outside the front gates. The two contractors at the gate turned to Cameron, waiting for the order.

Cameron checked his manifest. The license plate matched, but that didn't mean shit, not in this part of the world. The knot in his stomach tightened. He nodded tightly to the guards at the gate.

The two contractors slipped through the gate and told the driver to get out of the cab. The driver, a spindly Afghani with dusty jeans and exhausted eyes, quickly obliged and swung himself down from the driver's seat, leaving the engine idling. One contractor followed him around back to inspect the cargo while the other began to sweep under the truck with a long-handled mirror. All protocol.

Except something didn't feel right to Cameron. Why had the driver left the engine running? All of the delivery drivers had been thoroughly vetted and trained, and they all knew to kill the engine upon approach. Had this one simply forgotten? Was he drunk, lazy? Or had been gotten to, like so many broke and starving fools before him? Was he a relative of some poor farmer that the Taliban paid a visit to one night? Most times, they would let the family decide who amongst them would give their life in a suicide attack so the rest of the family could live.

The fire in Cameron's gut was burning hotter now. He rubbed his face again, chasing away the bright flashes that never seemed to stay away for long. That damn ringing in his ears was back, louder than before. He shook his head, the sunlight cutting brightly in his eyes.

This isn't Yemen, he told himself. *This isn't Yemen.*

But fuck if it didn't *feel* like Yemen. Why hadn't the driver turned off the goddamned truck?

Cameron watched as the contractor continued to sweep the underside of the chassis. He was chatting with the other contractor as he went, bullshitting about this or that. Those guys got paid good tax-free money to be out here. They had better be professional.

Cameron threw the cigarette to the ground and stamped it out. His hands were starting to shake.

The contractors kept chatting, even as one of them casually inspected the cargo. The driver stood off to the side, smiling. Apparently he knew enough English to get in on the joke. Or did he find something else funny?

Cameron took a step forward, the sound of a Nissan Atlas exploding in his memories, followed by the cries of Yemenis and Americans bleeding out in the sand.

The contractor with the mirror hocked a wad of phlegm and spit it in the dirt. The other one laughed at another joke. The driver kept smiling.

Then the driver's eyes locked with Cameron's. Cameron had seen that look before. It was the same look of the old man behind the wheel of another Nissan Atlas, right before he cut down seventeen people in a blaze of fire and improvised shrapnel.

In an instant, Cameron had his pistol drawn.

"You!" Cameron cried, the ringing in his ears deafening the world around him. He covered the distance to the truck in a heartbeat. His hands were fully shaking now. "Yes you motherfucker, get down! Get down now!"

The Afghani driver paled at the sight of a Barretta barrel lunging toward his face. He dropped to the dirt and covered his head, praying and begging in Pashto. Cameron didn't speak it, but he knew the word "Please." The man said it over and over and over.

"You think you can try to fuck us over, huh?" Cameron hissed, digging the gun into the back of the man's head. "You think we're stupid enough to let you in here?"

"Whoa, Cam—" one of the contractors said, but Cameron wheeled on him.

"Shut up! Go kill the engine. I want this truck taken apart, you hear me? Get the EOD team out here now!"

The two contractors shared a nervous glance as Cameron stood over the cowering Afghani. Back in the compound, a crowd had gathered but kept their distance, unsure of whether to take cover or watch the spectacle that was unfolding.

One of the startled contractors had just shut off the engine when Cameron was pulled out of his blind rage by the sound of his name on his boss's angry lips.

"McNeil! Let these guys take care of this. I need you in my office. Now."

THE WHITE SPOTS had finally faded from his eyes by the time Cameron stepped into the command hut. The fire in his gut had turned to ash, but the ringing in his ears was still there, far away and incessant.

His hands were trembling as he sat down across from his commanding officer, Special Agent Stan Juszczyk.

"Jesus Christ, Cameron," Juszczyk said as he threw himself into the chair. "You want to tell me what the hell that was all about?"

Cameron tried to steady his hands. He couldn't even remember what had set him off. One minute he was taking a smoke, the next he had a gun to some poor bastard's head.

"I don't know, sir. When I looked at the driver I—I got a bad vibe."

"A bad vibe?" Juszczyk parroted in a low voice. "C'mon, McNeil, we all get bad vibes. I can't even drop a good deuce 'cause I think the toilet seat is booby-trapped. But you know the protocols here as well as I do. You get actionable intel, and then you make a rational informed decision. You don't call out the fucking explosive ordnance disposal team just because someone looked at you sideways."

"They might find something."

Juszczyk made an exasperated noise. "Look, I listened to you the first time you thought a bomb was inbound. I listened the second time, too. But this shit has got to stop. You take your job seriously, I'll give you that, but you can't keep sending the base into lockdown on a hunch."

Cameron tried to slow his breathing. He didn't know what to say. A slow wave of guilt was creeping its way up his spine. It wasn't supposed to be like this. He was supposed to have left all this shit behind him. Yemen was supposed to stay firmly in his past.

Juszczyk must have read his face, because he blew out a jet of air and said in a calmer voice, "Look, I get it. We all have bad days."

Cameron's hands tightened on the chair. "No, sir, we

don't. LeBron James can have a bad day, but if *we* have a bad day, people die. We don't have the luxury to miss our free throws."

"That's real fucking poetic. I'm gonna miss your brilliant insights."

Cameron's face registered his surprise.

"That's right, you're being reassigned."

"What, why?"

"Because you're an asshole and you're going to get somebody killed."

Cameron gritted his teeth.

"Relax, I'm screwing with you. Look, this new assignment just came in," Juszczyk continued. "I need to send someone, and you're the one I chose."

"And what if I don't agree to go?"

Juszczyk didn't flinch. "It's an order, not a suggestion. See it as a chance to step away for a bit, get a fresh perspective on things."

"I don't need a fresh perspective."

"Well, then, use it as a time to get to know your new partner."

Cameron blinked. His ears were still ringing. "Partner? What do you mean partner?"

Juszczyk helped himself to a wide grin. "She's a real stunner. Blonde, young, loves long walks in the park and eats kibble." He leaned back in his chair. "You're perfect for her."

SHAWANDA

One year ago

IT WAS WINTERTIME again, and the rain had come back to Bedford Hills Correctional Facility, but Shawanda didn't mind at all as she stood at the front doors to the prison, four beautiful young labs by her side.

For the first few litters she had had to say goodbye inside, but after five years and dozens of happy dogs trained, Shawanda had earned the respect of the guards. This time they let her outside of the prison to see the "D" litter off into the future.

As the rain dripped off the overhang that sheltered the front door, Shawanda knelt and shared some kisses with her yellow babies.

"You all be good, you hear? Don't give your new people no trouble."

Deja set her wet nose against Shawanda's cheek. Dover sat close by, smiling widely. Disney and Dolly waited their turn for a hug, which they happily accepted.

Shawanda loved each and every one of them. It broke her heart to see them leave, but she knew that they each had a bright future ahead of them.

She stood as the van pulled up, ready to take them to

Virginia and the next step on their journey. She stepped back and clasped her hands over her chest as they were all leashed up and led out into the rain, tails wagging.

One of the female guards put her arm around Shawanda's shoulder as the dogs hopped into the van and then drove off down the road.

Shawanda Jackson never cried, but her eyes betrayed her as she watched the taillights.

She had learned how to say goodbye to her family of puppies, but then and there, she vowed to never let herself lose her real family—her sisters and little brother. Once she got out, she'd make it right.

BRADFORD

7:27 a.m.
Federal Canine Training Facility
Front Royal, VA
July 2019

IT WAS ALREADY hot when ATF Agent Thomas Bradford pulled up to the small guard shack. When he lowered the driver's window, the humidity hit his face like a hot washcloth. The checkpoint was manned by an overweight guard in his early sixties—he looked like a retired cop, definitely past his prime. After a half-assed check of Bradford's credentials, the red-and-white-striped gate lifted.

The AC in his rental smelled like stale cigarettes and new car, but Bradford had it blasting all the way from the cheap motel in Winchester where he stayed the night before. The program director had given him a quick orientation briefing over the phone, so he knew to book the room for only one night after his flight from Philly. Apparently, they were going to have all the new handlers stay in dorms here at the facility, just like in the academy. Back when he was still a young man who had his whole life ahead of him.

He pulled into a spot and put the car in park. The big white training facility stared back at him.

What the hell are you doing here, Bradford?

He popped the door and stepped into the sweltering heat. He'd been to the Shenandoah region before—he'd even hiked a good chunk of the Appalachian Trail, taking five days from Compton Gap to Turk Gap—but he'd done that in May before all of Virginia turned into a furnace. He scanned the green ridge behind the facility, looking for signs of the trail. He knew it ran right next to the property, and he half expected to see hikers trekking just on the other side of the chain-link fence.

A part of him dreamed of setting out and walking from here all the way to Mount Katahdin in Maine, but instead, he threw his duffel bag over his shoulder and made his way inside. Four tee shirts. An extra pair of jeans. A sweatshirt. Socks and underwear. That and his gym bag was all he brought for the next thirteen weeks—everything else he'd need would be provided courtesy of Uncle Sam.

The main building of the facility was a large white structure with sliding doors like a hangar. They were all open to catch the morning light.

Inside he found an expansive training floor, divided into various sections by cones and obstacles and low cinderblock walls. The place was spotless. The polished concrete floor didn't show a single clump of fur, but he could smell the unmistakable odor of Labradors.

There was a group of people already standing in the center of the room. Even though he was three minutes early, clearly he was late. As usual.

"You must be Agent Bradford," one of them called out.

He was a tall black man dressed in dark blue BDU pants, combat boots, and a tight gray polo emblazoned with the US Department of Justice seal. The words *National Canine Division* were stitched above and *Instructor* below. "Glad you could join us."

"I don't have anywhere else to be," Bradford said as he swung off his bag. Then he remembered that for the next three months, he was basically a rookie again. Why did he have to put in that damn application? He added a moment too late, "Sir."

"I'm Instructor Adams," the man said, clearly unimpressed. "I'll be your lead trainer for this class."

"A pleasure, sir."

"I'm sure it is," Adams said flatly. He nodded to the three other people standing with him. They were all wearing civilian clothing.

"These are the other trainees in your cohort. This is Sherry Fry, she works Customs Border Protection out of Texas."

Bradford extended his hand. Sherry was a young woman, late twenties, fit and serious. She shook his hand firmly. He could feel her wedding ring dig into his hand—he noticed it not because he was looking for it, but because it was obvious that she had switched it to her right hand. He could tell that she meant business. He liked her right away.

Instructor Adams motioned to a clean-cut Latino man who wore an easy smile. "Jason Hernandez, out of the

Marshal's office in New York."

"Hey, man, nice to meet you," Jason said, shaking Bradford's hand like a car salesman. "I've heard a lot about you."

Bradford immediately figured this guy worked with someone, who knew someone, who made a phone call and found out all about him. That's the government way. No secrets. It also worked the same way when you fucked up. Everyone and their grandma knew what you did even before you found out.

"So I hear you've trained dogs before, right?" Jason continued.

Despite himself, Bradford thought back to the cabin on Lake Muskesin where he buried Copper.

"That was a long time ago."

"Maybe you can keep an eye out, make sure I don't screw up. Yeah?"

Adams cut Jason down with a glance. "You leave the instructing to me, Marshal. You screw up, I'll be the first to know about it. Understood?"

"Completely, sir," he said, dropping Bradford's hand and taking a step back.

Lastly, Adams turned to the man who hadn't moved a muscle the entire time. He was built like a soldier and had the eyes of someone who had seen the inside of a firefight. "And this is Security Specialist Cameron McNeil."

The man didn't extend his hand. Bradford could smell the ego on this guy from across the room.

"Security Specialist?" Bradford asked, sizing him up. "You CIA? State Department?"

"Specialist McNeil is with us at the request of the DOD," Instructor Adams said, steering them away. A middle-aged woman was approaching, her shoes clicking on the concrete floor. She was dressed in smart business attire and had an assistant at her side.

"Everyone," Adams said, "allow me to introduce you to Deborah Bender, the director here at the facility."

Adams stepped aside, and she smiled at them with genuine warmth. "Let me welcome you to Front Royal, the Mayberry RFD of Virginia. On behalf of the entire staff here at the National Canine Division, we appreciate your dedication as you embark on this next phase of your careers. Canine training has served a vital role in law enforcement in this country for over one hundred years. As a matter of fact, this place was the US Army's canine training camp in World War II. The NCD is proud to have trained hundreds of the world's best handlers right in this very facility."

To Bradford it sounded like a stump speech, but there was no denying the credentials of this place. It had a reputation for producing the best dogs—and the best handlers. Those that didn't flunk out.

"As you may know," the director continued, "the government has designated ATF as the lead training body for a host of federal, state, and local agencies across the US and fifty-three foreign governments all over the world. Your respective agencies have decided to utilize this facility, its trainers, and its canines to accomplish their mission regarding the detection of explosives. You are here because you represent the best and brightest of your agencies."

Director Bender motioned to the far wall, which was lined with many plaques of handlers with their dogs. "As you know, this program receives thousands of applications for handler training from across federal law enforcement and other agencies, but we only graduate thirty handlers a year. Once you've completed your training here, you will be among one of an elite group at the front lines of bomb and firearm detection. We look forward to seeing what you can do."

Instructor Adams stepped forward, setting his heavy boots in a wide stance. "You know what it took to get here. The training staff has reviewed your applications and your service records. We interviewed your supervisors and your co-workers, and you each passed the in-person interview with top scores."

As Bradford listened to the pep talk, his stomach turned to knots. For him, he'd jumped through all those hoops three years ago, back when he actually wanted this assignment. But then the red tape got in the way. He'd never been good at politics in the bureau, and he pissed off the wrong higher-up by taking charge of a sting operation without the proper clearance—and by opening his damn mouth during the inquiry hearing. He managed to keep his badge, but his application had been shelved. So much had changed since then. Why the hell hadn't the past stayed where it belonged?

Adams leaned forward, towering over their group. "You four have made the cut, but the difficult part is just starting. For the next thirteen weeks, you will be here seven days a week, ten hours a day. No days off. No trips home to snuggle with the missus. No bullshit." He cut another glance at Jason. "The dogs you will be paired with have already received six weeks of exemplary odor-recognition training here at the facility, and they have each performed flawlessly. They know their stuff. I can personally guarantee you that if they are not finding explosives, *you* are doing something wrong. Understood?"

He was met with a chorus of "Yes, sir."

"Good." For the first time, a hint of a smile showed on his lips. "Now let's meet your dogs."

CAMERON

7:43 a.m.
Federal Canine Training Facility
Front Royal, VA
July 2019

Instructor Adams turned his head and shouted, "Okay, bring 'em out!" and Cameron McNeil watched as four fifteen-month-old yellow Labs trotted out of a back room. Their tongues lolled in their mouths, as if they were smiling at the four new recruits who would—hopefully—become their handlers. He could almost feel the excitement coming off them.

The problem was, Cameron McNeil wasn't a dog lover.

He watched with a flat expression as the four young dogs came to a halt beside Adams. The assistant holding their leads gave them a gentle tug and a simple sit command. They all sat, grinning and panting and looking sharp.

Cameron suddenly craved a cigarette. *What do they have to be so happy about?*

"Ladies and gentlemen," Adams said, not unlike a proud parent, "meet your new partners."

The boss lady stepped forward and gave them their assignments. Dolly went to Sherry, the Border Patrol officer. She took Dolly's lead and smiled. Disney went to the

Marshal, and Jason bent down and ruffled the dog's head.

"Well look at you, sweetheart," Jason said, rubbing Disney's cheeks.

Deja was the most serious dog of the bunch, and she went to the ATF agent, Bradford.

Match made in heaven, Cameron thought.

That meant Dover was his. The assistant walked him over and handed his lead to Cameron. The large dog sat and looked up at him with big, dark eyes.

"So can we change the names?" Jason asked, still giving his dog a rub down. "I mean, Disney's a great name and all, but it's a little kiddie sounding, you know?"

"What's wrong with that?" Sherry asked.

"It just doesn't say *law enforcement* to me."

Sherry laughed. "You want something meaner? How about Hitler? Now there's a name that says this dog will chew your leg off."

Jason winked at her. "How about Boomer?"

"That's not going to happen," Adams said, putting an end to the chatter. "These dogs have already gone through numerous forms of training since they've been weaned from their mothers. They all know their names by heart, so there's no changing it now. Besides, these names were chosen by the women who raised them."

"You mean the convicts?" Cameron asked, hooking his fingers through his belt loops.

"You obviously read the material that we forwarded to

you," Adams replied sarcastically. "Those women did a damn fine job with these dogs, and they deserve our respect."

Both Sherry and Jason seemed impressed, but Bradford's face didn't change. Cameron had been watching him the whole time—watching him from the moment he strolled in late like he owned the place. Cameron knew the type. Men who were good at their job but didn't give two shits about the people on their team. He'd seen enough of those guys in the Company. The CIA was full of cocky guys who couldn't get their heads out of their own asses. And more often than not, those were the guys who put everyone else in danger. Cameron swore he'd never be like that—not after Yemen.

"Now that we're all getting acquainted," Adams continued, "you should know that these dogs have already undergone the most rigorous canine odor recognition training in the country. And the second half hasn't even started yet. They were selected based on the bloodline of their odor-detection ability. They went through a year's worth of obedience training in the correctional facility, and then spent weeks here at Front Royal getting trained on the six food groups."

"The what now?" Jason asked.

"We call them the six food groups," Adams repeated. "They are the six families of chemical structures that nearly all explosives fall into." He began to count off on his fingers without missing a beat. Cameron was sure the man could do it in his sleep. "Nitroalkanes, that's your C-4 and plastic explosives. Nitrate esters, your dynamites, commercial explosives, and gun powders. Then there are the nitraromatics, which includes TNT and military explosives. Nitramines, which are primarily detonation cord. Acid salts, which are mainly black powder and all your pyrotechnics, and finally, peroxides. That's the nasty shit. We'll brief you on that later when you get a class on IEDs and what the terrorists are using nowadays."

Cameron suddenly felt hot around the collar. He reached up and touched his neck. He tried to fight it, but sweat started to bead on his palms.

"So it is true that we'll be working with actual explosives?" Jason asked. "Live dynamite and C-4 and all the rest?"

"That's affirmative," Adams replied. "Our program trains dogs exclusively on actual explosives, just as they would be found in the field." He looked them all in the eye. "And you will be tested on all of them."

"But isn't that dangerous?" Sherry asked.

Adams shook his head. "Not if you follow orders and don't do anything stupid."

Don't do anything stupid . . .

A bright light flashed in Cameron's eyes. A Nissan Atlas truck turning into a ball of searing fire. His ears ringing like a bell had been struck. The haunting tar-like smell of Symtex, the mushroom cloud and burning tires. The scalding rush of the high explosive shock wave compressing the air in his lungs.

And then, just as quickly as it came, it was gone. He looked to the other handlers, hoping none of them had noticed where he'd gone. They all seemed oblivious. He breathed a small sigh of relief.

Then he noticed Dover. The dog was watching him with curious, processing eyes, as if he had sensed what the others missed.

Don't you even go there, dog.

Adams was talking again. "By learning the six categories, these dogs have the ability to detect over 14,000 explosive formulations, everything from firecrackers to TNT. They already know what they're searching for. For the next twelve weeks, what you and your canine partners will learn is *how* to search. We will teach you how to search planes, trains, automobiles. We'll clear sporting venues, luggage, people, crowds, backpacks, anywhere someone might hide explosives. And for those of you charged with finding guns and ammo, your partners will do that too, and do it extremely well. Remember, gunpowder *is* an explosive. Depending on environmental conditions, I've seen dogs find shell casings that were fired six months prior."

Jason gave a low whistle.

"We will instruct you on the current ATF training methodology. We wholeheartedly believe in food reward, which means that the only time these dogs eat is when they find explosives."

"So there's no other feeding schedules?" Sherry asked.

"No, these dogs will have their nose on explosives every

single day of their working lives, and they will only eat when they hit upon an explosive odor. As long as these dogs are active duty, their training is a seven-days-a-week, 365-days-a-year commitment from you."

Cameron couldn't believe what he'd just heard. "Wait, you're saying that these dogs only get fed when they're training, and we have to train them all day, every day?"

"That's right."

"No days off?"

"No days off."

Cameron could feel his frustration rising. "You do know my agency has committed me to this assignment for the next three years?"

The corner of Adams's mouth ticked up. "Then you better get comfortable. Look, take any Olympic athlete or hall-of-famer and ask them how much they train to get to their peak. It's no different with these dogs."

Cameron suddenly found himself cursing Juszczyk for cooking up this batshit idea. For the first time in his life, he wished he was back in Jalalabad.

DORMITORY

8:19 p.m.
Federal Canine Training Facility
Front Royal, VA
July 2019

FRONT ROYAL WAS a tiny town with only grubby roadside motels, so they were all put up at the dormitory building two miles from the main facility. It was a step above a barracks but a step below a college dorm room.

"I feel like a twenty-year-old," Jason said as he hauled his duffle up the stairs to the shared hallway. "Beer pong anyone?"

Bradford shook his head, but Sherry laughed.

"I'll raincheck on that one," she said.

Jason shrugged and gave her another wink. "Your loss."

The day had been long and stressful—Instructor Adams had seen to that—so they all filed into their rooms, bringing their new partner inside with them.

Jason immediately started to wrestle with Disney on the bed, while in the room next door, Bradford set up Deja in her bed in the corner.

"Stay," Bradford said, pointing firmly in Deja's face. Her head cocked to the side, and she watched him as he cleaned his gun on the bed, but she did not move for the rest of the night.

One room over, Sherry was playing with Dolly on the floor, trying not to think about Darryl—and wondering why she kept thinking about Jason.

And in the last room down the hall, Cameron McNeil, the soldier who didn't like dogs, was already asleep on his bed with Dover curled up next to him.

JASON

9:43 a.m.
Federal Canine Training Facility
Front Royal, VA
July 2019

"A DOG'S NOSE is one of the most sensitive instruments on the planet."

They were all sitting in a cramped classroom that was adjacent to the main training hall, listening as Instructor Adams paced at the front of the room next to a digital projector. Jason drummed his fingers on the desk, just like he did back in the Marshal's academy—and in college and high school before that. Hell, he probably did it all the way back in the third grade and drove his teacher mad. Instructor Adams seemed to ignore it, but Cameron, the mysterious security specialist, kept glaring at him.

Jason had done a bit of research on all the other handlers in the DOJ database before he got here—one of the perks of being a Federal Marshal—and he knew that Cameron McNeil had been a Marine assigned to embassy duty in Budapest, Hungary before he was tapped for a joint program between the DOD and State Department. But Jason couldn't find any more details after that. The records were all highly classified.

He's definitely CIA, Jason thought as he met Cameron's glare and returned it with his usual confident smile. He kept drumming his fingers.

"Your average canine has over thirty million olfactory receptors in their nose," Adam was saying, "compared to only about six million for humans. The part of their brain responsible for processing these signals is forty times larger than our own." Adams clicked the projector remote and a black-and-white drawing of a dog's brain appeared on the wall. Nearly half of the left lobe was shaded red. "This is called the rhinencephalon. Translated from the Greek, it literally means 'nose brain.' As you can see, a canine's rhinencephalon makes up a large majority of their overall brain mass. Our rhinencephalon, in comparison, is about the size of a garbanzo bean."

Jason inexplicably found himself thinking about hummus. He glanced at the clock. They'd already been in here most of the morning. Every break he would head to the back of the room to refill his cup with that black syrup they called coffee. And it wasn't helping.

"A dog's entire world is rendered through its sense of smell," Adams continued. "Canine eyesight is limited, and some studies have indicated that they only see a very narrow range of color."

He clicked the slide. It was a row of brightly colored traffic cones, each one a different color—yellow, orange, green, and pink.

"If I were to tell you to pick out the pink cone, you'd have no trouble whatsoever. You could even do it at a hundred yards. That's how strong your eyesight is. It's effortless for humans to pick up visual cues like these cones. That's because we see in full spectrum. Dogs, on the other hand, can use their noses to *smell* in full spectrum. So let's say I blindfold you and pop the top of a can, and I ask you what you smell. You say, easy, it's beer. When a dog smells that, they say it's malt, barley, yeast, carbon dioxide, water, aluminum, etcetera. Each one is a separate and distinct layer. Dogs do it just as easily as you or I can pick out that neon pink traffic cone from the row."

Sherry made an intrigued sound as she scribbled notes in the next seat over. From the moment she walked into the training facility yesterday for their first orientation, Jason had been struck by her. He'd never expected a border patrol officer to be . . . cute. Sure, she was married, but Jason had seen the way she looked at her phone. He was good at reading people, and he could tell that all was not right in the Fry household. Now, sitting in that cramped room, the smell of her perfume kept distracting him. *Guess my rhinencephalon works just fine*, he thought as he tried to catch her eye. No luck. He took another sip of black syrup.

Adams clicked the slide again. This time it was a swimming pool.

"A dog's nose is so sensitive that it can detect a single teaspoon of sugar diluted into a body of water the size of an

Olympic swimming pool. We're talking odor detection down to the parts per million."

Jason leaned over and rubbed Disney between her ears. She beamed him a wide, wet grin as her tail thumped the floor.

"See, I knew you were a genius," he said in his squeakiest voice. "Who's my genius? Yes you are. Yes you are!"

Disney melted under his praise and affection, and even Sherry cracked a smile at him.

Jason took the opportunity to whisper, "Still think I should have named her Boomer."

Sherry stifled her laugh and turned her full attention back to Instructor Adams, with an extra eyeroll thrown in for effect.

Score, Jason thought, leaning back in his chair. He glanced at the clock. Nearly ten-thirty. Time to get out of this godforsaken classroom and hit the training floor. He was excited to work with Disney, and he was excited to be here in the program, but classrooms were always a special kind of hell for Jason Hernandez. Real work was not done behind a desk.

Like an older brother, his partner Bill Simmons would constantly say he was a dumb sack of shit, but that had never fazed Jason. Jason was one of the best Marshals in the field, and he had the stats to back it up. He knew the answers and aced every test he ever sat for—he just didn't see the point sitting around inside when the action was *out there*. He'd been that way for as long as he could remember. His seven years in the Marshals Service proved that out. The guys you always saw in the office never lifted a finger. The guys you never saw were out there getting fugitives off the streets.

He came from a poor family who moved to Newark back in the eighties. His parents were both from El Salvador, and they had instilled in the family a work ethic that only the children of immigrants could understand. They wanted the best for their three boys, and they'd given them all American names to help the boys achieve more than they themselves ever could. As the eldest, Jason had taken the brunt of that expectation, but school had always bored him to tears. It wasn't just his third-grade teacher whom he'd given gray hair—it was his parents, too. They'd threatened him with everything under the sun. Groundings. Taking his car keys. Military school. None of it stuck. Every time he'd come home with detention for being the class clown, or a note about not doing his homework, his dad would always say the same thing in his rough Salvadoran slang: *No lo jodió. Don't fuck it up, Jase. You only get one shot at this life.* He'd heard it so many times, he started wearing it like a badge of honor.

He had skated through high school with a GPA hovering just north of three-point-zero, so in senior year when he strolled into the family kitchen with its smells of epazote and cooking rice and announced that he'd gotten into NYU, his parents were stunned silent. It helped that he'd gotten over fifteen hundred on his SATs and ran varsity track, but his parents had no idea he'd even applied. It was not the last time that he was full of surprises.

"Are you listening, Marshal?"

Jason shook himself out of his memories. "Yes, sir. Absolutely. I'm just itching to get out in the field is all."

"We'll see about that." Adams shut off the projector. "Alright, everyone out to the training floor. Time to run some drills. This morning we'll be starting off on the block wall, then onto luggage."

The four handlers got up and made for the door, but Adams stopped Jason.

"I'm going to get these three set up. You wait here."

There was something in his voice that told Jason he'd crossed a line.

No lo jodió, Jase.

Adams followed the other handlers onto the training floor. Cameron gave him a condescending little smirk as he led Dover out of the room. "Uh oh," was all he said, and then he was gone.

Asshole.

Disney sat patiently as Jason fidgeted by the desks. He thought about his last big case, and about the legendary sting operation at the ballroom he'd pulled off just before he got this assignment, but none of that could keep his attention for long. He hated that he was on time-out while everyone else was working.

Looking through the window with its half-closed vertical blinds, he could see Adams lecturing the other three handlers on the training floor. He restlessly made his way over to the long cabinet on the far wall. It had airtight metal drawers labeled with various explosives and chemical compounds that the dogs would test on. This is where the instructors prepared the training aids for the day and was signed *Hot Area - Access Limited.* Jason perused the drawers with labels like "ANFO" and "PETN" until he came to one label that read, quite conspicuously, "NG DYNAMITE."

His curiosity got the better of him, and he opened the drawer. Sure enough, in a zip lock bag, there was a characteristic red stick.

"No shit . . ."

Unzipping the bag, he picked it up gingerly with his thumb and forefinger. He half expected ACME to be printed on the side, but then he realized he'd seen too many Roadrunner cartoons when he was a kid. As he held it, he couldn't believe that something so small could do the amount of damage that he saw in the video that was shown to the class.

He was smart enough to put it back and close the drawer before Adams returned.

"Marshal Hernandez," he said officiously, not bothering to sit—and not inviting Jason to, either. He came uncomfortably close. "Do you want to be in this program?"

At least Jason could trust Adams to get straight to the point.

"Yes, sir. I do."

"Then you had better start acting like it. We have thirteen

long weeks ahead of us, and there are hundreds of applicants from across the federal government who'd love to take your spot. I expect you to follow orders, and I expect you to pay attention when I'm delivering a lecture. Do I make myself clear?"

"Completely, sir."

"Good."

Then Adams turned and went back out to the training floor, motioning for Jason to follow.

The other handlers were already gathered around a thirty-foot long, waist-high cinder block wall with quart paint cans placed in many of the openings. All the cans had five holes punched in the lids.

"For this exercise," Adams explained, "you will have your dog sniff along this wall. Our NCD trainers have hidden black powder in two locations. Your dogs know black powder—just keep them moving, slow and steady, not too tight on the lead. Guide them with your free hand, making sure their noses investigate the high blocks as well as the ones along the floor. There are several hundred openings in this wall, and you will not be able to put their noses on each and every block, so you will need to look for changes in their searching behavior to indicate they are close. They will be a little confused because they are used to putting their nose right on the explosive. Today, they may or may not give a clear detection signal. You have to pick up the change that says, *I'm close but not right on it.* This is where teamwork comes in."

Bradford, the ATF guy, was up first. He gave a low, long *seeeek* command, just as they had been instructed so that the dogs never confused the command with a short, sharp negative, like *no* or *out*. Then he and Deja set off. Deja started scouring the wall, running her nose along each cinder block and across the can lids. Bradford seemed totally in control, like he had done this a hundred times already, whispering soft commands like "gooood dog" and "atta girl." He brought his hand up to the higher cans so the dog's nose passed by the punched lids, then down to the middle and lower cans.

That guy's legit, Jason thought as he held Disney's lead.

Deja proceeded down the wall until she hit on the smell in one of the topmost blocks. She immediately sat down.

"Good girl," Bradford praised her in a high-pitched voice. He reached into his food pouch and paid her with a bit of food.

Next up it was Sherry and Dolly, followed by Cameron and Dover. Both teams did alright, although Cameron struggled to keep Dover engaged. Dolly was really interested in a particular can, but Adams told Sherry, "Keep her moving, that's not it." Most likely the kibble distractor.

After the wall was reset again, it was finally Jason's turn. He loosened his grip on Disney's lead and gave her the command.

"Seeeek."

He motioned to the uppermost block to begin the exercise.

Disney stood and started to move forward, but then she hesitated. Almost immediately, she sat back down again.

That was strange. None of the other dogs had done that. They had only given the "passive alert" of sitting when they hit on explosive substances, just like they'd been trained.

"Disney, seeeek."

Again, the same. Disney stood, moved forward, then stopped as if she was confused. She sat and stared at him.

Don't tell me I got the dud . . .

"Come on, Disney, seeeeeek!"

"Stop right there, handler!" Adams boomed, striding over. "Stop giving that command."

Jason froze. "Something's wrong. She looks confused."

Adams took one look at the situation. He seemed like a man who had seen it all.

"Is she? Did you handle your firearm this morning?" Adams demanded. "Any of the substances or sniffing containers? Did you touch anything in the Hot Training Aid area?"

Oh shit.

Jason's look must have said it all.

Adams pointed to the lead, a look of frustration and disappointment on his face. "Your hands are contaminated. The smell is all over the dog's lead, so she's hitting as soon as she gets the command. The dog is right. You're wrong."

"Sorry, sir. I—"

Adams cut him off sternly. "Go kennel your dog and

decontaminate your hands immediately. And take the lead with you." He shook his head. "Our little chat back there was a warning, Hernandez. But this is strike one. Now go."

As Jason headed for the bathroom, he could hear Adams saying to the others, "Let Handler Hernandez's mistake be a lesson to you all. Nothing will ruin a dog's future career faster than contamination. That's why we go to every possible length to keep the six explosive food groups separate, and we never, *ever*, mix them. If you pay a dog for hitting on the wrong smell at the wrong time, you can undo months of work."

As Jason made the long walk across the training floor, he kept thinking:

Well, Jase, looks like you fucked it up after all.

SHAWANDA

Two months ago

SHAWANDA JACKSON SAT in the hallway on a rickety wooden chair and stared at her hands. They were worn and calloused. Much older than her twenty-four years. They looked like her grandmother's hands. Hands that had seen hard labor. Hands that couldn't roll back the clock.

She ran her finger along a scratch on her palm. She hadn't felt it happen, but one of the dogs must have nicked her when they were playing in the training room. She had a new batch of puppies—the "E" litter—and she worked the dogs hard, training them on their commands for hours at a time. Didi liked to call her "Sarge," as in "Drill Sergeant," but Shawanda knew that dogs needed playtime to unwind and integrate all the lessons. You couldn't work a dog nonstop. They needed to breathe, to just be a puppy for a while.

That was an opportunity she never had, so she was damn sure the puppies would get it.

"Ms. Jackson?"

Shawanda looked up to see a young black woman in a tweed skirt standing in the doorway across the hall. She couldn't have been much older than Shawanda, but she seemed so young and clean. Like she'd never seen the streets.

"Yeah."

"They're ready to see you."

Shawanda smoothed her hands on her pant legs and forced a swallow.

Behind the well-dressed woman, another inmate walked out of the room and slunk down the hall. It was like an assembly line—one in, one out. Shawanda took a deep breath and walked across the hallway, knowing it was the threshold between her future and her past.

Inside the room, there were three men and two women seated behind a long table, each dressed in a suit or other professional clothes.

Shawanda tried to keep her pace measured as she walked to the lone chair in front of the table. Too fast, and she'd seem weak. Too slow, and she'd seem like a thug. Everyone was watching her. She knew the game—you had to play your part if you wanted to get ahead.

She sat in the chair and looked them all in the eye.

"Shawanda Jackson," the man in the center said, looking down at a file in front of him. "You come before this parole board requesting early release having served five years and four months of your ten-year sentence for aggravated battery and possession of narcotics with intent to distribute."

He said it like he was ordering a hamburger at McDonald's. Shawanda shifted on her chair.

"You are aware that these crimes are categorized as violent felonies and require seventy percent of the sentence before parole can be requested?"

Shawanda nodded. "Yes, sir."

"I see here that you have been commended for good behavior many times since you've been here at Bedford Hills. And with the exception of three minor infractions, your behavior while at this institution has been remarkable. I also see that you have taken up a leadership role in the Puppies Behind Bars program. Your file contains a very complimentary letter here from a Mrs. Errico, who states that you have done an exemplary job in that program." He looked up at her, peering over his glasses. "And you feel that you meet the standards for early parole?"

"Yeah. Uh, yes, sir. I do."

One of the ladies behind the table made a note on her legal pad.

"Can you tell us a bit about your experience with the Puppies Behind Bars program?" Another man asked. "How did you get involved with it?"

Shawanda tried to sit up straight. "Well, uh, you know, it just kinda happened. It was right after I got here. I saw this flyer one day in the cafeteria, and it said they were looking for a new person to help out with the dogs. I'd seen the other ladies around the prison with 'em before, but I never thought I'd be able to work on the program, you know. Everybody wants to be on it."

"But you were able to get assigned to the program?"

"Yeah, that's right. Got lucky, I guess."

"Did you have a passion for animals before this?"

"Not really," Shawanda said, uncomfortable under all of their gazes. "I mean, we never had no animals when I was growing up. My ma, she didn't like the mess."

"How do you feel about animals now that you've worked on the program for five years?"

For the first time in a long time, a shadow of a smile came to Shawanda's face. "I mean, I love 'em. They're everything to me."

To her surprise, the men and women on the other side of the table softened.

"It says here that you have helped raise and train four litters," the man continued, "and that your dogs have over a ninety percent acceptance rate into the Federal Canine Training program."

Shawanda paused. "Is . . . that good?"

"Yes, Ms. Jackson," the man replied with his own shadow of a smile. "That is very good."

The woman made another note.

There was a silence that opened up. Shawanda wasn't sure what it meant, but she didn't like it. These five people stood between her and her home—but what would she find when she got there? Chareece and Erikah would be in their twenties now, and little Isaac would be almost fifteen. They came to visit her once, during her first year inside, but they were sad and quiet and it didn't go well. They sent a few letters after that, saying that Isaac still needed medicine for his lungs and that things were tough. They were staying at their grandma's house in High Bridge, but she only had

Social Security and the wages from a few odd jobs—nowhere near enough to support a family of four.

But then the letters stopped, and Shawanda had no idea what was happening outside.

The man behind the desk took off his glasses and looked at Shawanda for a long, uncomfortable moment.

"You were arrested because you were involved in some pretty serious gang activity, Ms. Jackson. Your attorney at sentencing made it clear that you were not the main assailant in the battery of Mr. Samuels on the night of January 10th, 2014, but you were nonetheless involved in a beating that left a man fighting for his life. You were then arrested with three other individuals in a stolen car with four ounces of heroin packaged into one-hundred-and-eighteen bundles for distribution. You pleaded guilty to these charges, is that correct?"

Shawanda met his stare. No one had forced her to get in that car. No one had forced her to sling those bags of heroin. She had made her choices, and she had paid her dues.

"That's right. I took responsibility for my actions."

"And what assurances can you give this panel that you will not engage in these activities again should you be granted early release?"

Shawanda fell silent. She stared at her shoes for a long moment. There was a clump of Emma's yellow fur on her left toe. She was always the puppy in the "E" litter who shed the most.

"I can't change what I did," Shawanda said after many seconds had passed. "I did things that I thought were right at the time, but now I know I was wrong. My time in here has shown me that." She paused, her throat catching. "I was supposed to be the one to take care of my family. And I let them down. There ain't no way I can make that up to them, but I can at least try to make things better going forward. But I can't help them if I'm in here. I want to get back to my family, sir. And there ain't no way I'm going to jeopardize that again."

She forced herself to make eye contact even though her tears were threatening to fall.

"I ain't never going back to that life."

The parole board put their heads together for a moment, and then they asked her a few more questions. She provided a few more answers. The whole thing felt like a dream. And then, after ten minutes and an eternity had passed, she heard the words that she had hoped for and dreaded for so long.

"Shawanda Jackson, your parole is granted."

BRADFORD

12:17 p.m.
Federal Canine Training Facility
Front Royal, VA
August 2019

FOR ONCE, THE fresh air felt good on Bradford's face. He and the other handlers-in-training had been cooped up in the main training facility for weeks, running exercise after exercise. Most of the time the dogs had to sniff their way along cinderblock walls or training wheels or obstacle courses of unused paint cans, but today they were finally outside.

Adams had brought the handlers out to what he called "the back 40," which was in fact a three-hundred-acre tract of rolling hills and sunny fields behind the facility. Long before the federal government trained dogs here, and even before its time as a training camp in World War II, this piece of land was a horse farm and a fruit orchard. Bradford could even imagine Old General Stonewall Jackson marching his Army of Northern Virginia through these hills during the Civil War, gorging themselves on apples as they went.

The four handlers were gathered with their dogs on the side of a winding paved road that ran through the expansive property, not far from the canine memorial that was tucked back among the trees. The road was entirely within the training grounds, so they were the only souls in sight.

"Today we'll be conducting roadside searches," Adams said, standing next to an unmarked Ford Taurus from the early 2000s. Classic boring Fed car. "When it comes to firearm retrieval, this will be your primary mode of recovery. You'd be surprised how many guns get tossed from a car window, so this is one of the most important exercises we run here at NCD. Marshals and Border Patrol canine teams do these kinds of roadside sweeps all the time, and ATF is constantly getting called by the locals. Everyone will be doing roadside searches in one form or another—guns, shell casings, even roadside bombs." He turned to Cameron and gave one of those *this means you* looks.

Behind his Oakleys, Cameron's face was unreadable. Even though his hands were clasped together behind his waist, like a soldier at ease, Bradford could easily envision the M4 slung across this guy's chest, with one hand on the grip and his trigger finger alongside the frame, ready.

It was a full five seconds before Cameron replied. "We don't look for guns in Afghanistan. Just the guys that point them at us."

Sherry and Jason both looked at each other and smirked, like two high schoolers sharing a secret.

Bradford cracked a smile—not just at Cameron's jarhead BS, but at the sexual chemistry that Sherry was trying so hard to ignore. It had taken him some time, but Bradford was actually starting to like these people. Even macho-man Cameron McNeil.

Next to him, Deja also started to smile—or maybe the day's heat was making her pant.

"Why don't they just use a metal detector?" Jason asked, peeling his eyes off Sherry. "We use 'em all the time with the Marshals when we get a warrant on some fugitive's property. People bury all kinds of shit in their backyards."

"You ever seen the side of a highway, Hernandez?" Adams asked bluntly. "You know how much crap builds up along the side of a road? You wouldn't get five feet before that detector picked up every beer can, lug nut, hose clamp, and hubcap. A canine sweep is your only option."

Jason swatted at a fly on his neck.

"To search efficiently with the canine," Adams continued, "you want to zero in on where the gun would likely be. There's no point tromping through a cornfield if the firearm isn't there. Thankfully, there's only so far a gun can go when it's thrown from a moving vehicle. How far do you think that is?" He looked around, waiting for an answer.

"Seventy-five feet? Maybe?" Sherry fielded.

Adams shook his head. "Not even close. Anyone else?"

"One fifty," Cameron said, still standing like a soldier. "Tops."

"Wrong. From a vehicle moving fifty-five miles an hour, it has been scientifically proven that a gun can travel approximately thirty-five feet. That's it."

Jason did a fake cough that engulfed the word, "Bullshit."

"I shit you not, Marshal. Between the difficulty of getting

a good angle from the car's seat, the onrushing air, and the poor aerodynamics of the gun itself, it doesn't matter if you're a housewife or Tom Brady. That gun is only going to go about ten yards." He gave one of his rare smiles, his strong teeth flashing in the hot afternoon sun. "But don't take my word for it. Come on, let's take a ride."

And with that, he climbed in the driver's seat of the Taurus. The handlers all looked at each other in surprise, and their dogs felt the excitement in the air, their tails suddenly thumping on the pavement. Even Cameron couldn't keep the corners of his lips from turning upward.

Adams leaned out the window. "Who wants to go first?"

One by one, each handler was instructed to glove-up and climb in the backseat with their canine partner. Adams would get the car up to speed on the winding road and hand back a 9-millimeter Sig Sauer semi-auto, slide back and magazine out to show it was unloaded and safe. The handler would toss the gun from the passenger side out the open window. Some of them tried it like a frisbee, some did it underhand. Some put their fingers around the barrel, others around the handle.

Bradford went last. He knew a good baseball player could throw a ball three hundred feet from palm to glove. Bradford had played in college, but when he wound up and tried to fling it sidearm, he only got it twenty-five feet.

"Dammit," he swore as Adams stopped the car. He peeled off the latex glove that he'd worn when handling the gun. "It was this damn glove. I could've gotten it a lot farther if I was barehanded."

Adams smirked at him. "If you say so, Agent Bradford. Maybe next time we'll get a government convertible, that should help your distance. Now get out there and find that gun."

Bradford climbed out of the car with lead in hand. Deja dutifully hopped out right behind him.

"I swear it was the glove," he muttered as he bent down to make sure his disappointment didn't affect the dog.

Deja gave him a quick kiss on the cheek, as if to say, *I know. Now let's play hide and seek.*

He felt a stirring in his chest as he got to his feet, but he quickly set it aside. The corner of his eye caught the flag in the distance. He'd tried not to look at it ever since they'd first arrived, but he unconsciously looked to the canine memorial up on the hill, with its bronze statue of a Labrador, nose to the ground and on the job. He knew that the ashes of hundreds of retired law enforcement canines had been scattered there. Once a handler and canine were teamed up, they were together for the rest of the dog's natural life, even long after the canine retired from service. Like family.

Every time Bradford looked at the memorial, it made him wish he'd done more for Copper than stick an old wooden cross in the ground beside the cabin. How could he ever let another dog into his heart after Copper had already stolen it away for good? No—training a dog was like doing shooting drills at the range, caring for them like cleaning a gun. Love didn't need to factor into it. These dogs were different. They were government-owned. They weren't pets, and they most certainly were not hunting buddies. They were tools, placed on this earth to do a job. Plain and simple.

"Come on," he said to Deja. "Probably best that I wore that glove. I don't want you smelling *me* out there."

Bradford had spent the better part of the last decade training dogs, and he knew for certain that dogs were cheaters. It was no fault of their own—they were just hardwired to find the reward the easiest way possible. When he was training hunting dogs, it was the same thing. He'd go out into his backyard, walk to the edge of his property, and toss a dummy covered in duck scent out into the weeds. Then he'd bring the dog out, make it sit, and with a vertical flat hand, point the dog in the proper direction to find the training dummy. When training the more experienced dog, he'd deliberately send it off line. He'd smile and shake his head when the dog would put its nose to the ground, pick up *his* scent, and follow it to the spot where he threw the dummy, bounding into the weeds and getting a head start on the search pattern to find the reward. Conniving little bitches.

That's where distractor training came in, and that's why the class had spent hours over the last four weeks working with scent cans full of latex gloves and other smells Deja might associate with a person instead of an explosive. Any time Deja would get confused and sit in front of one of those cans, she wouldn't get fed. Over time, she slowly made the connection that those smells were not the ones she was looking for. That way, on an exercise like this, Deja would be searching for the gun not based upon the smell of the latex glove that Bradford had been wearing, nor any of his other smells, but only on nitrate esters, the "food group" associated with gunpowder.

He held Deja's leash tight as they stood by the side of the road, looking out over the tall grass moving in the hot breeze. She was alert, focused. He could see the intensity in her eyes, in her demeanor. He could tell this dog was a worker. Deja's look became even more intense as Bradford adjusted the kibble pouch attached to his utility belt, causing the dog's soft yellow floppy ears to move slightly upward. She really was one of the sharpest dogs he'd ever seen. It was just dumb luck that they'd been paired up, but had Bradford been given a choice, he would have picked Deja.

He glanced up at the memorial on the hill.

Don't you fall for her, Bradford. This pup is just a tool.

Then he said, "Seeeeeek," and Deja was off on the hunt.

SHERRY

3:57 p.m.
Federal Canine Training Facility
Front Royal, VA
September 2019

THE PHONE IN Sherry Fry's pocket buzzed like a mosquito that was out for blood. At first she paid it no attention, letting the texts go unread. Then the vibrations started signaling incoming calls that kept coming, sometimes late at night, just after her exhausted brain hit the pillow in the drab cinderblock dorm room. She knew who it was, but she still had to take a look to make sure it wasn't her mom or brother with a family emergency.

But the name always read *Darryl,* and because he never left a voice message, she would answer them occasionally. She and her husband of seven years would have a hollow conversation about how hot it was back in San Antonio or about how many hours she was putting in at the training facility. Sherry would tell him about what she and Dolly were working on, and he'd tell her about the latest detail he'd be assigned with the Federal Protective Service, but there would be miles of space between their words. A silence hovered around the edges, lurking, waiting to overtake them and force them to admit things they weren't ready to admit. Waiting to dig up a past they both would rather keep buried—but it was easier to ignore the past, just like it was easier to ignore the incoming call.

She didn't know if it was Darryl calling this time, but she didn't even bother to look. She silenced her phone in her pocket and focused again on Instructor Adams.

He was, as always, dressed in his dark blue BDU pants, combat boots, and a well-fitted gray polo. She'd never seen him with even a single hair out of place. Everything about the guy was tight-laced and by the book. Somehow, he didn't even break a sweat, not even when they were out in the blinding sun of the afternoon.

Over the last eight weeks, Sherry had developed a deep respect for the man. He was like a father to them as they tried to shepherd their pups from floppy-eared prospects to sharp-eyed explosives hunters. The whole process had been more challenging and more demanding than Sherry could have imagined, but she was grateful that Adams had been there to guide them.

"Your dogs are not invincible," he was saying. "They are flesh and blood, and out there in the field, they will rely on you to keep them safe. Remember, *you and only you* are responsible for the safety of your dog." He turned to Cameron. "McNeil, what does that mean in practice?"

The soldier reached down and petted Dover, who raised his head and nuzzled him back. "It means that we can always refuse a search if we deem the environment to be unsafe."

"That is correct," Adams said with a curt nod. "No matter what agency you work for or how pissed off your boss is, no matter how much pressure some cop puts on you to find evidence for *his* career case, a handler always has the final say if they conduct a search or not."

He's clearly never met Jimmy Gonzalez, Sherry thought, remembering all the ass-chewings her boss back in Quemado had given her over the years.

Just then, her phone buzzed again in her pocket. She knew the vibrations were always the same, but this one felt more insistent, as if Darryl was somehow trying to call harder.

Jesus Christ, Darryl, she thought, pressing the silence button as firmly as she could, hoping he'd feel it on the other side. *Just leave a fucking message.*

Sherry Fry sighed. Though she hated to admit it, she knew it was her fault. She had trained Darryl to keep calling like this—he knew that if he persisted long enough, eventually she'd answer. She suppressed a smile at the thought of Darryl, another helpless "D" name in the litter of pups. Instructor Adams had made it perfectly clear that feeding the dog even one time outside of a training context could ruin the dog's ability to work, and Sherry couldn't help but wonder if she'd ruined Darryl by answering after she had told him not to call. Maybe training a dog and living with a husband wasn't so different after all. Or maybe that was the problem—that everything in her life had been boiled down to routines and expectations. The irony was not lost on her that she had spent the last eight weeks instilling good habits in Dolly, and yet she couldn't even begin to build good boundaries in her own life.

Instructor Adams snapped up her attention. "This afternoon, we are going to be drilling on first aid procedures for you and your dog. Pay attention, because these next few hours could help save your dog's life out in the field."

He motioned for the training assistants, who came onto the training floor with stuffed dummies the same size and shape as their dogs. These medical practice dummies had airways and Velcro enclosures to simulate wounds. There were even bones that could be disengaged to simulate compound fractures. Their K-9 partners, kenneled up in their crates along the wall, curiously eyed the stuffed dummies being inspected by their human partners. Dolly couldn't take it anymore and let out a high-pitched whine followed by a deep bark. Dover followed suit with a series of low woofs.

Adams proceeded to show them how to hook up an IV in the field, either a saline drip in the tuft of fur between the shoulder blades if the dog got dehydrated in hot weather—something Sherry particularly made note of given her work on the border—but also plasma transfusions in veins, if necessary. They worked with the dummies first, then brought out the dogs.

"Dolly," she chided sweetly as Dolly kept licking her hands as she felt for the veins along the inside of the dog's front inner leg. Dolly always had a way of making her melt, even when they were supposed to be working. Sherry had never met a sweeter dog in her entire life. She'd had a dog growing up, a beagle named Butch, and her brother had a German Shepherd that was super smart. But Dolly was different. She was not only smart, but analytical. Sherry—who had been trained to decide in ten seconds if a person crossing the border was a dangerous smuggler or a nervous worker—could tell that before Dolly undertook a training problem, the dog would seemingly think it through. She would pause and weigh the options before forging forward. Sherry had never seen anything like it in a dog.

Adams then led the class through a series of scenarios with the dummies, starting with what to do in case the dogs were lacerated out in the field. He demonstrated proper bandaging techniques then moved on to larger wounds.

"The dog's belly is the most vulnerable part on its body," Adams was saying. He pulled his finger slowly up from his belt buckle to his stomach. "If a dog is climbing over rubble or debris, a shard of glass or piece of metal could open up them and eviscerate them on the spot. You need to be prepared and act quickly. Now grab your staplers."

Sherry's hands went clammy as she practiced stapling the dummy's stomach closed. Adams explained in nauseating detail how they needed to ensure that the intestines were pushed down and in while they stapled the wound closed with their other hand.

Dolly watched the whole thing with a curious expression on her face, her head turned sideways as Sherry worked.

Sherry tried to focus on the task—and tried even harder to not think about this happening to Dolly. They'd only been together for eight weeks, but already she couldn't imagine what she'd do if Dolly got hurt.

Thankfully they moved on to mouth-to-snout resuscitation after that, and Sherry was able to put the image of Dolly's blood on her hands out of her mind.

Clearly Jason also felt the need to lighten the mood, because he gave a sudden shout—"About time we got to the good stuff!"—and proceeded to hump the dummy.

"Hernandez!" Adams interjected with a tone of exasperation. "Knock that shit off."

Jason complied, but not before he cracked a smile at Sherry.

She laughed despite herself. It was the most juvenile thing she'd ever seen, but she'd grown accustomed to Jason and his middle-school antics. At first, he was nothing but annoying, but as she got to know him, she started to suspect that there was more going on beneath the surface than Jason Hernandez let on.

Just then, her phone buzzed again.

Without missing a beat, Sherry Fry took it out of her pocket and turned it off completely.

BRADFORD

8:57 p.m.
Federal Canine Training Facility
Front Royal, VA
September 2019

IT HAD BEEN another long day on the training field, and Thomas Bradford was beat. But when Jason knocked on his dorm-room door and suggested running into town to grab a beer with him and Sherry, Bradford found it hard to say no. After all, he'd been working with these people for nine weeks. They had developed an understanding that only comes when you spend countless hours in the presence of the same people.

"You two head out," Bradford said, wanting to take a quick shower. "I'll meet you there."

He took a quick two-minute rinse, got dressed in jeans and a t-shirt, then got Deja situated in her kennel. She looked like she didn't want him to leave, but she didn't protest as she lay down in her crate.

"Good girl," he said softly.

Car keys in hand, he stepped out into the hallway. He was halfway down when he spotted Cameron, climbing the stairs with a bag of cheap Mexican takeout.

"Hey, Cameron," Bradford called out. "The rest of us are grabbing a beer down in Winchester. You wanna join?"

Cameron's expression didn't change.

"Hernandez already asked me," was all he said as he beelined for his room.

There was something in his answer that set Bradford on edge. It had been weeks of the silent treatment, and Bradford had had enough. He called down the hall, "You got a problem, McNeil?"

This drew Cameron to a stop. He paused at his doorway, then cast a look at Bradford.

"What did you say?"

"I said, do we have a problem? We've been here for weeks and you've said, like, ten words to us."

"And your point is?"

Bradford bristled but tried to level with him "You don't want to be here? Well, you're not the only one. Man up, and make the best of it."

Cameron moved the Mexican food to his other hand and opened the door to his room. Apparently he hadn't kenneled Dover, and the dog rushed into the doorway to meet him.

"Look, Bradford, with all due respect, I was assigned to this detail, and that's the end of it. Once we pass our certification, I'm heading back out into a warzone while you get a cush job sweeping football stadiums. So I'll skip all the getting-to-know-you BS."

And with that, he stepped inside and shut the door.

Bradford blew a jet of air through his nostrils.

I guess that's what I get for trying to play nice, he thought as he made his way down the stairs to his car. What an asshole.

CAMERON

6:23 a.m.
Federal Canine Training Facility
Front Royal, VA
September 2019

CAMERON MCNEIL CLIMBED into the waiting van with sand in his eyes. Not even his Oakleys could spare him the sharp pain of the early morning sun. In the Marines, getting up at the asscrack of dawn was standard operating procedure—but that was a lifetime ago. After nine weeks of the same van ride with the same people to the same training facility, each and every morning without fail, Cameron McNeil found himself fantasizing about sleeping in until noon.

Enough of this groundhog day shit, he thought as he settled into the seat, nursing the same watery coffee as always from the single-cup coffee maker next to the sink in the dorm.

"Hey there, sunshine," Jason said as Cameron and Dover slid in next to him. "Missed you at the bar last night."

"What are you all smiles about?" Cameron asked, taking a sip of coffee. How he wished he had a smoke to go with it. The two siblings, Dover and Disney, sniffed each other's ears, their whip-like tails beating against the backs of the front seats.

Their early morning energy made Cameron feel even shittier.

Jason shrugged. "Just another beautiful day in paradise." He bent his face close to Disney and rubbed her sloppy cheeks. "Isn't that right, sweetheart," he said in his gooiest voice. "Isn't that right. We love only getting four hours of sleep. Yes we do. *Yes we do*."

"You're nuttier than squirrel shit," Cameron said flatly. "You know that?"

From the back, Sherry suppressed a laugh. Cameron was surprised she was even listening. Most mornings she was totally engrossed in her phone. Rumor around the facility was things were not so hot back in the Fry household. But unlike the others, Cameron had no interest in learning about these people's lives. As far as he was concerned, they were momentary distractions until he got back to the mission— back to Afghanistan.

Bradford was the last to arrive, trotting over from the dog run located next to the dormitory building. The driver fired up the van once he and Deja had climbed inside. Cameron made it a point not to look in his direction.

Bradford didn't say a word about the night before.

I guess he finally got the message. Good. That old man needs to mind his own business.

The van trundled out of the dormitory parking lot and took the same route to the training facility about two miles away.

But once they passed the security gate, they instead took a left turn and headed out on one of the private back roads behind the facility.

"Not starting in the classroom today?" Jason said, leaning over the driver's shoulder.

"Nope, range day," was all the driver said in reply.

In minutes, the van pulled into a gravel parking lot next to a wide field surrounded by tall green trees. The grass was cut short and bare spots were spread out in no apparent pattern. Some of the spots revealed different-sized craters. This was the training facility's explosive range.

Instructor Adams and several of the trainers had already arrived and set up. With them was Chief Petty Officer Marcus Wade, U.S. Navy Explosive Ordnance Disposal, retired. Chief Wade, a civilian contractor, presented the explosives class the first week of the training program. The guy was probably sixty but looked forty, rugged and fit, right out of central casting. He mentioned that he was a diver charged with recovering ordnance from the ocean floor. Definitely the guy you wanted on your side during a bar fight.

The handlers and the dogs stepped out of the van and joined Adams and Wade and the other trainers. Thankfully someone had set up a folding table with some decent coffee and donuts.

"Good morning, handlers," Adams said as they ate and drank. "Today we're going to be doing live detonations. You've studied these materials for weeks, and each of your dogs has done admirably in seeking out these compounds and obeying your commands. Now we need to put their startle reflexes to the test—and show you what these compounds can do in practice rather than in theory.

"The startle reflex can bounce the best dog from the academy straight into someone's home—hopefully in a new role as a service or comfort animal, but more often, because of the stress, just as a pet. Many a pure-bred hunting dog have had their careers ended because of this dreaded condition. Back in the prison training program, the raisers were instructed to clap, stomp their feet, or make some type of sharp noise to start the conditioning. Here at the NCD facility, the trainers first employed cap pistols, then moved onto blank cartridges in larger and larger caliber guns. Just like all their odor training, conditioning the dogs for loud noises was done gradually and with repetition. Too much too fast could have induced a bad reaction. Before you arrived, we even took the dogs to the Fourth of July parade in Winchester so they could acclimatize to the loud reports from fireworks. We did everything we could to prepare the dog to keep working in the most challenging conditions like parades, sporting events, and even combat, if necessary."

Chief Wade stood behind the table covered with different types of ordnance—commercial explosives on the left and military on the right. All of the substances they had studied for weeks.

Wade started with a demonstration card that held different types of dummy detonators. "Detonators, or as we call them in the military, blasting caps, contain primary high explosive, similar to the nitroglycerine like you used to see in the old Western movies. Primary explosives are the most sensitive and the most susceptible to heat, shock, and friction. It's also the classification of certain types of homemade explosives like triacetonetriperoxide, or TATP, and all your peroxide-based bombs. Very bad stuff." He went on, "While this stuff is an effective high explosive, its sensitivity makes it impracticable for use in the field, as they could easily be set off inadvertently."

He motioned to the table, with the familiar blocks of C4, military TNT, and sticks of commercial dynamite.

"That is where these secondary high explosives come in. These are less-sensitive materials that can be stored and handled with relative safety. They will only generate an explosion when triggered by a shockwave from a detonator. In other words, secondary explosives are safe to handle and safe to train with. You will be issued secondary high explosives when you depart the academy for daily training with your canines. When you are not training with these items, they will be stored in an explosives magazine that will be shipped to your duty stations upon your graduation from the academy. That being said, always treat these materials with respect, but without a detonator, you really just have a stick of chemicals." Wade waived around a stick of trenchrite like it was a tube of Jimmy Dean breakfast sausage.

Lastly, he motioned to a white sack that looked like a

long sandbag.

"And finally, we have our tertiary explosives, or blasting agents, like ammonium nitrate fuel oil, or ANFO. Blasting agents like ANFO are the most stable, so they are used widely in industrial or commercial applications like mining or demolition. It requires both a primary shockwave from a blasting cap and secondary explosion from a high explosive to set it off. They are by far the most stable of all the explosive energetic material."

Wade immediately keyed upon the obvious looks on the students' faces and continued to brief the class. "What happened in Oklahoma City in 1995 was that McVey and Nichols used about three thousand pounds of this shit to bring down most of that building. The terrible end result was the murder of one-hundred-and-sixty-eight innocent people. They obtained the chemicals from a farming supply store. ANFO is nothing more than fertilizer mixed with diesel fuel—keep that in mind. Out of all the explosive training you have received during your time here, you need to recognize how easy it is for assholes to make bombs. You and your partners are the only thing that stands between innocent citizens and those who would do great harm."

With that, Wade stepped away from the table and headed to the range control tower.

Adams motioned them all to step forward to where several concrete lane dividers had been erected along the edge of the field. One of the trainers started handing out ear and eye protection. Cameron waved away the clear goggles, preferring to keep his ballistic Oakleys firmly in place.

"That brings us to today's demonstration," Adams continued. "When it comes to explosive materials, the main consideration is the balance between volatility and stability. Military-grade explosives are low-oxygen and highly stable, and they generate a black cloud on detonation. Most of your homemade bombs, or the improvised explosive devices cooked up by terrorists and militias around the world, are often peroxide-based, which makes them oxygen-rich and highly unstable. They will produce the biggest bang and the distinctive white cloud. You can spot the difference a mile away."

As he listened, Cameron noticed that his hands were starting to shake. The memory that he tried to keep buried was pushing its way to the surface, refusing to be ignored. Behind his Oakleys, Cameron watched as the white mushroom cloud rose into the blinding Yemeni sky, towering over the State Department complex that had just been leveled. He took off his glasses and rubbed his eyes, trying to chase away the memory, but it fought him like a stubborn stain that wouldn't fade.

"Let's get into position and demonstrate these explosives in action," Adams said.

Cameron's heart was suddenly pounding in his chest. He had gone from calm to panicked in the space of a single breath. He held Dover's leash tight, feeling like the world was tilting beneath his feet.

"Everybody set?" Adams asked once the group had assembled behind one of the concrete barriers. "Chief Wade, the range is yours."

Over the staticky PA system, Wade's voice crackled, "The range is hot. Detonation in three, two, one."

The flash was bright but there was no sound. Milliseconds later, the pressure wave hit the center of Cameron's chest like a quick shove from one of his Marine buddies when he wasn't looking. The ground rumbled and the loose dust that laid upon it became airborne, immediately followed by the sharp sonic boom. But something was terribly wrong. Why was there a person out there? Wait, there were several people walking near the seat of the large blast. Cameron saw burning truck parts rise high into the cloudless sky. He quickly stood up from his place of safety and wanted to shout out, warn them, but it was too late. It had already happened, and there was nothing he could do.

Suddenly he was back in Yemen, his ears ringing and dripping blood, dust blinding his eyes, sand and rocks and the debris of falling buildings pelting his CIA standard-issue black baseball hat. That white cloud towered over him, mocking him, telling him that he had failed. He scrambled through the dirt as fires erupted all around him. He saw the charred carcass of the Nissan Atlas truck, smoldering in the shattered heart of the compound. Even though his eardrums had been blown out, he could still hear the cries of the Yemeni and American civilians trapped and dying beneath the rubble. All because he hadn't done his job . . .

"McNeil?"

Cameron drew a ragged breath, and he found himself back in Front Royal, Virginia, sprawled on his ass in the bright morning sunlight.

Adams and the other handlers and the trainers were all gathered around him, looking down at him in concern.

But then Dover was there, coming to his aid, licking his face and nuzzling him back into the world. Like always, Dover had known where he had gone. Like always, Dover helped bring him back.

"Jesus, you alright, Cameron?" Jason asked, offering a hand.

"I'm fine," Cameron said, climbing to his feet without anyone's help. Dover was still glued to his side. "Just lost my footing is all."

Adams gave him a sideways glance. "And here I was thinking the dogs would startle. You good to go?"

He nodded. "Good to go, sir." But Cameron was still a thousand miles away. Only Dover by his side kept his feet on the ground.

SHAWANDA

Three weeks ago

HOW COULD ONE neighborhood change so much in five years? At first glance, High Bridge was still a bad part of the Bronx, but things were different. The brick walkups still looked tired and run down, but some of the bodegas and pawnshops had given way to cafes and juice bars. The boys on the corners and down the alleys were still rough, but on some streets Shawanda saw white women walking their dogs, as if the hood had completely evaporated from one block to the next. The city she knew so well—the city where she had been raised, the city where her parents had died, the city where she had made all of her mistakes—Shawanda Jackson hardly recognized it anymore.

She had her hands deep in her pockets as she walked down the familiar unfamiliar streets. New York was in the grips of a late summer, but she wore a baggy hoody that hid her body and her muscles and the small scratch marks that covered her hands and forearms. They were the last gifts the puppies from "E" litter had given her before she signed her parole papers and walked out the front door, but Shawanda never wanted those scratches to fade. She didn't want anyone to see them, either, so she kept them hidden beneath the sweatshirt. Those were her memories. No one else's.

Shawanda turned down one of the streets close to her grandmother's home. Her shoes felt strange on her feet. For years she had hated the prison-issue boots that made all the women look like lumberjacks, but now that she was back in the same pair of Nikes that she'd worn when she'd surrendered to Bedford Hills five years ago, she suddenly found them to be too loose, as if there was no support at all. As if she were falling straight down through the pavement.

She sped up down the street, passing by a new shiny condo with clean windows and a gym on the bottom floor. *What are they all running from?* she wondered as the sweaty bodies pounded the treadmills in the corner of her eye. She passed the old Chinese restaurant, and the old laundromat, and the alley where she and her boyfriend Jerome and two other teenagers had beaten a man nearly to death.

Before she knew it, she came to the small duplex where her grandmother lived. The gentrification had not made its way to this block. The narrow rowhouse was looking worse for wear, and the adjacent house looked completely abandoned, with graffiti and plywood over the windows. She walked up the creaky wooden steps, stepped under the sagging eaves, and let herself inside.

All the familiar smells came back to her. It was almost like going home.

"Wanda!" a voice cried out.

Shawanda had hardly made it through the door before her baby sister Erikah launched herself from the sofa and wrapped her in an embrace. Shawanda stiffened. It had been so long since she'd been touched, but Erikah didn't let go.

"Hey, sis," Shawanda said.

Erikah pulled away and rubbed away her tears, smearing her eyeliner. "Oh my god, I'm so glad you're here! I can't hardly believe it's you. When I got your letter, I got so excited that you was getting out! I thought it'd be a few more years."

"Well, you know, good behavior and all that," Shawanda said. The discomfort was almost unbearable. She looked around the house, trying to look anywhere but at her crying sister.

The house was trashed.

"I'm so sorry I didn't write," Erikah was saying, still crying and touching Shawanda. "I'm a terrible sister."

"No, no, don't blame yourself," Shawanda found herself replying. She didn't blame Erikah. After all, Shawanda herself had stopped writing two years into her sentence. There was only so much that could be said.

Erikah was starting to tremble. She was only fourteen when Shawanda had seen her last, but now she thought her baby sister looked so much older than her nineteen years.

"No, I shoulda done more," Erikah sobbed. "I shoulda been there for you."

"It's alright. You had to look after you."

Shawanda was starting to get antsy. She wanted to change the subject.

"Where's Isaac? He around?"

"He's at school."

That was a relief. Shawanda had worried about her baby brother every day she was in prison, wondering if his cystic fibrosis was getting worse. Wondering if they could afford all the doctor's bills that surely kept piling up.

"How's he doing?" Shawanda asked. "Must be in high school by now."

"Yeah, sophomore. He's alright. He's got this medicine that seems to help, but you know how it is. There's bad days and not so bad days."

Shawanda nodded, her heart starting to ache. "Where's moms?"

Erikah tucked a braid of hair behind her ear. "She's upstairs. Sleeping."

Shawanda blinked at her. "It's eleven o'clock. Moms don't ever sleep past six."

"She's not doing so good," was all Erikah said.

Shawanda knew it was worse than her baby sister was letting on. Her grandmother had always kept a tidy house, just like her mother had, but the place was now in shambles. Broken furniture. Discarded beer bottles. Trash piled in the corners. Something wasn't right.

"I'm so glad you're here," Erikah said, mirroring Shawanda as she looked at the disarray. "Chareece's been hittin' it pretty hard."

"What about me?"

A young woman had appeared in the doorway to the kitchen, arms folded across a lean chest. She had the same round face as Erikah and Shawanda, but there was an edge to her that Shawanda immediately recognized—an edge forged on the streets.

"Sup, Reecy."

"What's up with you," her sister replied, still in the doorway. "They let you out early or something?"

"Girl, you trippin," Erikah said. "Didn't you hear me when I told you she was coming home? I gave you her letter to read."

Chareece sucked her teeth. "Shit, I ain't about to read no letter. If Wanda wanted to talk to us, she woulda kept calling."

"Reecy, come on," Erikah protested. "You know it ain't like that. She—"

Shawanda interrupted her. After everything she'd been through, she wasn't about to let her baby sister stand up for her.

"Nah, it's all good, sis," she said to Erikah. "Reecy's alright to be mad."

A silence settled on the house as the three sisters stood there in the half-ruined living room.

"The place looks different than the last time I saw it," Shawanda said finally.

"Reecy and her man Tariq have been hanging out,"

Erikah said, not hiding the accusation in her voice. "Their crew is always up in here, and they don't take care of shit."

Chareece rolled her eyes.

"Tariq?" Shawanda demanded. "Tell me you ain't still hanging out with that boy."

"You don't know shit about him," Chareece fired back. "He takes care of me. Takes care of all of us. When you left, moms had to get a second job working nights, but then she got sick and couldn't work. Someone had to step up and take care of this family. Someone had to look after our baby boy, 'cuz you sure as hell ain't."

"What'd you want me to do, Reecy? Send you my ramen packets from commissary? What good was that gonna do?"

"All I know is, you wasn't around. Isaac needed me, so I stepped up."

Shawanda didn't like where this was heading. She knew Tariq was trouble back when he was just a sixteen-year-old hustling on the corners. She didn't want to think what he might be up to now—or what he was getting Chareece roped into.

Shawanda knew that path all too well. It was one she had taken herself. One she hoped she would never have to take again.

Shawanda's head was starting to pound, and she abruptly needed some air.

"Wait, where you going?" Erikah said as Shawanda stepped out the door. "You just got here."

Shawanda put her hands in her pockets and made her way down the front steps. "I'm gonna get some food. I'll be back in a bit."

And with that, she set back out onto the streets.

Nothing felt right out here in the real world, and she suddenly found herself missing the life she'd left behind in Bedford Hills. She missed the puppies with a fierceness that overwhelmed her. Life was simple when all she had to think about was her dogs. It was the one thing she could be proud of.

For a brief moment, she entertained the hope that she could get a job working at a pet store or something, something that would get her close to dogs again. Something to support her family and get them back on the right track.

But then she thought about Latisha's taunts all those months ago in the laundry room. Maybe Latisha had been right—no one out here gave a shit about what she'd done with those dogs. No one would give her a job just because she raised puppies behind bars. It wouldn't change the fact that she was an ex-convict, living life on the edge. As much as it pained her to admit, she had to face the facts: she had raised dogs to be police, and that made her a target out here on the streets. She would have to keep that part of her life hidden.

She walked with no destination in mind, treading her old neighborhood, tracing the fading scratches on her arm.

It was only her first day of freedom, and Shawanda Jackson already could feel her old life starting to pull her back in.

JASON

9:57 p.m.
Lou's Tavern
Winchester, VA
October 2019

"I CALL BULLSHIT!" Jason shouted, his voice cutting over the drawling country song that poured from the speakers. His beer jumped as he slapped the table. Down the bar, a few plaid-wearing construction workers shot unfriendly glances their way. Even though the handlers had been in town for months now, they were still "the feds" as far as the locals were concerned. They had not exactly been welcomed with open arms, but all of that would soon be behind them.

Tomorrow they would take their final exam, and somehow Jason had convinced them to come out and blow off some steam and celebrate before their last day. Sherry and Bradford were game, but Cameron shut the door to his dorm room in Jason's face. It was his loss.

Jason lowered his voice and leaned over their table.

"Like I said, I call bullshit. There's no way you arrested five drug runners all by yourself."

Sherry smirked and took a satisfied sip of her Coors. "Swear to god."

Bradford was sitting across the table, and he laughed as

Jason screwed up his face. The marshal's brain could hardly process what Sherry was telling them.

"But . . ." Jason stammered. "How does that even work? You've only got two hands. And those guys all had guns, right?"

"Sure did."

"How long before backup arrived?" Bradford asked as he took another handful of bar nuts.

"About five, ten minutes."

"And you cuffed them all yourself?"

"I used zip ties on three of them, but yes, I did."

Jason whistled and ran his hands through his hair.

"What, you surprised or something?" Sherry asked, taunting him. He loved it when she looked at him like that. "Didn't you bag like forty fugitives in that hotel ballroom?"

"Well, yeah, but . . . But I had *help*. It's not like I busted out forty sets of cuffs and took them all down myself."

Sherry shrugged and smirked again. "Then it looks like I win."

Bradford laughed again. "I think she's got you beat."

"I'd say," Jason said, leaning back in his chair. "You're a badass, you know that?"

He gave Sherry another one of his winning smiles and toasted her with his beer. There was no doubt that Sherry Fry was one tough woman, but for a moment, he thought he saw a bit of a blush appear on her cheeks as he smiled at her. Maybe—just maybe—he had a chance.

"So what about you, Bradford?" Jason asked, knowing better than to try his luck with Sherry just yet. "What's the craziest thing you've ever done on the job?"

"Me? Well, nothing as exciting as that."

Jason would not settle for that answer. "Oh, come on. I always wished I woulda put my X in the ATF box. You guys do more undercover than all the other agencies put together."

Sherry decided to also goad Bradford into a war story. "I don't see Tom here as the UC type," she said. "I mean, where's the long hair, beard, tat sleeves?"

With a wry smile, Thomas Bradford addressed his doubters. "Never judge a book by its cover." He took a long sip of his beer, and to Jason's surprise, began to regale them.

"A few years back," Bradford said, "there was a huge influx of shiny new guns all over the far south side of Chicago. Not only the gang-bangers, but everyone—and I mean everyone—was carrying, from school kids to grandmas. All the serial numbers had been professionally removed, and they ground those bitches down deep. Every time we recovered one, the lab did their best, but they came up empty every time.

"One day, we grabbed a guy who popped a convenience store owner and fled with eight cartons of Marlboros. Same old story. Serials numbers ground down. But this time the lab was able to come up with a partial number. After tracing every gun with that possible combination of numbers and backtracking every single one, we got a positive trace. The guns were coming from a pawn shop in Arkansas, so I headed down there and hooked up with the boys from the Little Rock office. They knew the shop. Junior's Pawn Shop in Bald Knob, Arkansas. It was owned by Junior Polk, all three-hundred pounds of him."

Sherry set down her beer and leaned forward. "This has got *Deliverance* all over it."

Of course, Jason couldn't pass up the opportunity to be a smart ass. "You know you got a real pretty mouth, Bradford."

Bradford gave a mock laugh and continued. "Sixty miles north of the Little Rock ATF office, we pulled in behind an abandoned warehouse just outside of Bald Knob. The senior agent, a good ol' boy named Walter-Glenn Jordan, looked at me and basically said, 'Step back, Yankee, we got it from here.' Now, we got this thing in Chicago: you catch a runner, you cuff him. You do the case, you bash the door. The same goes for undercover work. You develop the suspect, you do the UC. Jordan knew he wasn't going to win this battle. He actually started laughing and said, 'This should be entertaining.' They wired me up, and as I got in my Alamo rental car, he said in his deep southern drawl, 'We're going to have to stage pretty far away 'cuz this is a small town. I hope they don't beat your Northern ass too much before we get in there to rescue you.'"

Sherry interrupted, "Wait a minute. You at least put on some overalls, right? Maybe a straw hat or something?"

"Nope. I went in just like I got off the plane. Khaki pants, blue polo, and a gray windbreaker. I was taught that the closer you stick to the real you, the more believable you'll be. There's no way I coulda said I was from down there. My plan was to say I was from Chicago, visiting my wife's relatives a few towns over, and I was telling family members that I'd like to get a gun or two to take back home for protection."

Sherry followed up with a look of disbelief. "And you honestly thought that he was going to believe that story?"

"The one thing these guys have in common is they all want cash. Even the ones you arrest right after the deal say, 'Man, I knew you were a cop.' They talk themselves out of their suspicions because they want to close the deal and make their money.

"So I stroll into this dirty, crappy pawnshop, and behind the counter is a young hillbilly chick with bad teeth. She couldn't have been more than sixteen, and I ask her if Junior was around. She tells me he's in the pool hall across the street. Great. I could almost hear the Little Rock boys laughing from there. They were probably figuring out the over-and-under on how many times these hicks were going to shoot me. As I take the long walk across the street, my mind is churning up all these different scenarios about what could happen next. I decided to stick with my story.

"As I walked up to the open door, I see four guys standing around a pool table. Two young, two old. The doorway blocked my view, but there had to be at least a couple more in there. Along the wall to the right of the pool table, sitting on a tall stool, was a big man in his forties. Had to be Junior. I took a deep breath and whispered into the wire that I was entering the hall and that I saw at least five males.

"As I walked into the hall in my city slicker outfit, every eye turned to me. I was waiting for that scratch-across-a-record sound that instantly stops the music, followed by complete silence and crickets chirping."

Sherry and Jason broke the tension with a laugh.

"I walk in, and to nobody in particular, I say, 'I'm looking for Junior.' Big man slides his fat ass off the chair and strolls over and says, 'I'm Junior, whatchu want?' He's eying me up and down, no doubt checking out my Dockers. Turned out there were three more tobacco-spittin' mother-fuckers by the other pool table and a bartender reading the paper. This was it, do or die. I spoke up loud and clear and told him, 'I'm from outta town and I was asking around where I can get a piece, and everyone says I gotta see Junior.' I swear, it seemed like ten minutes before Junior bellows out, 'You've come to the right place,' and starts walking toward the door. I followed. Everyone in the joint went back to doing what they were doing."

Sherry's jaw dropped, "That's it? You mean, he accepted you that easy? Is this guy an idiot or what?"

Bradford shook his head. "UC work isn't like how it is in the movies. Junior wasn't an idiot, he just wanted to close a sale. When he saw me, he probably thought he could take me to the cleaners on an over-priced Colt. If you act like yourself, people don't suspect you. They have their own filters on the world, and in Junior's world, I was an easy mark.

"So anyway, on the walk over to the pawnshop, he asked where I was from but never asked who my 'relatives' were or where they lived or anything. So I go into the shop and he brings me in the back room and shows me a shitload of guns. I ended up walking out with six guns, all with ground-out serial numbers. The dude was brazen. He was probably the sheriff's brother or something and had no fear of getting caught. Oh, and the sixteen-year-old? Turned out that was Junior's wife. Can't get more trailer trash than that."

"Did you arrest him on the spot?" Jason asked.

"Nah, I left that up to the Little Rock boys at the proper time. We needed to identify all the gun-runners first, see who was helping Junior, then see what the US Attorney wanted to do. In the end, they all went to prison."

Sherry still wore a look like she couldn't believe it. "So, you walk in looking like a fed and he just sells to you?"

"It's not always that easy. One time I was buying an M-60 from a guy who was stealing them from the military. This guy was not only hinked up, he was smart. He wanted to see my wallet, he wanted to see my keys, he wanted me to lift my shirt. I told him I wasn't carrying. He said, 'I don't give a fuck if you're carrying. Hell, I got three guns on me right now, I want to see if your wearing a wire.' Then he wanted to see my belt to see if it had scuff marks from where a cop carries his gun and badge."

Jason asked, "Why the keys? What was he looking for?"

"I asked him that, he said he was looking for a handcuff

key. This asshole was scary. Needless to say, I was trained by ATF agents who were the best at UC. The guy that trained me infiltrated the Hell's Angles. I learned to go over everything from head to toe before going in."

"What about your wire?"

"No worries there. I had a tiny camera inside a shirt button and a transmitter in my watch. No more taped wires to your chest. That's old school. We used to use special cell phones but someone ran into a guy that wanted all cell phones left in the cars. So, the techs had to come up with something new."

Bradford concluded his story, and just as fast, his mood swung the other way. He sat there for a moment, staring into his beer. Jason could almost see his mind working, thinking about his long and storied career—a career that, somehow, never took him into management. Jason had done some digging on each of the handlers before they arrived in Front Royal, and he knew that Thomas Bradford had been up for promotion three or four times, but always turned it down.

Jason had always wanted to know why, and now that he had a few beers in him, he figured now was as good a time as any.

"So, Bradford, I gotta know. Why'd you never move up into management in ATF? I mean, the paygrade must have been, what, a GS-14 step seven? We're talking six digits." Jason took another swig. "Why'd you give that up just to stay a field agent?"

Bradford was quiet for a long time, and Jason suspected

he'd touched a nerve. You didn't hunt down fugitives for a living without recognizing when someone wanted to run from their past. And he had a sneaking suspicion it had something to do with the former Ms. Bradford.

"I just like it better out in the field," Bradford said finally. "I like being in the thick of it. Driving the mahogany squad car all day, managing other agents' caseloads, dealing with the pinheads in the front office, that's a special kind of hell for a guy like me."

Sherry smiled. "So you're a real lawman at heart."

"Well, I don't know about that. I know it sounds hokey, but I really want to make the world a better place by getting the idiots that ruin it for everyone out of society for a while. I'll leave the management to the guys who wear the suits."

"So why'd you apply to the canine program?" Jason asked. "I heard you applied a few years back but didn't make it in."

Bradford looked up at him. "How'd you know about that?"

"Come on, I can sniff a fire hydrant for information, too. Figured I better know who I was up against."

Bradford clearly didn't like people rooting around in his private life, but he shrugged all the same. "Yeah, I applied a few years back, but it all got wrapped up in a bunch of red tape. Then a few months ago, I get the call, out of the blue. Next thing I know, I'm packing my bags and heading out here to spend every waking minute with you assholes."

"Well, I for one am glad you're here," Sherry said. "It's been amazing watching you with Deja. You clearly have a connection with that animal."

Bradford drained his beer. "You've trained one dog, you've trained 'em all. They're just like any other tool. If they could invent a small portable bomb-sniffing machine that could analyze odor in a hundredth of a second, it would be more efficient and cheaper than our dogs."

Jason suddenly felt like he'd been punched in the gut. All evening he'd been missing Disney, who he knew was waiting patiently for him to return to their drab dorm room. She had wagged her way straight into his heart.

"How can you even say that?" Jason shot back. "Machine? *These machines* have emotions, they have heart. They're living beings, just like you or me. They're not some hammer you can just toss in your toolbox when you're done."

"All I'm saying is that working dogs have a job to do," Bradford said, "just like we've got our jobs. It doesn't need to get any more complicated than that. Besides, if you start worrying about *their* emotions and feelings, you're going to miss what you're looking for."

Jason's bullshit detector was starting to go off again, but he was in too good of a mood to get into it with Bradford. So instead he laughed and drained his beer in kind.

"You've got a heart of stone, man. Shit, even Cameron gets all melty when Dover gives him a kiss. You see him out on the range the other day? It looked like that dog was the only thing he cares about in this world."

"Speaking of our absent CIA buddy," Sherry said, dropping her voice conspiratorially. "What'd you find out about him? You know, in this fancy database of yours."

Jason shook his head. "Very little. Dude's like a ghost. He was in the Marines, did a few tours in Iraq. Picked up a Bronze Star. He was honorably discharged in 2011, but after that, his file is paper-thin. He did some work in Budapest contracting for the State Department, but there's nothing about that detail, or the one he's working now in Afghanistan."

"Definitely CIA," Sherry said.

"Definitely," Jason agreed.

Bradford pushed himself back from the table. "Ok, Sherlock. You too, Holmes. I'm going for another round. You two want another?"

"No, two is plenty for me," Sherry said. She smoothed her hands on her pants. Jason could tell she was nervous about their big exam. "I want to be sharp for tomorrow."

Bradford nodded and pointed at Jason.

"Sure, get me another Heineken."

And with that, Jason was finally alone with Sherry.

But just as fast, she was on her phone, texting with a frown on her face. It seemed like she was on it whenever she had a spare moment, and it never seemed to make her very happy.

"Trouble at home?" he asked, surprised by his own directness. He guessed the liquid courage was kicking in.

She slipped the phone back into her purse and sighed.

"Sorry. Yeah. I was just texting with my husband."

Jason winced internally. *Ouch. Dropping the H-bomb right off the bat. Maybe this isn't such a good idea, Jase . . .*

But the three Heinekens were already fast at work, and Jason decided to try his luck.

"I don't mean to pry, and you can tell me to take hike if it's none of my business, but it looks like things aren't going so well."

Sherry gave a short, wry chuckle. "Yeah, you could say that. With my job and his work with FPS, we never seem to be in the same place at once. We haven't seen each other in months." She sighed again, her eyes distant. "We never really talked about it, you know. It just kind of . . . happened. And now—well, I don't know what's gonna happen next."

Jason took a deep breath.

"Does he make you happy?"

Sherry gave him a surprised look. Then the corners of her mouth turned up.

"Go take a hike."

Jason laughed. "Fair enough." He was glad Bradford was still at the bar, but he could use that next Heineken right about now. "Look, I know we probably shouldn't mix our personal lives with work, but if you ever want to talk about it, I'm here for you. I've been told I'm an excellent listener."

She softened. "Thanks, Jase."

He ratcheted his courage and gave his most charming smirk. "I've also been told I'm a great kisser. Probably not as good as Dover, but definitely up there."

To his great relief, she laughed loudly.

"So what do you say?" he asked.

Bradford was making his way back to their table, and Sherry looked at Jason with glittering eyes.

"Let's just get through tomorrow. Then we'll talk."

BRADFORD

8:32 a.m.
Federal Canine Training Facility
Front Royal, VA
September 2019

"HANDLERS, YOU'VE MADE it to the very end."

Instructor Adams was standing in the center of the classroom, looking as commanding as ever. His three assistants and a new person the handlers had never seen before were all lined up alongside him, and the tension in the air was palpable. Today was the day. It all came down to this. Every morning, the van dropped off the teams at the double steel doors and they proceeded onto the large training floor to start the day's training activities. But today, they were ushered through a side door and directed to the classroom. They walked past the large picture window that allowed the occasional visiting dignitaries to view the training area. Bradford immediately noticed the curtains were drawn. They had always been open since their first day, all those many weeks ago.

Nobody bothered to sit once inside the room.

"You have all conducted yourselves admirably during this process," Adams continued. "This training program is the most rigorous of its kind in the country, and you four have

made it through twelve long weeks to make it here today."
Adams moved the clipboard behind his back. "But all of that
only matters if you pass this final examination. Today we will
be testing you and your canines on everything that we've
learned up to this point. Failure is not an option. If your dog
fails to identify explosive materials at any point during this
exam, just one miss, you will be immediately disqualified,
and you will be going home. Your canine—and I mean the
government's canine—will either be recycled or be
reassigned."

Bradford felt a twist of worry take hold in his stomach.
They had all been warned that the final test was serious, but
he had no idea it was a sudden-death situation. In so many of
his other tests in the bureau, the talk was tough but there was
always a little wiggle room. Everyone gets a Mulligan.

Next to him, Deja was looking up at him with a
concerned look on her yellow face. Her perceptive eyes
searched his, looking for a signal, looking for reassurance that
everything was alright.

She can probably feel my heartbeat, Bradford thought.
*Hell, she probably can even feel my blood pressure shooting
up.*

He knew that after these twelve long weeks of working
together and bonding and learning to trust one another, Deja
could sense the minutest change in his demeanor. She could
easily smell the difference in stressful perspiration as opposed
to his everyday sweat from the Virginia heat. She could read

him almost as well as his former wife—or even as good as Copper.

"You will be tested in four stages," Adams explained. "The first two stages will be administered here in the training facility, and the final two will be conducted at pre-selected field sites. We're in for a long day, people."

Bradford looked at the other handlers. Sherry and Jason were standing close together, their dogs parked side-by-side. He could have cut the chemistry between them last night with a knife, but this morning they were both stone-faced and completely focused.

He then looked to Cameron, expecting the same steel-jawed expression that he'd grown so accustomed to. But to Bradford's surprise, even the tough ex-Marine looked like he was staring down the barrel of a gun.

I'll be damned. Looks like the jarhead gives a shit, after all.

"The tests will be administered by one of our chemist technicians, Shweta Lakswendra," Adams said, motioning to the assistant they had never seen before. "She will run you through each stage and then take those same explosive samples back to the ATF lab where she will use a mass spectrometer to certify the chemical compounds your canine alerted on. That way if you are ever called to court, you can testify that your canine positively identified all the major explosive categories." For once, Adams cracked a small smile. "And since I'm not running the exam, you know you won't get preferential treatment or any hints." He cut his eyes at Jason. "Or my boot up your ass."

Bradford had to stifle a laugh.

"Following completion of this stage, you will exit the double doors, give your dog a break in the dog run, and wait in the van for everyone to complete this stage. I fully expect to see four canine teams in that van and onto the next test."

With that, Lakswendra stepped forward. She was a petite Indian woman in her forties, but her accent was from the South. If Bradford had to guess, he'd say Georgia. Her demeanor was pleasant and her smile warm, a total contrast to when Adams ran a search problem. Bradford could tell she was a dog lover and probably had volunteered for this.

"In the first stage, you will have your dogs run through three rows of cardboard boxes and locate the explosive materials hidden in a number of boxes. The boxes not containing explosives have distractors in them. As Mr. Adams mentioned, if your canine misses any explosives, it is an immediate fail."

Bradford forced a swallow. Deja moved closer to his leg and gave a nearly inaudible whine.

"We'll proceed with the examination in alphabetical order," she said, looking at her clipboard. "Thomas Bradford, you're up first."

With a deep breath, Bradford led Deja out to the floor.

"Good luck, brother," he heard Jason saying as the door to the classroom was shut behind him.

Shweta Lakswendra moved efficiently as she led both

handler and dog to three long rows of cardboard boxes, just like you'd find in any warehouse or shipping facility. Bradford tried to count the boxes quickly, but he was too nervous. It looked like there were about twenty in each row.

"Agent Bradford, you will need to proceed down the line of boxes and find any and all explosive materials hidden inside. Your dog's sit signal and a verbal notification by you will be taken as a positive indication of explosives. You may go back with your partner to double-check any box, but once you indicate completion, the test is over." Lakswendra's tone became deathly serious. "If your dog misses an explosive substance and does not give the proper signal, you will be immediately disqualified. Do you understand?"

"Loud and clear," he said, tightening his grip on Deja's lead.

Any nervousness the dog had felt earlier was now replaced by a sharp focus. Deja knew what to do—now it was up to him to keep *his* focus and not break her concentration. He knew that all emotions, all thoughts, all doubts traveled down leash, and if he didn't get his stress and emotions in check, he could confuse her and force her into a dumb mistake. After all, Deja didn't really care about bombs or guns or PETN or black powder. In the end, all she cared about was the love and affection she got from him—and, of course, the handful of kibble. He had to be on his A-game for her.

"Proceed," Lakswendra said.

Bradford chose the row on the left first. He liked starting

to the left whenever they had the option. He would work that row, find the explosives, come down the middle then finish up on the last row to the right. He had his game plan, but like George Foreman once said, "Everybody has a game plan until you get punched in the face." He gave the *seeeek* command, and Deja took off for the long row of boxes.

She set her nose to each one, working quickly and efficiently with fast, sharp movements. A low grunting sound emitted from her wet nostrils as she pulled in an endless stream of molecules and parsed them down into their individual olfactory components. She would draw the air through her nose, making minute adjustments to the shape of her palette and nostrils to alter the flow of odor and the way it spread across her millions of individual scent receptors. As she exhaled, she closed off the alar folds to alter the direction of the exiting air to the sides, stirring up more scent that could be explored on the next inhale. She could smell the lingering pine tar in the pulp that had gone into the cardboard, and she could even tell that the tree had grown in rocky soil at high elevation. She could smell the latex of the gloves on the hands of the man who assembled the box that morning, the cigarette that he smoked after breakfast, the smoke laced with traces of maple syrup and bleached flour. And of course, she could smell the distractor inside. In this case, it was that black plastic material with the adhesive smell. She remembered back during a search when it was wrapped around those sticks. But in the millisecond of smelling those odors and processing everything, Deja did not smell the odor that paid, just the black plastic. No explosives in this box. No kibble to be had. Move on to the next.

Bradford followed along after her, guiding her and working with her as she went from box to box. They worked their way down the row, sometimes moving fast and sometimes slowing down for an extra sniff on a particular box.

Several times Bradford was sure they had a positive. He could tell Deja was about to sit whenever her back hocks quivered, but each time it happened, she stayed on her feet and moved on to the next box.

By the time they were down to their final three boxes in the row, Bradford was starting to panic.

"Deja, come on girl," he said softly. "Seeeeeek."

Deja redoubled her efforts on those last boxes, but again, no sitting.

Bradford swallowed and looked at Lakswendra. She had been so cheery back in the classroom, but out here on the training floor, the woman was inscrutable. He had no idea if they'd already missed the explosives—would she stop the test and fail them on the spot, or would she let them get all the way to the end of the last row before telling them to pack their bags?

By the time they came to the penultimate box, Bradford was already thinking that an early retirement didn't sound so bad. September at the lake cabin was glorious, now that the heat had broken and the mosquitoes were getting killed off by the cool, frosty mornings.

He was just starting to wonder what would happen to Deja when they came to the final box. Would she get shipped off to another program? Maybe she'd go to some local PD who needed a good K-9 dog, even if she couldn't cut it at the highest level. Or maybe she would retire into civilian life, becoming the prized dog of a grade-schooler out in the country . . .

Before he knew it, Deja had come to the end of the row. She was still standing on her paws, waiting to make the turn and continue on to the middle row.

Lakswendra approached with her unreadable face.

"Do you wish to conclude this row?" she asked directly.

Bradford looked down at Deja, and she looked up at him.

There was a part of him that was sure he'd blown it, that he hadn't had his head in the game—and Deja had been thrown off because of it. Maybe he shouldn't have had that third beer last night. Maybe he should have just stayed in Philly and never gotten involved in any of this. Maybe Deja would be better off without him. Should he ask to re-search that box in the middle, the one where he thought she wanted to sit? At this point, he couldn't even recall which box that was.

But despite all of his doubts, in that moment, he knew he had to trust his dog.

"Yes, row complete."

Lakswendra nodded and made a note on her clipboard.

"Excellent, continue on."

Bradford gave a mighty sigh of relief.

"You mean . . . all the boxes were dummies?"

Lakswendra nodded. "Correct, there were no explosives in this row. They do that to test *you*. A lot of people want to force their dogs into finding something. A false indication at a big event is not a good thing."

Her seriousness melted, and her chuckle relieved some of the tension in Bradford.

They just had to throw a curveball on the first pitch, didn't they?

He led Deja on to the next row.

"Okay, okay, you were right," he whispered to her. "But don't let it get to your head."

He gave the lab a good rub between her ears.

"We've still a long way to go."

CAMERON

4:28 p.m.
Federal Canine Training Facility
Front Royal, VA
September 2019

CAMERON STARED DOWN the long corridor like it was the last hallway in the entire world. Rows of lockers marched towards the empty gym, the shadows playing against the folded accordion bleachers. Behind him, the cafeteria stood empty and motionless, lined with pennants and banners from school victories in years past.

It was just like the high school he attended back in Ohio—the same sights, the same smells—but it didn't bring him any comfort. The sweat was beading on his forehead and pooling along his spine. He and Dover had already been at it for twenty minutes, and he knew their time was running out.

"Come on, buddy. Seeeek. Find it."

Dover worked his nose quickly along the lockers, feeling his person's tension and trying to do what was asked of him.

The entire school was empty, and the four handlers had spent the last few hours doing sweeps of the campus, one by one. At first, Cameron wondered why they scheduled the final exam for a Saturday, but when they pulled up to the school for their fourth and final stage of the exam, it all made sense.

The first stage had gone pretty quick. Each handler had run their dogs down the three rows of shipping boxes. Simple enough, although Dolly did false indicate at the end of that negative row. Sherry was pissed that they staged a negative row on their final exam, but she admitted to the other handlers in the van ride over that it was totally her fault. Sherry decided to work the rows right to left, and on the final three boxes, she swore Dolly wanted to sit on the second box from last. Sherry slowed them down and insisted the dog sniff again, and she described how Dolly looked at her, confused, and then sat. They were instructed time and again in training that the dogs believed that this was just a game of hide-and-seek—holding them up on something that didn't have explosives was just as confusing as if you pulled them away from something that did have explosives in it. Thankfully Sherry had realized what happened, and she didn't give the verbal confirmation to Lakswendra. Bullet dodged—but it served as a lesson for them all.

For the second stage, Instructor Adams had taken them to the garage attached to the training facility and had them run sweeps of cars and trucks, searching for explosive materials hidden in wheel wells and deep inside trunks. Jason and Disney had nearly missed a tin of nitroamines hidden inside a small slit in one of the passenger seats, but Disney sat her butt down just as Jason was about to call out that they were finished. If Disney had not hesitated when exiting the vehicle, giving Jason time to let her go into her passive alert, they both would have been headed home.

The third stage was a field sweep, where Adams's assistants threw firearms into the high grass and had the dogs track them down. Dover and Disney both took longer than anyone would have liked, but they made it under the wire. But Deja, Bradford's dog, hit on the gun in fifteen seconds flat. Cameron knew Bradford trained hunting dogs, so he figured the ATF agent had some kind of bloodhound magic that he was able to pass along to Deja.

Either that or he just got lucky, Cameron had thought from behind his Oakleys as Dover wagged his tail by his side.

But then all four handlers and dogs boarded a van, and they were brought here to the high school for the fourth and final stage.

"This is the hardest test of all," Adams had said as they all lined up in front of the entrance. "Mission sweep. You will have twenty-five minutes to locate an explosive material hidden somewhere inside this building. If you do not locate the explosives within the allotted timeframe, you will be immediately disqualified, so you must conduct your sweep quickly but efficiently. We have separated the school into four distinct areas, one for each handler, to rule out any false positives from the scent of the other dogs." Adams looked each one of them in the eye. "Time to make me proud."

Time to make me proud, Cameron repeated as Dover finished searching one row of lockers and moved into the adjacent classroom. Cameron glanced down at his watch. Five minutes to go. They had all started at the same time, so they would all be exiting the building in a few minutes. Time to see who made it and who went home.

"Come on, buddy," he said, urging Dover forward even though Dover needed no urging. The dog understood what was expected of him, even if he didn't know what was at stake. All that mattered to the dog was that his person was nervous—and that he needed to find whatever Cameron wanted him to find.

They swept the classroom as quickly as possible. Dover hesitated on a few spots, sniffing deeply, but it was probably just a familiar distractor.

Cameron urged him out of the room, but he could feel time running out.

Down the hall, two of Adams's assistants watched his progress, making notes on their clipboards and checking their watches.

I'm going home, Cameron thought, his spirits sinking. *We're toast.*

But Dover kept on searching. He worked his way furiously down the hallway, heading back toward the gym even though they had already swept it at the start.

Cameron was going to lead him back to a classroom they had rushed through earlier, but Dover leaned against his leash in the other direction, insisting on scanning the hallway one more time.

Trust your dog.

Cameron glanced down at his watch. Under two minutes.

"We've already been down here, buddy," Cameron said as Dover pulled down the hallway. Part of him wondered if Dover had lost his focus, choosing this hallway because of the all the high school smells of cheap food and sugary lip gloss and old gym shorts tucked away in the lockers.

Trust your dog.

But Dover seemed more focused than ever, as if he could sense the ticking of Cameron's watch.

Trust your dog.

Finally he came to a janitor's closet, one they had passed on their first sweep fifteen minutes ago. Like last time, Dover hesitated, sniffing the door deeply. The first time this had happened, Cameron had dismissed it as just another distractor—probably the ammonia or the bleach inside the closet.

But this time, Dover gave a little whine and tried to nudge the door with his nose.

"You want to go in?" Cameron asked, feeling a sudden hope.

The door was slightly ajar, and he pushed it open.

Dover shot straight in, working the four-by-four space in a matter of seconds. He set his nose on a small unmarked cardboard box and immediately sat down.

Cameron felt a flood of relief. He thought he had learned to trust Dover completely, but it still amazed him how much he could stand in his own way. If he had just listened to Dover from the start, he could be sipping a margarita by now.

He bent down and gave Dover a giant handful of kibble and a big hug.

"Good boy," he whispered in his ear. Then he stood up and called out to the assistants, "We've got a hit in here."

They appeared at the door with their clipboards.

Shweta Lakswendra smiled at him.

"That's a positive identification. And with not a minute to spare. Well done, Specialist McNeil. You can step outside and reward your dog, we'll finish up here."

Cameron failed to mention that he had already provided the well-deserved food reward to Dover, and gave him another handful under the watchful eyes of the evaluators. After all, Dover deserved a god-damned Big Mac for his accomplishment this day.

Cameron felt like he was walking on air as he made his way to the parking lot, Dover by his side. He pushed open the big double doors and found everyone waiting for him, their dogs standing happily by their sides.

They all had passed.

JASON

11:03 a.m.
Daniel Patrick Moynihan US Courthouse
New York, NY
October 2019

"COME ON, MAN," Marshal Bill Simmons was saying, "show us what she can do."

Jason Hernandez was standing in the middle of the bullpen, the wide-open office space on the ninth floor of the US Courthouse on Pearl Street. The building was a big granite tower plunked down not far from Ground Zero in Lower Manhattan, and while Jason had always thought it was uglier than hell, it was good to be home.

"Easy, easy," Jason said, soaking in all of the attention. "She's not some carnival attraction. She's a US Marshal, just like you or me. She's even got a badge, look. And from what I've seen, she works a lot harder than most of you."

Several marshals and admin staff had left their desks and were gathered around Jason and Disney. She also seemed to be enjoying the attention, and her tail wagged eagerly across the tired, high-traffic carpet. The badge on her collar reflected the fluorescent lights overhead.

"Yeah, sure, Jase," one of the marshals goaded him, hanging his elbows over the edge of his cubicle. "Talk is cheap. Let's see all those tax dollars at work."

Some of the others chimed in, urging him on.

Jason loved it.

"Alright, if you insist."

He dropped to one knee, rubbed Disney's head, and told her to stay. Then he went over to his cubicle and, looking like a surgeon preparing for an operation, donned a pair of latex gloves from a box on top of his desk. Next he unlocked his desk drawer and withdrew two small bags of gunpowder from a plastic ammo box. He handed one to his long-time partner, Bill Simmons, and one to another marshal.

"Hey, where's our gloves?" Simmons asked. "Should we be touching this stuff?"

Jason chuckled. "Relax, it's just a bag of gunpowder. The gloves are just so Disney doesn't track *my* odor." He bent down and clipped on Disney's lead. "Ok, you two hide those somewhere in the office, and then Disney and I will come back in and show you the magic."

"Ok, ok," Simmons said. "But let's make this interesting. If Disney finds the bags, I'll do your fugitive update reports for the month. If she doesn't, you owe us all a round of drinks tonight."

That was music to Jason's ears. There were few things Jason hated more than paperwork.

"You got yourself a deal," he said, shaking on it.

And with that, he led her out into the hall.

The other marshal sprang into action like a kid playing hide and seek. He ran over to a filing cabinet, put the cloth of powder inside the middle drawer, and silently closed it. But Simmons stood there, holding the bag and looking dumbly around the bullpen.

"Oh Jesus Bill," Emily, one of the Investigative Assistants in the office, said with exasperation. "You're like a truck with its headlights out."

She snatched the bag from his hand and marched to her cubicle down the main hall. The other employees followed, some of them giving Bill an elbow or two.

"What? I'm not good on the spot," he protested, straightening his tie.

Emily pulled the chair out from under her desk, kicked off her heels, and climbed onto the desk. She pushed one of the drop-down ceiling panels aside and slid the gunpowder inside.

"There," she said, sliding the panel back in place and hopping down. "Now that is how you hide something."

The marshal by the door stuck his head out and called Jason back in.

"Well, that was fast," Jason said, leading Disney. "Hope you all are taking this seriously."

He scanned the crowd, seeing some poker faces but also some snickering.

"Ok, Disney," he said, speaking close to her ear. "Let's show 'em what we've got. Seeeek."

He unclipped the lead from Disney's collar, and just like that, she went zipping around the office, her nose glued to the floor. Her head was down, her movements sharp and precise. It was like she was a magnet, drawn towards the smells they had trained so hard for those twelve weeks.

Jason watched with pride as she beelined for a cubicle halfway down the room. She whipped inside, and everyone followed, eager to see her in action.

Inside the cubicle, Disney sat down in front of the filing cabinet and looked at Jason expectantly.

"Is it in the cabinet?" Jason asked.

The marshal who took the first bag laughed and sighed at the same time. "Sure is. And I hid it deep in there, too."

Jason bent down and praised Disney, giving her a small handful of kibble from the pouch on his belt. "She could smell it a mile away. Literally."

"So is it really true that she only gets fed when she's working?" one of the secretaries asked. "Like, you never just pour her a bowl of dog food after you've had your dinner?"

"That's right, she only gets fed when she finds an explosive. So that means we're training three, four, even five times a day, come hell or high water."

Bill Simmons whistled. "That sounds like a pain in the ass."

"You're a pain in the ass," Jason replied. "Alright, we've got another bag to find. Ok, Disney. Seeeek."

Once again, the dog took off like a shot. She zigged into one cubicle after the next, then zagged across the hall. She searched desks, garbage cans, bookshelves. She sniffed chair after chair after chair. One minute passed, then another. Then another.

"Looks like your pup might be stumped," Simmons said, leading the throng of employees as they followed Disney in her work. She zipped ahead, going into yet another cubicle.

"Just give it time," Jason said. But inside, he was beginning to wonder if they really had managed to thwart her. That certainly wouldn't look good. In fact, he'd never live it down.

Maybe they flushed it down the toilet. Or threw it out the window. I wouldn't put it past these clowns.

It was starting to look hopeless. He was ruing the fact that he'd have to splash out a hundred bucks on drinks tonight when they all rounded the corner and found Disney sitting patiently in Emily's cubicle.

She was looking up at the ceiling.

BRADFORD

1:52 p.m.
ATF Field Office
Philadelphia, PA
October 2019

TRY AS HE might, Thomas Bradford just could not escape the bane of paperwork. He and Jason had bonded over their contempt for the bureaucratic horse crap that came with this line of work, and the two of them had frequently swapped managerial horror stories as they ran through the endless drills that Instructor Adams put them through. It had only been a few weeks since they had graduated from the National Canine Division program, but much to his surprise, Bradford found himself missing that goofball of a US Marshal. And Sherry. And Dolly and Disney and Dover. Hell, he even missed Cameron McNeil, inasmuch as you could miss an angry pair of sunglasses.

There was no doubt that they all had bonded over their journey together, but that felt like a million years ago. Now he sat here in his eight-by-eight cubicle, filling out ROIs. The Report of Investigation, Form 3270, was the main reporting vehicle for everything an ATF agent did. Some supervisors wanted an ROI detailing your morning dump. People's careers were significantly advanced by how many 3270s were generated in their computer case files. For the bean counters in HQ, quantity mattered—and that pissed Bradford off, especially when quality took a back seat. Real life always had a way of catching up with you.

Under his desk, Deja slept soundly, her head resting on his right foot. He could tell she was dreaming by the twitching of her back paws. He wondered if she was running down a long row of boxes, trying to zero in on the smells that had been so deeply ingrained into her. That was the life she knew—the life she had trained for. Or maybe she was dreaming of running through a bright, sunny field and splashing through a clear stream, chasing after frogs. Even though she was raised in a sterile correctional facility and had spent so much of her life preparing for a career in law enforcement, sometimes Bradford wondered whether she shared memories with all the other dogs that came before her—some kind of genetic well that they all drank from, all the way back to the first brazen wolves who took a risk and cautiously made their way into prehistoric human camps, looking for scraps of food. He would see it sometimes in Copper when they were out in the woods, when his nose went from air to ground and back again. And he saw it in Deja, too. A look in the eye that said, "I've done all this before. It's what I was put on this earth for."

Just then, Deja's ears pricked back, and she was alert and awake.

Only a few moments later, the big boss appeared, casting

a shadow over the cubicle. Philly Special Agent-in-Charge Richard W. Rawlins was a tall man with a crisp suit and tie.

"Hey, Tom," the boss said, urgent and focused. "Get Deja ready. There's been an officer-involved shooting just over the state line in Delaware. The Wilmington office is requesting the dog."

"What happened?"

"The details are still sketchy, but it looks like an officer was ambushed in her squad car last night. Officer was DOA." His pause was full of gravity. "Assholes took her weapon and shot her with it. They need to find that gun."

"Christ," Bradford said. It was the request you never wanted to get—but on the other hand, if it did come in, Bradford wanted it to be him they were requesting. While every search was important, there were some that exceeded the scale, and this was one of them.

"Get up with a Detective Stevens when you get there. He'll bring you up to speed. He's doing interviews right now, so don't bug him on the way there."

Bradford stood and grabbed his equipment bag from the top of his credenza. In it was everything he needed for three days on the road. After that, it was on the government credit card.

"We're on it."

BRADFORD PULLED UP to the police department in Newport, Delaware, the lights still flashing on his unmarked black Suburban. I-95 had been mostly free of traffic, and even with the rain, he'd made it in just over half an hour.

The station was off the main drag, bordering a quiet neighborhood with sleepy houses and tidy yards. Old trees lined the quiet streets, slowly turning yellow and orange in the cool, damp air. It was the sort of place where people settle down to raise a family once they get tired of the hustle in the bigger cities up and down the Eastern Seaboard. It was just a few minutes south of downtown Wilmington, but it looked just like any other quaint small town that Bradford had seen before.

He climbed out of the Suburban and threw on his ATF jacket. He reached back into the SUV, grabbing his extra badge from the console. This one was on a chain that he slipped over his neck, letting the gold shield hang down low on his chest. He had the experience to know that on a major incident, tensions would be running high. And what with everyone and their fucking uncle running around, the sooner the cops knew who he was, the better.

He got Deja out of the back and clipped on her lead, and together they made their way across the slick parking lot, blinking the rain out of their eyes. He normally wouldn't bring the dog out for an initial meeting, but in some strange way, Bradford wanted Deja to absorb the seriousness of what was going on.

Inside, Bradford walked up to the bulletproof glass partition and spoke up so that his voice projected through the small opening. "ATF Canine here for Detective Stevens."

The young officer started to ask for identification, but Bradford had already whipped out his wallet with credentials and pressed it up to the glass. Bradford remembered back when he was that young. He wondered what the veteran officers had thought about him, looking like he had just graduated from junior high.

As the kid studied Bradford's ID, a side door opened.

A tired face appeared. It was an older man in a wrinkled white shirt with a full salt-and-pepper beard.

"Thanks for getting here so quick. Detective Bob Stevens," he said.

"The name's Thomas Bradford. And this is Deja. We're here to assist you however we can."

"Good, good," Stevens said, holding the door open. Bradford was so used to people immediately making a fuss upon meeting Deja, reaching down for a quick head scratch or a question about how old, but Stevens hardly noticed. This was a man with a million things on his mind.

Bradford and his canine partner followed Stevens down a hallway. They passed several offices, one marked *Chief Bukowski*. Bradford's thoughts shifted to what this chief must be going through right now. This was a small department—twenty or thirty officers at most. Bradford could tell it wasn't just a police department. It was a family. He followed as Stevens walked past an interview room with the placard flipped to "In Progress" and stepped into the next door.

"Come inside. We're just wrapping up our questioning. We're taking five at the moment."

Bradford entered the cramped, dark room. He directed Deja to an out-of-the-way corner and let the leather lead fall to the floor beside her. A tall detective with a Delaware State Police badge on his belt and another uniformed officer were inside, watching the interrogation room through a one-way mirror. The officer was taking notes, and there was a video camera on a tripod next to him. There was a man sitting alone in the interrogation room, sipping a can of Coke Zero, obviously waiting for the interviewer to return.

"So you want to bring me up to speed?" Bradford asked as he shut the door behind him.

"At two-twenty this morning," Detective Stevens said, "Officer Ellen Donahue was shot outside her squad car in the parking lot of a 7-Eleven in downtown Newport. She usually took her lunch break in that spot. It looks like she was either getting into or exiting her vehicle when she was shot in the chest, just above the collar of her vest, and then five more times in the face. Her service weapon was taken. We're working forensics now, but it looks like she was shot with two different weapons. Her service weapon was a Glock 40. We recovered five .40 caliber casings on the pavement around the squad, and one nine-millimeter casing about eight feet away. No guns were recovered at the scene, including hers. Nothing else was taken from either her person or her squad car. The only thing the store clerk heard was the shots—no yelling, no fighting, no anything. He made the 9-1-1 call."

Bradford's stomach turned. "That's awful."

Stevens's face was grim. "Looks like a straight-up ambush. First shot knocks her down, then the offender takes her service weapon and puts five in her face."

Bradford started to speak, then stopped. He nodded to the camera in the room.

Stevens picked up on it immediately. "We're good. It's miked up to the interview room."

"Is this the boyfriend?" Bradford continued, motioning to the man sitting at the table in the interrogation room. He was an athletic man in his mid-thirties, wearing an expensive button-down shirt with the tie untied. He looked utterly exhausted, but from Bradford's quick glance, he seemed like he was cooperating with the other detective who just entered the interrogation room and sat down across the table from him.

"Peter Donahue," Detective Stevens said. "He's Ellen's husband, but they've been separated for about nine months."

"Gotta start there," Bradford said, watching Donahue answer questions through the glass. Donahue's eyes were red, but he was making eye contact and answering the interrogating detective directly.

"We can't find anything about anyone she was seeing since they separated," Detective Stevens said, his voice clipped and strained. "She moved back with her folks, and he got to keep the house, the truck, pretty much all of it. As far as she ever talked about it with us here at the station, the split seemed pretty amicable."

"What's his alibi?"

"Said he was at home asleep, and before you ask, the camera at the 7-Eleven doesn't show the north side of the building where she parked. We watched when she went in, got her coffee and a bran muffin, chatted it up with the clerk, then left. Nothing out of the ordinary."

"Do you believe him? How far does he live from here?" Bradford studied Donohue's face through the glass. "What about traffic cameras? Home security cameras?"

Stevens stared through the one-way mirror. "He lives fourteen miles from the crime scene. We're still checking with area businesses along the possible routes. This is a small town. We don't have any traffic cams. And the state police are pulling the cell tower pings for his phone locations right now."

On the other side of the glass, the interrogating detective continued his line of questioning. Bradford and Stevens watched.

"And you say that you haven't seen your wife in how long?" the detective asked, tapping his pen on a notepad. It was mostly blank.

"Uh, it's been a few weeks, at least, but I call her a few times a month to see how she's doing," Donahue answered, his hands shaky as he rubbed his cheek. "But the last time I physically saw her . . . I can't really remember. I think it was two Tuesdays ago. She had to come by the house to pick up some of her clothes."

"And how did that interaction go?"

"Fine, I guess. You know, I mean, it's never easy when we see each other, but it was fine. She just came in, got her clothes. We talked a bit about work, and then she left."

"So there was no argument? No incidents of any kind?"

"No, none. It was perfectly fine. It just always bums me out to see her, you know?"

"She was the one to end the relationship, correct?"

Donahue nodded. "Yeah, she wanted to leave."

"And why was that?"

He sighed deeply and sat back in his chair. "Man, if I knew that, maybe she would've stayed. But you know Ellen. She was never one to really open up about her feelings, you know? I could tell something was different for months, then just one day, I come home from work, and she's sitting at the kitchen table, all 'We need to talk.' And just like that, she packed her bags and left."

"And you wanted her to stay?"

"Hell yeah I wanted her to stay. She's my wife, you know." Donahue's face clouded, and he leaned forward again. He seemed genuinely distraught. "Or was. I guess. Fuck, I can't believe she's gone."

He set his head in his hands, and Bradford turned back to Stevens.

"What do you think?"

"I think he's cooperated so far," Detective Stevens answered. "He's saying all the right things. He didn't lawyer up. He even let Detective Richards here"—he motioned to the interrogating detective—"take a team and do a voluntary search of the house this morning."

"They find anything?"

"Not a hair out of place. Far as we can tell, the guy's clean. He did have some guns and ammo in there, but just rifles and shotguns. His one pistol was still in the nightstand, it's a .380."

There was something in Stevens's voice that gave Bradford pause.

"But . . .?"

"But there's something about it that just doesn't sit right," Stevens answered. He clenched his jaw, which made his beard look even grayer. He looked like a cop who had seen a thing or two. "Like I said, it could be nothing, but when we called him to notify him that Ellen had been shot, he didn't sound surprised. He didn't even ask if she was alright. He just asked which hospital she'd been taken to, and asked if there was anything he should do. It was like he already knew she was dead, even though we didn't tell him that right away."

"Shock can make people do some strange things," Bradford offered. "I've seen murderers blubber on the 911 calls after they've killed their spouses, and then other times, the wives or husbands hardly batted an eye even though they had nothing to do with it. Those are tough reads unless you really know the person."

"Yeah, I get that, but . . ." Stevens sighed, and for the first time, he looked down at Deja. He patted her between the ears. "I just want to do this investigation right. For Ellen. So if you have any ideas, I'd like to hear 'em. No egos on this case. ATF, State Police, FBI, I'll take whatever advice gets us closer to making an arrest. Now, as far as you're concerned, I heard good things about your dog. That her specialty is finding guns. There are several wooded areas between the 7-Eleven and Donahue's house, not to mention all the grassy roadsides and a couple of ponds. I want you and your partner to sweep those locations. If the ex is the perp, he could have tossed one or both of the guns along the way."

Just then, through the glass, Donahue and Detective Richards stood up. Another uniformed officer entered and escorted Donahue out of the room. The departure was cordial, with Richards placing an understanding hand on the grieving man's shoulder.

A moment later, Detective Richards entered the observation room.

"You letting him go home?" Stevens asked the other detective.

"Of course I am. I ain't got shit to charge him with." With just a few words, Detective Richards filled up the whole room. He was a barrel-chested man in his early forties, with thinning hair and a square jaw. He looked like a bull ready to stamp his feet, but then he noticed Bradford and Deja. "I'm sorry, who have we here?" It must have taken his eyes a moment to adjust to the dark room, because it took him a second to read the letters on Bradford's jacket. "ATF? Do we need the feds?"

"I called them," Stevens said, not backing down even

though the other detective was twice his size and fifteen years his junior.

"And why the fuck did you do that? I told you we got this covered. Forensics is running the ballistics now, and we've got squads canvassing the area. Something will turn up soon. I guarantee it. GSR should be back any minute, and the state is running Donohue's phone."

"I wanted to cover all the bases, Richards. We need to find the guns. We could send out a hundred boy scouts to search the woods on foot all day, but we'll just be wasting our time. A dog is the only way. And you know as well as I do that Wilmington PD just has patrol and drug dogs. Besides, the dogs at the ATF are the best. They're trained to find guns, just guns. Agent Bradford here can save us dozens of man-hours."

Detective Richards seemed unimpressed. "We didn't need to get the feds involved. When we catch the shooter, he'll tell us where the guns are. The feds always try to come in and take over. It's a shitshow every goddamn time." He glanced at Bradford. "No offense."

Bradford shrugged. "None taken. But I can assure you, I'm not going to step on your investigation. I'm just here to help."

"Where are you gonna have him search?" Richards asked Stevens.

"The road between the 7-Eleven and Donahue's house. I also want to search the woods around the property."

Richards sighed. "I think you're wasting your time, and wasting the time of this very highly-paid agent here. But do me a favor—don't bother Mr. Donahue, will you? I've got him talking and cooperating in the investigation. If someone pisses him off, he's going to hire an attorney, and then we get shit."

Bradford could feel Deja fidgeting by his side.

Easy girl, he thought, rubbing her neck. *We'll get to work soon.*

SHERRY

11:14 a.m.
Eagle Pass – Piedras Negras International Bridge
Eagle Pass, TX
October 2019

SHERRY FRY WORKED her way along the row of idling cars as the sun beat down on her neck. She wore her forest-green bulletproof tactical vest with *CBP Border Patrol* and *Federal Agent* emblazoned in block yellow letters—not the most comfortable thing to wear in ninety-seven-degree heat. Dolly trotted alongside her, wearing special boots to protect her paws from the sweltering tarmac. Below the bridge, the green water of the Rio Grande glittered in the sun.

Sherry worked her way along the cars and trucks waiting to cross the border as Dolly diligently sniffed the wheel wells, door seams, and back bumpers. From several of the cars, she could hear the low bass of *norteño* music reverberating through the concrete of the bridge.

She was always friendly and professional as she engaged with the drivers, sometimes in English and sometimes in Spanish. There were delivery trucks carrying produce. Families going to visit relatives. People going to work, going on about their daily lives.

She came to a rusty Toyota coupe and signaled for the driver to roll down his window. The old man squinted up at her sunglasses.

Sherry gave him a smile. "Anything in your car my dog is going to like?" she asked in Spanish.

He sensed her humor, and he relaxed a bit. "Ai, no, *señora*. I'm going to work. I have no drugs."

No drogas.

If only she had a dollar for every time she heard those two words.

It was no secret that Piedras Negras, a town of over 200,000 people, had been largely taken over by members of the Gulf Cartel, just as they had done in most cities in Coahuila and Tamaulipas states. This infamous band of drug runners and killers had set up shop from the Gulf of Mexico all the way to the Big Bend of the Rio Grande, controlling hundreds of miles of border and doing more than a billion dollars in business a year as they supplied the north with cocaine, heroin, and fentanyl. Murder, extortion, corruption—these were just a way of life for the many Mexicans living under the bloody shadow of the cartels.

And things had been getting worse over the last few years. In addition to buying off policemen and politicians, the Gulf Cartel had also recruited a large contingent of corrupt special forces soldiers from the Mexican Army back in the '90s, but enticed by the untold riches waiting for anyone willing to kill for it, these ex-soldiers broke off and formed their own rival cartel, *Los Zetas*. In many ways, the Zetas were worse than the cartel they left behind, and by 2012, they had devolved into any crime that would bring in the cash, from smuggling to outright human trafficking. By 2015, they had suffered some major setbacks and splintered into smaller groups after their two leaders were arrested, but just this last year, one of the splinter gangs had moved into Piedras Negras and declared war on the Gulf Cartel.

Ninety-seven people had been killed since January, and there was no sign of it slowing down.

Sherry Fry had grown accustomed to seeing the exhaustion and the fear in the eyes of many who were crossing the border, and the old man in the rusty Toyota was no exception.

"Travel safe, *abuelo*," she said.

She tapped the side of his door before moving on, and he nodded to her.

"Thank you, *señora*."

Then he leaned out of the window to watch the dog move on to the next car.

SHERRY WAS SWEATING profusely by the time she made it back to the port of entry on the US side of the bridge.

She stepped under the shade of the large awning behind the main office and poured some water into a portable bowl for Dolly. The dog lapped the water eagerly, sloshing it on the pavement. Nearby, the cars moved slowly through the lanes and approached the booths with waiting CBP officers.

Sherry took a drink from the water bottle, then she pulled the phone from her pocket, as she always did whenever she took a few minutes for herself.

Darryl hadn't texted in days, but that was not why she was checking.

A small smile spread across her face as she saw several texts from Jason.

soooo bored. you?

hey what do you think is better, empanadas or chimichangas? remember i'm salvadoran so if you answer wrong I may have to kill you

yes i'm hungry and no it is not lunch yet

so when can I come visit???

She shook her head and texted back, trying to not laugh and draw attention to the fact that she was using her phone on duty.

Can't talk now. I want to see you soon.

She slipped her phone back into her vest, feeling a new type of warmth that had nothing to do with her sunburn.

But then Darryl appeared in her mind, as he always did, and Sherry felt a stab of guilt. She had rationalized it to herself so many times. Darryl wasn't around. She wasn't around. Too much had happened between them. He was probably off having an affair of his own. They were all adults, they could make their own choices. And on and on it went.

Unlike other times, this time it did little to make her feel any better. Flirting was one thing. Having Jason fly out to Texas was another matter entirely.

She sighed and took another long drink of water.

She knew Jason was lonelier than he let on. All of the bravado and all of the showing off—she knew it was because there was something sad inside. A part of her wanted to fix him, but that sounded like the last thing she needed right now. She had too much to fix as it was.

Sherry tightened the leash abruptly, drawing a surprised look from Dolly.

"Sorry, girl," she said, rubbing her ears. "Come on, let's get back to work. Your mom is done with her phone for the day."

CAMERON

2:15 p.m.
Forward Operating Base (FOB) Davidson
Nangarhar Province, Afghanistan
October 2019

THE BLADES OF the UH-60 Blackhawk cut through the blinding afternoon sky, thundering over the dry mountain pass and sweeping down into the Kunar River valley. Cameron sat next to the door gunner, watching as the Hawk flew past the meager farmsteads with their dry mud walls and their skinny goats. He saw men and children dashing for cover as the helicopter approached low and fast. Cameron couldn't help but wonder what they were thinking as they scattered, what memories those thundering blades whipped up inside them. No one in this part of Afghanistan had fared well in the war with America, which had now dragged on for a second generation. Cameron knew that they were fighting a new crop of Taliban recruits who had been born long after the twin towers fell—desperate, angry youths who had known nothing but war to make them men.

As Cameron watched the little children run and hide as his Hawk raced overhead, he couldn't help but wonder if any of them would pick up a rifle in the weeks and years to come—or how many would plant a bomb on the roadside.

Cameron gave a heavy sigh. Whenever he started to think like this, he needed a smoke to clear his head. Next to him, Dover was strapped into his tac harness and secured to the airframe. His usually floppy ears were shielded by special canine earmuffs, and he wore goggles over his eyes. They had trained in helicopter procedures for several days at Andrews AFB in Washington DC, and then again after arriving in Kabul before deploying to the forward operating base—and while Dover wasn't too fond of his headgear, he took to it like a pro. Cameron was impressed with how well Dover was handling the noise, wind, and bumps of the UH-60. There was no way the convicts could ever acclimate the dogs to this.

"You're a born aviator," he said loudly, knowing that Dover couldn't hear him above the noise of the turbines, but he knew that Dover could feel the praise and the love. Dover gave Cameron a quick lick on the exposed skin between Cameron's shirt sleeve and glove, then resumed his intense focus out the door, anxious to get to work in this war-torn country.

Like handler, like dog . . .

Cameron could only imagine what Dover was thinking as he explored this new world that they found themselves in. The sights and smells were nothing like home—even the dirt smelled different here, more ancient than back in Michigan, as if the many empires that had risen and fallen in this desolate corner of the world had all left their mark and changed the very land itself. He wondered if Dover could smell the history here. Could he smell the Russians and the Mongols and the Greeks before them? Could he smell the twenty years of American and coalition soldiers who had fought for this strip of land tucked up next to the Pakistan frontier? Could he smell the frustration that victory was still no closer at hand?

What the fuck are we even doing here? Cameron found himself wondering, and a small part of him wished that he had never let Dover lead him back to that janitor's closet in the final test. If they had flunked out, he'd be back here in his old position and Dover would be back somewhere safe in the states, rather than flying into an active warzone. For months all Cameron had wanted to do was come back here and get back to work, to protect the men and women who were his responsibility—but now that he had Dover with him, he found himself worrying for the dog in a way he'd never worried about anything else before. If something ever happened to Dover out in the field . . .

He drove the thought from his mind. Dover was tough, and Cameron knew the dog could handle whatever came their way. Cameron just didn't know if he could handle it himself.

You've got a mission to do, he told himself, tracing the outline of the cigarette pack in his pocket. *You and Dover have to keep these guys safe.*

The notion gave him some strength. If he and Dover could even stop one bomb, save one single life, then everything that came before would be worth it. Perhaps, finally, Yemen wouldn't haunt him like a shadow and he could finally move on.

The Hawk raced across the dry valley, and in minutes they approached FOB Davidson. The base spread out across the valley bottom, a collection of Quonset huts, cargo containers, and concrete T-walls surrounded by a double perimeter of razorwire fence. The rotor blades of the chopper roared as the pilot maneuvered to the landing site, kicking up huge plumes of dust as they swooped down.

As soon as their Blackhawk touched down, Cameron unclipped Dover's harness and together they hopped out and raced across the dusty, wind-whipped landing pad. Dover looked all business in his tactical goggles.

Cameron started to make his way to the office to report to his boss, Stan Juszczyk, but there was an Army soldier waiting for him. Like all the other members of the Explosive Ordinance Disposal team, he wore desert fatigues and a heavy combat vest emblazoned with the letters EOD on his left shoulder. He wore a Beretta M9 sidearm on his hip, and on his chest was a patch with a bomb atop two lightning bolts— the special insignia that the EOD team reverently called "The Crab."

"McNeil!" he shouted. "'Bout time you got your ass back here."

Cameron broke into a genuine smile. He pulled out a cigarette and tried to light it despite the wind from the chopper. He said to Ken Delgado with the smoke between his lips, "Glad to see you didn't surrender the place to the enemy."

"Fuck no. I just kept the place warm for you."

Cameron laughed and went to shake Delgado's hand, but Delgado blew him off and went straight for Dover.

"Dover!" he shouted, rubbing Dover's cheeks despite the earmuffs and goggles. "We've heard so much about you. Are you a good boy? Are you a good boy?"

Dover's tail thumped wildly in the sunbaked dirt, and Cameron shook his head. Even in a warzone, a dog could turn a grown soldier into a bowl of jelly.

Then and there, Cameron vowed that he'd never let any harm come to this dog. Not here. Not anywhere.

BRADFORD

4:48 p.m.
6000 Block of Old Mill Road
Newport, DE
October 2019

THE RAIN HAD eased off over the afternoon, but the woods were still dripping and damp. Many of the ash and beech trees had shed their leaves, but the sugar maples were still vibrant orange. Behind the unsettled clouds, the sun was starting to set.

Bradford, dressed in rain pants and a Gortex jacket, worked his way methodically down a culvert that stretched along the north side of Highway 4, leading a soggy Deja as she scanned the piles of muck and brown leaves and discarded trash by the roadside. They had checked three separate woodlands, including the grassy areas along the two-lane road between here and the 7-Eleven where Officer Ellen Donahue had been murdered with her own gun.

Bradford shivered under his jacket as he worked. It felt like the first snow of the season might not be far off, but that was not what was troubling him. He just couldn't imagine a police officer, a woman who was loved by her colleagues and by the community, being killed in such cold blood. And the way she was killed. Bradford couldn't help but think about that first shot, a nine-millimeter blowing a hole in her trachea and severing her cervical spine. He prayed to God that it was over right then and there and she felt nothing else.

It just didn't seem senseless or random—it seemed targeted. He knew this one was solvable, but he also knew he'd better have the hard evidence to prove it.

In federal court, case agents get to sit at the prosecution table to assist during trials. Bradford knew that during voir dire, the questioning of potential jurors, every single juror expects there to be a fingerprint found on every gun and the case to be wrapped up in an hour. Most potential jurors have watched a lot of TV crime shows, and none of them trusted circumstantial evidence. Television had raised the bar for a conviction, so first and foremost, the detectives needed to develop a credible suspect in this case. They were right to look at the ex-husband first and totally clear him before moving on to the next potential. After all, there was always the possibility that this was a random hit. Some cop-hater or psychopath who was just passing through. Absolutely no connection between victim and offender other than the tragic crossing of two random paths. Those were the tough ones.

It made Bradford think of the infamous Lane Bryant shooting back in Chicago. One February morning, a man walked into a Lane Bryant boutique, rounded up four customers and two employees in a back room, and shot them all. Only one survived to give a credible ID, but even though the sketch artists were able to provide a detailed likeness of the killer, they never found the guy. Maybe it was a robbery gone bad, or maybe he was just out for a drive and something snapped. It happened over a decade ago, but the case was still unsolved. Bradford knew that when it came to the mind of a murderer, anything could happen. But right now, Bradford was committed to his assignment—finding the guns that ended an officer's life.

He shook his head quickly, as if to fling away that motion picture of Ellen Donahue's death. At this point it was a distraction, and he might miss a subtle change in Deja's behavior. Over his time training with her, he had come to learn the minute changes in the way she searched. They were only noticeable to the person who worked with the dog every day, much the way long-time married couples can tell exactly what's wrong from the slightest glance or tone of voice. Bradford had learned that a change in behavior occurs in detection dogs when they detect odor but not enough to activate the passive sitting response. If the handler misses these hints, they could easily pass up the find and never know it.

Like an old married couple, Bradford was in tune with Deja's behavioral changes from the start. Her main cue (which Bradford had trouble even verbalizing to others) was that her tail went from a playful hide-and-seek wag to a slightly slower now-I'm-not-so-sure wag. No one else would even notice, but this was Bradford's signal to slow her down, add some high-pitched verbal praise, and circle her back to that area. He would even widen the search area to give the dog every opportunity to find it. Most times, the dog's curiosity was satisfied and no target odor was found, and the regular search could resume. But every once in a while, doubling back over the area gave Deja a moment to figure it out. Then her tail would go crazy. She would take in larger amounts of air, her actions would become more focused—and bingo! A full-on ass-planting, followed by that unmistakable look of accomplishment. And, of course, a nice food reward.

Bradford was hoping Detective Stevens could witness that very scene as the detective walked the gravel shoulder above the culvert, watching as he and Deja worked the grassy roadside and the first twenty-five feet of woods.

He had asked Bradford if he could jump in the K-9 vehicle with him to show them the areas to be searched. Bradford knew that Stevens needed to get away from the PD for a bit to clear his head.

Bradford and Deja made it to the end of the woods where the cross-street intersected, thus ending that search area. The phrase "needle in a haystack" kept repeating itself in Bradford's head as dog and handler made their way up the slick embankment to the shoulder.

"Nothing?" Stevens asked.

"Just a lot of McDonald's wrappers and beer cans," Bradford said in displeasure. "It's a frickin' junkyard down there, but no guns."

"Could the rain and cold air be throwing her off?"

Bradford shook his head. "Real cold air has an effect on vapor, but this is nothing today. If there was snow on the ground, she'd have to really get her nose down, but she'd still find it. Did you ever wonder why they put ice in urinals? It's to draw the odor downward and not up into the air."

"Huh, no shit." Stevens stuffed his hands in his pockets. "So what's next?"

"Actually, Deja could use a little food about now."

Bradford reached nonchalantly into his jacket pocket and slipped Stevens a ziplock bag that contained an empty shell casing.

"Don't let the dog see, but take out the shell and throw it into the woods as far as you can."

Stevens seemed to appreciate being included, and he tossed the casing when Deja wasn't looking.

Bradford led Deja back down to the grass, unclipped her lead, and with a long and low *seeeek* command, sent Deja in the opposite direction of where the casing landed. The dog bounded forward, showing no lack of energy despite just completing a two-hour search. With nose to the ground, she worked her way about a hundred feet to the south, then swung around into the wind and turned back to where she had started, working in a zig-zag pattern that included both the grassy area and woods. She passed Bradford and Stevens, and then abruptly abandoned the back-and-forth search for a straight beeline ten feet into the woods. She skidded to a sitting position on the wet leaves.

Bradford hurried over, using the verbal bridge technique that Adams had taught them—the loud, high-pitched "gooooood doggggg"—until he got to his partner. The casing was not visible, so Bradford gave the zeroing-in command. "Show me."

With that, Deja buried her nose into the leaves and came up looking for her reward, never leaving her sitting position. Bradford reached down where her nose pushed aside the leaves and came up with the casing. Like always, Bradford gave a handful of kibble.

"Impressive," Stevens said. "You guys are good, just as advertised."

"She's just like any other highly calibrated tool you'd use," Bradford explained, trying not to notice the love and excitement in Deja's eyes. "We keep training to keep her sharp."

Stevens gave him a look out of the corner of his eye, as if he wondered if Bradford was really so by-the-book. "Well, no use freezing our asses off until it's dark. I think we need to make another stop before we call it day."

They started to walk back to the K-9 vehicle.

"What have you got in mind?"

"While you were out there, I got the GSR results back from the state lab. We swabbed Pete Donahue's hands this morning for gunshot residue, and, well, it came back positive on his right hand and forearm."

Bradford was surprised. "But you said he owned guns, right?"

"Yes, several rifles and a .380 handgun."

Bradford wanted to be polite, but he had to ask the

question. "When you were swabbing him, did you ask when the last time was he fired a weapon?"

"No, I'm afraid we didn't. But what's the harm in clearing up that question right now?"

It seemed like the fresh air reenergized the detective. His eyes were bright and he had a plan—even though that plan was in direct disobedience to Richard's request.

When they got to the car, Bradford grabbed a towel from the back to dry Deja off before they climbed inside.

"We were also able to obtain some footage from the high school," Stevens continued. "It's four miles from us on this very road. The patrolman who viewed the video said the camera covers the main entrance, but you can see the roadway in the distance. The quality is grainy, so he can't say for sure, but at 2:20 a.m., there was a light-colored late-model pick-up going west. Guess who lives west of the school and whose second vehicle is a white Silverado?"

"You're kidding me."

"I shit you not. I think it's a good time to have another chat with Mr. Donahue. But there's some bad news."

"How bad?"

"His cell records came back. His phone was pinging the tower a quarter-mile from his house all night."

"So what? Ever run out of the house and forget your phone?"

"Good point. I'll do the talking, but feel free to jump in if I'm not getting anywhere."

•

TEN MINUTES LATER, Bradford, Stevens, and ATF Explosive Detection Canine Deja pulled the unmarked Suburban down a long gravel driveway. They came to a stop in front of a clean, charming country house tucked back in the woods. It was a picturesque spot with long porches and bright white shutters.

"Nice place," Bradford said as they got out. At Stevens's suggestion, he brought Deja with them. Her nose flexed as they got out of the K-9 vehicle, drawing in the cool evening air through her nostrils, picking up hundreds of different markers and clues.

"Pete's some kinda finance guy," Stevens explained as they walked up the front path. "Works at a bank up in Wilmington. Went to Rutgers, I think."

"You seem to know a lot about him."

Stevens's expression was flat. "Hell, I've had beers with the guy at shift parties."

Bradford could see the competing emotions running across the detective's face, but it was all business when he rang the doorbell. The brass lamps on either side of the door kept back the growing night.

A few moments later, Peter Donahue appeared at the door. He was dressed in a clean button-down, but unlike before at the station, he seemed fresh and alert. And surprised.

"Bob, hey," Donahue stammered. He couldn't help himself from leaning out the door and looking up the driveway. It was as if he were expecting someone else.

"Hi, Pete," Stevens replied. Despite the stone-straight face behind the gray beard, Bradford could hear the barely contained emotion in the detective's voice. He struck Bradford as very much a father-figure type, and Bradford wondered if he was taking Ellen's death harder than most. He seemed to know the house well—maybe it brought back memories of her.

"Look, sorry to drop in on you like this," Stevens continued, "but we've got to ask you a few questions."

Donahue stood in the doorway, his shoulder against the frame. "I already talked to you guys all morning and into this afternoon. I went over everything with Detective Richards. Twice, even. Besides, I was just on the phone with my parents when the bell rang. I have to call them back." Then he glanced at Bradford. And Deja. "Who's this?"

"This is Agent Bradford, with the ATF. He's here to assist in the investigation."

Bradford watched Donahue closely. He studied the athletic face that had seemed so tired this morning. He watched for any signs of tension, any involuntary motions. Any body language that might reveal what Donahue was thinking, even if he wasn't saying it out loud.

"Oh, good, good," Donahue muttered, nodding and looking Bradford in the eye. "All the help we can get to find Ellen's killer. Just let me know what I can do."

"May we come in?" Stevens asked without missing a beat. "I really don't want your neighbors hearing what we're talking about."

It was a good tactic, but Donahue hesitated.

"I don't know, the place is ... Your guys really left it a mess today. I'm a bit of a neat freak."

"That's ok, there are just a couple of things we need to clear up. Shouldn't take long. We really appreciate all the help. Sometimes it's the little things that break these cases."

Brad was impressed with the small-town detective's style.

"Uh, well, ok. Just for a minute, you caught me at a bad time. But, um, the dog . . ."

Bradford still was having trouble reading this guy. Situational discomfort, distrust, deception? Peter Donahue was a potpourri of expressions.

Bradford decided to break the ice. "Don't worry, the dog's friendly."

"No, it just looks like he's been in the rain. Don't want him to shake or anything."

"No problem, sir. I'll just have *her* lay right down on this rug by the door. She won't move."

Donahue wavered in the doorway for a moment before he finally relented. He stepped aside to let them in, but he cast one last glance up the darkening driveway before he shut the door.

Stevens got the conversation back on track as the three stood in the living room. "Pete, remember when you were at the station this morning and I took some swabs from your hands?"

"Yeah, sure."

"That was to see if you fired a gun recently. Pete, we got a problem." Clearly Stevens knew when to leave a line hanging to elicit a reaction. Stevens looked directly into Donahue's eyes "The test was positive."

Bradford studied his face for a reaction. Nothing.

"Yeah, ok. Oh, wait, you think because . . ." Donahue let out a short breath and gave a grin. "Guys, the day before yesterday I was at Fox Valley Rifle Range. People saw me there. I was shooting my 30-06 and my shotgun. Oh man, I'm sorry for that. You should've called, I would've told you that."

Stevens did not find the omission funny. "But didn't Detective Richards go back over the last three days in detail? As a matter of fact, if I recall, the day before yesterday, you said you were at work all day, then stopped for pizza with your friends on the way home and went straight to bed after that."

"Yes, yes, but I had my guns in the trunk. I was supposed to go the day before, but it rained. I got off early, had time to kill, and went to the range. Then I met up with my friends."

"That's a pretty important piece of information to leave out, don't you think?"

Peter Donahue ran his hands over his face. The strain and exhaustion were creeping back. "I'm sorry. It's just that with everything going on . . . Look, I'm not hiding anything. I understand you got a job to do, Bob, but why would I hide that? A bunch of people saw me there. I even think they got video of all the ranges. Check it out if you like."

"We'll do that," Stevens said matter-of-factly.
Donahue blinked. Apparently, he expected a different reaction from Ellen's old colleague. "Am I still a suspect or something? Detective Richards cleared me this morning, said I could come home."

"Detective Richards released you pending the results from forensics. The investigation is still ongoing." Stevens spoke brusquely, not giving Donahue a chance to reply. "You don't mind if Agent Bradford here does a sweep of your property and house with the dog, do you? It shouldn't take more than half an hour. Then you can get back to your evening."

"Guys, I—"

Just then a cell phone buzzed on the table in the hall. The sound reverberated loudly in the quiet house.

"Give me a second, would you?" Donahue said as he stood. "It's probably my folks. I was on the line with them when you rang. They're taking this pretty hard. They loved Ellen . . . We all loved Ellen."

He walked into the hall, disconnected his phone from the charger, and made his way into the kitchen.

From her spot by the door, Deja watched him intently as he vanished out of sight.

Bradford had been in these situations before, and he knew better than to make chit-chat with Stevens. They would debrief when they were outside, but not here.

Stevens was on the same page, and they stood there in the living room, taking in the house with the trained eye of seasoned investigators. True to his word, Peter Donahue kept a clean and tidy house. The decor was tasteful and well-thought-out, not the usual big-box-store stuff. The furniture was expensive and hardly used. The hardwood floors looked like they got a regular cleaning.

That was why Bradford was so surprised when he saw the small pile of broken drywall on the floor in the hallway. He hadn't noticed it at first, but there were chunks of drywall and white dust beside the table where Donahue kept his phone. And sure enough, there was a hole in the wall directly above it.

Bradford motioned to Stevens with his eyes, but Donahue appeared back in the room. He looked flustered, and he held the phone to his chest.

"Look, Bob, it's my mom. She's a total wreck. I—I can't . . ." Donahue's face contorted. "Can we wrap this up?"

Detective Stevens made a placating motion with his hands. "Sure thing, Pete. Thanks for your time. We'll be in touch, ok?"

Donahue nodded and turned his back, speaking quickly into the phone as Bradford and Stevens led Deja outside.

The gravel crunched beneath their shoes as they made their way to the Suburban. The forest was now almost completely dark.

"You see that hole in the wall in the hallway?" Bradford

asked as they climbed inside.

"Sure did."

"So what do you think?"

Stevens's eyes were fixed on the house as Bradford started the car.

"I think our friend Pete is hiding something."

SHAWANDA

2:34 p.m.
New York, NY
October 2019

SHAWANDA JACKSON STOOD at the sink, trying to clean the grime off her grandmother's favorite pan. It looked like it hadn't seen a brush in years. Shawanda had always hated pulling dishwashing duty back in Bedford Hills, but now she found a certain satisfaction in it. It was almost like a meditation. Besides, someone had to start cleaning up this place.

She still couldn't believe that this was actually her grandmother's house. Before she got locked up, this place had been the hub of the family, the glue that held them all together even as things kept on getting harder and harder. Their grandmother had been their rock after their parents had died—but now she could hardly get herself out of bed.

Erikah and Isaac were sitting at the kitchen table behind Shawanda. Isaac had walked home from school and went straight to his homework, but even fifteen minutes after his walk, his breathing was still labored as he pored over the textbook in front of him.

"So what you gonna do next?" Erikah was saying,

swiping on her phone and talking to Shawanda at the same time. "Lord knows we needed some help around here, but you can't just scrub dishes all day."

Shawanda had been home for a week, but she hadn't started looking for a job. Part of the parole agreement was that she would actively look for work, which included writing up a resume and applying for jobs. But whenever she started to think about heading down to the library to use their computer and printer, she would suddenly find something else to clean or another project around the crumbling house. Anything to keep her hands busy.

"Oh, you know how it is," she said, scrubbing harder on the burnt crust on the pan. "Ain't much work out there."

"Uh-huh," Erikah said in an *I've heard that before* tone.

It set Shawanda on edge.

"Look, you know it ain't easy for a convict to find work. I can't just walk into a Whole Foods and ask for a job. Most of the baggers and cashiers in there went to college. What have I got? A prison GED. Shit, ain't no one gonna hire me."

Erikah swiped absently on her phone. "Least you could try."

Isaac snorted a laugh.

"Oh, you think it's funny, huh?" Shawanda said, not unkindly.

"Just trying to imagine you working at Whole Foods," Isaac said, grinning over his homework. "You'd bring home all sorts of kale and shit."

Shawanda waved her scrubber at him. "And I'd make you eat it, too."

Isaac laughed again and went back to his geometry. It made Shawanda so happy to see him doing well in school. She'd spent countless hours in prison worrying about him, wondering how he was doing, wondering if he could still breathe. She couldn't even begin to measure the relief she felt that he had grown into a capable young man. He would never go on to run track or play football, but at least her baby brother had a shot at life.

As long as he gets his medicine, she thought as she turned back to the dishes. As usual, the knot in her stomach ratcheted tighter. *How the fuck we gonna pay for all this?*

She glanced over at the door to the living room, where the sound of the TV blared. She could see Chareece and Tariq's legs as they lounged on the filthy couch. He had his big sneakers up on the coffee table, which she had spent a good half an hour trying to get clean yesterday.

"That boy ain't got no respect," she muttered, realizing how much she sounded like her grandmother.

"What you say?" Erikah asked from the table.

Shawanda went back to her scrubbing. "Nothing."

"Hey, how do you find the hypotenuse of a right triangle?" Isaac asked, looking up from his worksheet.

"Shit, you asking me?" Erikah said, leaning away from him. "You're the brainiac around here."

"Let me see your phone," he said, clawing toward her.

"Nuh-uh!" she said, fending him off. "I ain't lettin you cheat on your homework. You gotta figure it out yourself."

"Come on, come on!" he insisted, giggling as she slapped his hands.

It warmed Shawanda's heart to hear them laughing and connecting like this. She had missed this more than she had known.

Just then, Tariq hauled himself up from the couch and swaggered into the kitchen.

Erikah and Isaac fell silent. Erikah dropped her eyes to her phone, and Isaac sunk back into his homework. Both of them suddenly seemed much smaller.

Shawanda felt a cold bolt run down her spine. It was the same feeling she got whenever Latisha came around.

Tariq seemed to relish the effect he had on this family, and he walked over to the fridge in no particular hurry. He pulled out a beer, cracked it, and took a long slow drink in the middle of the room.

Shawanda stood still at the sink. She could hear him drinking behind her.

She wished it was as easy to get rid of him as it was to clean up a crusty pan. But Tariq had always been the tenacious type.

After he drained his beer, he got another one from the fridge and leaned on the counter next to the sink.

"Sup, Wanda."

She didn't respond.

"Me and your baby sister about to roll outta here. We got

some business to take care of. You wanna come with?"

Shawanda knew Erikah and Isaac were listening intently even though they were pretending not to hear. It was no secret what Tariq got up to, and try as they might, none of them could convince Chareece not to get involved. Shawanda had warned her that the path of guns and drugs only led to death and suffering, but Chareece wouldn't hear it. As far as she was concerned, she was putting food on their table, which was more than Erikah or Shawanda could say.

Shawanda bit her tongue and got back to scrubbing.

"Nah, I'm good."

"You sure? We could use some muscle."

Shawanda clenched her jaw, and Tariq laughed in her face as if he was the funniest motherfucker in the Bronx.

"Shit, baby girl, I'm just fuckin' wit' you."

He drained his second beer and tossed it in the sink.

"How bout you get some food going for when we get back." He reached into his back pocket and slapped down a few twenty-dollar bills on the countertop. "And I don't want none of that prison shit you cook. Go out and get us some cheeseburgers or something."

And with that he went back into the living room, where Chareece was waiting by the door. They laughed as they headed out to the street.

The kitchen was quiet after that. Neither Erikah nor Isaac said a word.

All Shawanda could do was take out her anger on her

grandmother's favorite pan. She scrubbed until her knuckles turned red.

After all, she knew all this was her fault. Erikah and Reecy hadn't had someone to support them when she was locked up, not in the way they needed. Shawanda knew it was up to her to make it right—to be the mom that their family had lost all those years ago.

CAMERON

8:53 p.m.
Forward Operating Base (FOB) Davidson
Nangarhar Province, Afghanistan
October 2019

THE SUN HAD set hours ago, sliding past the western mountains that separated the Kunar River Valley from Kabul, eighty miles away, but it was still unbearably hot. Winter wouldn't come to the valley for another few weeks, and this part of Afghanistan was still topping out in the nineties every day, without much relief at night.

CIA Specialist Cameron McNeil and EOD Sergeant Delgado walked into the large sand-colored metal Quonset hut, where a dozen military and para-military types were seated in chairs around a PowerPoint projected onto a drop-down screen. Some of them were CIA operatives, while the rest were active duty Army like Delgado. At this FOB, like many front-line bases around Afghanistan, counterintelligence and field operations went hand in glove. That wasn't to say that the relationship was comfortable—the Army liked to move first and ask questions later, while the CIA guys were great at gathering information and crap at sharing it. But out in the field, both needed the other if they had any chance of winning this interminable fight.

Cameron supposed it wasn't too unlike his relationship with Ken Delgado. Cameron worked well with the spooks when it came to gathering and utilizing intel to protect the base, but he'd never told anyone about his past or about what he'd seen when base security gets breached. He never talked about Yemen or his shaky hands or the nightmares that still haunted him—not even to Delgado, who was the closest thing he had to a friend. But neither Delgado nor anyone else pressed Cameron about his past—he was CIA, and just like at Front Royal, everyone knew not to broach the subject.

Cameron and Delgado took their seats, and Dover laid by Cameron's feet. A few of the other soldiers gave the dog their attention. In the few days since reporting, it was evident that everyone liked having a K9 unit on the team. It made everyone feel safer. Cameron saw the faces of the gate guards when he would run the dog around vehicles entering the FOB. The young twenty-year-old E-2 privates felt confident when Dover was on duty. They had a swagger in their step, as if they had to up their game to keep pace with the dog. From the machine gunners lining up the vehicle in their gunsights to the Afghani soldier charged with interrogating foreign-speaking drivers, everyone looked sharp. Just the way Cameron wanted it.

"Alright, everyone," Supervisory Agent Stan Juszczyk said, drawing the meeting to order. He was dressed in the standard CIA field outfit—khaki 5:11 pants with a gray polo. One of the MPs stationed outside closed the door to the Quonset. "As those of you in this room with clearance already know, the Agency has been engaged in a top-secret operation in this region for the last month, where we intentionally let munitions fall into the hands of enemy combatants."

"Well that's a brilliant fucking idea . . ." Delgado murmured under his breath, only low enough for Cameron to hear. Dover also heard it, and he looked up curiously. Delgado grinned and rubbed him between his ears. "You know what's up, don't you, boy?"

Juszczyk's announcement wasn't news to Cameron, however. He'd been briefed on the operation before he left Langley. It seemed like a dicey proposition. More munitions meant more risk for the base—but everything in war was a calculated risk.

"We embedded tracking beacons in cases of small arms ammunition that were left in strategic locations for Taliban fighters to recover," Juszczyk continued, illuminated in blue light from the blank PowerPoint projection. "The objective was to have the enemy recover these tracked shipments and bring them back to the locations where they store their other munitions, including the big stuff that they're using against our guys. For those that would question this tactic, it has paid off big time in other provinces. And we expect it to do the same here."

Juszczyk signaled to an agent sitting behind a laptop, and the slide changed to an aerial image of an Afghani farmhouse. It was a typical layout, with a main building surrounding a central courtyard, flanked by outbuildings, livestock pens, and acres of dry fields.

"Three days ago," Juszczyk said, "we staged some of the tracked munitions outside of Chaharbagh. They were quickly recovered by the Taliban, and we were able to track the signal to this farmhouse five klicks north of Kuz Kunar." He used his laser pointer to highlight one wing of the farmhouse. "But the signal became intermittent upon arrival, which means that either the battery is weak or the transmitter is crapping out . . . or it might mean that it's under a whole shitload of ordnance."

Juszczyk paused, letting his words land. The agent with the laptop advanced the slide, showing a topo map of the region with assembly points and lines of approach on the farmhouse.

"Either way, we know that our ordnance has been brought to this house. The objective here is for the team to find it, destroy it, and grab whoever is in that farmhouse."

As Cameron listened, his pulse was starting to quicken. He'd gotten back into the swing of base duty, but this was the first time he'd be outside the wire since he'd been back in Afghanistan. His hands started to shake, and he reached for his pack of smokes only to remember where he was. He glanced at Delgado. His friend had seen his jerky movements and gave him a *what the fuck* look.

Juszczyk turned to the Army officer standing next to him and yielded the floor. "Major."

Major McNamara stepped forward. He was a short, powerful man in his mid-thirties, dressed in clean, crisp army

ACUs complete with gold cloth oak leaf in the center of his chest. A career Army type.

"Thank you, agent. Ok, G-2 has this as a pretty quiet sector, which as you know means absolutely fucking nothing out here. If this is where their cache is hidden, you can expect booby traps. Check your fives and twenty fives when dismounting. Extra eyes out for trips, and remember, if you didn't drop it, don't pick it up. Lieutenant, I can have my EOD sergeant brief your security and entry team if you like."

"Yes, sir, I'll get up with him after the briefing."

"Ok, we will form up at the front gate at 0430 hours, depart at 0455. That should put us on target thirty minutes before 0610 sunrise. Three squads from 2nd Platoon will be your security. Lieutenant Fisher, you will be with me in the command eleven-fourteen as lead vehicle, followed by our two MRAPs, then the EOD rig. Sergeant Kelliher, you will be protecting our six with the third squad, and Sergeant, make sure your turret gunners keep eyes on these foothills to the west. I don't even want a fucking goat walking up on our guys when they're in that house."

"Yes, sir."

"EOD will have at their disposal one Explosive Detection Canine should you need a dog search of the area. Specialist McNeil will ride in the EOD JERRV."

Agent Juszczyk flipped closed the laptop, killing the PowerPoint. The hut darkened, illuminated by a few LEDs.

"Alright, you all have your orders. Get your gear checked. And gentlemen, be careful out there. Dismissed."

The soldiers and operatives stood and shuffled out into the hot night, heading back to their huts to prepare for the mission and grab a few hours of shuteye. Delgado stayed behind to work out a few more details with Juszczyk and the EOD team.

But not Cameron. He felt like he could jump out of his skin, and he left the Quonset at full speed. After a quick training session with Dover on Semtex, TNT, and single-based smokeless powder, he was done for the night. But then he was too wired to sleep, so he headed toward the outer perimeter wall instead of the Conex container he called home.

Delgado must have seen him passing by the command hut on his way to the wall.

"Hey, slow down, man," Delgado called after him. "Where the fuck you going?"

Cameron slowed down enough for Delgado to catch up, but he kept walking. Dover must have sensed Cameron's tension—he kept looking around nervously, his tail low and motionless.

"Can't sleep," Cameron said, pausing next to a dirt-filled Hesco barrier to set a cigarette between his lips. His hands were still shaking, but sparking the lighter helped give him something to do.

Delgado gave him another sideways glance. "You sure you alright, man? You look like shit."

"I'm fine," Cameron said after a long drag. They got to

the perimeter fence and stood next to the metal supports of a guard tower. Cameron stood, looking out in the darkness. He could almost make out the dry gullies and the low farmhouses in the distance. Threats coming from all directions.

"You sure you're up for this?" Delgado asked. He had bent down and was giving Dover a rubdown. The dog seemed to calm under his touch. "You're freaking us both out."

Cameron flicked his cigarette and went to light another. Delgado had it all wrong.

"I'm not scared to get out there. I want to get out there *now*. I'm tired of waiting around this base, searching cars, sitting on my hands." He looked out into the darkness. "It's about time we're more proactive. We've gotta take the fight to them."

As he spoke, Cameron tried not to think about his flashback on the explosives range in Front Royal. Now that he was back in a position to keep the base safe, he could feel Yemen getting closer and closer, as if the memory were only inches away at any moment. Back then, he and his superiors had only been reactive, focusing solely on defending the State Department annex against unauthorized entries, guerilla skirmishes, and mortar attacks. They hadn't gathered enough intel in the area to learn about the IED attack before it happened—before the Nissan Atlas truck full of scheduled food deliveries and other supplies also brought in eight 152 millimeter Russian Howitzer artillery shells, each containing 4.4 pounds of TNT. The driver had the bomb triggered with a dead man's switch, which was a button he held down as he drove through the checkpoint. The vehicle-born IED, or VBIED as they became known, would detonate if the pressure was let off the button. It didn't matter if the front gate guards were ready and aiming on the driver—if they killed him, the bomb would still go off. The only way to stop a terrorist like this was before they got into the truck that morning. If not, people would die. Even if the bomber had a change of heart, nothing could be done.

When faced with a threat like this, Cameron knew the best defense was a good offense—and he knew FOB Davidson needed all the defense they could get against the resurgent Taliban in the region. He couldn't let these people down. Not like before.

Delgado was still crouched with Dover. He looked up at Cameron. "What's up with you, man? Ever since you got back you've been acting all jumpy and shit. It's like you're trying to run from your own damn shadow."

"It's nothing. Don't sweat it."

"Fuck you, I *am* gonna sweat it. Your safety is my responsibility, and I don't like the way you're talking right now. If you go out there tomorrow with a point to prove, you're gonna get your ass killed. And you might just get me and Dover killed along the way, too. So you can spare me the 'It's nothing' routine. You're gonna tell me where your head is at, or I'll go to McNamara and get you off the team."

Cameron sighed. He was in no mood to tell his whole damn life story, but he knew Delgado was right.

He owed him the truth.

"Look, something happened on my last detail. There was a security breach, and . . ." He trailed off. "It was down in Yemen."

Delgado's eyes widened. "Shit. You mean, Yemen, like, the State Department annex?"

Cameron nodded. Seventeen dead. Over a hundred wounded. International news. All because he hadn't done his job and kept the compound safe.

"Fuck . . ." Delgado mumbled. "I had no idea, man." He hooked his thumbs through the loops in his tac vest and looked down at the dirt. "Were you on base security?"

"I was, yeah." It was all Cameron had to say. Anyone who had been in combat knew that you didn't talk about the shit you'd seen. Or about how many people died because you made a mistake.

Cameron *did* have a point to prove. He had to prove that he could keep the base safe, even if it meant tracking down every hidden cache of explosives in the entire goddamned valley.

Delgado was quiet for a while. Then he spit in the dirt and gave Cameron a hard punch in the arm. "Well, can't do shit about it now. Just keep your head on straight. Now let's get the fuck outta here, yeah?"

In a strange way, it was just what Cameron needed to hear. It was a soldier's way of saying, *I understand. And I've got your back.*

And with that, Delgado walked off to his bunk in the EOD hut.

With Dover faithfully by his side, Cameron stood at the fence for another half an hour and worked through five more smokes. He couldn't help but feel the danger that lurked beyond.

When he finally headed back to his quarters, Dover padded alongside him in the dirt, close and attentive. He licked Cameron's hand reassuringly, flipping his hand up with his wet nose.

Sometimes it felt like this dog was the only thing holding him together.

BRADFORD

9:24 p.m.
Newport Police Department
Newport, DE
October 2019

BRADFORD SAT AT the unfamiliar desk in the unfamiliar police station and watched as his coffee got cold. He'd been on hold now for over twenty minutes, and his wrist was starting to ache from holding the receiver to his ear. He wasn't trusting the speaker feature, fearing he would not hear when the other line picked up. Deja was sleeping at his feet, her paws twitching. Stevens was sitting at the desk behind him. Since returning to the police department, the pair had been watching the fuzzy black-and-white security video from the high school over and over, trying to zero in on the make and model of the grainy vehicle driving down a dark road at 02:20:38. It was light in color, and as the patrolmen had said to Stevens, it could be a pickup. Then again, it could be a full-size four-door. Whatever it was, it was driving west, 14.6 miles and eighteen minutes and twelve seconds from a homicide.

They needed to do an immediate thorough search of Peter Whitmore Donahue's residence, and this was all they had as far as probable cause to get in there with Deja. Bradford knew

this would never be enough probable cause at the federal
level—no federal judge would ever approve a warrant on just
a grainy video, but this was New Castle County, Delaware,
and you never knew unless you tried.

As he waited on hold, he looked over at Stevens, who
stared blankly at the paused video frame of the unknown
vehicle. He was lost in his thoughts, no doubt reliving the
moment he arrived on scene and found Ellen Donahue, his
good friend and fellow officer, murdered in a 7-Eleven
parking lot. And now he had to work it like it was someone
else's homicide. Bradford learned that the Delaware State
Police had offered to take over the case out of respect, but the
Newport PD chief, whom he had yet to meet, had insisted that
his department call the shots—no matter how personal, no
matter how painful.

Bradford knew all about wrestling with ghosts. You
didn't spend twenty years in law enforcement without seeing
things that burned themselves upon the surface of your mind,
never to be forgotten. He knew the toll that this line of work
took. He had seen death. And those who caused it.

Bradford glanced at his hand, noticing the tan line on his
left ring finger. Even after all this time, the skin was still
white, as if the wedding band he once wore had left a
permanent mark on him. Jennifer had passed away a few
years before he transferred to the Philadelphia office, and he
had never found another way to fill the void that she had left
in his life. They had both wanted kids, but after years of
trying, they went to an IVF specialist only to discover that she

had Stage III ovarian cancer. She hung on for a few more years, but in the end, her body finally gave out. Just like Copper.

Bradford knew that it takes a special kind of spouse to understand this job—and he knew that no one would ever understand him the way Jennifer had. From the moment he joined ATF, he signed up to respond to chaotic scenes of mass death at places of worship, businesses, schools. Recovering guns from the stiff hands of dead shooters where the police had taken them down—or where they'd turned the guns on themselves. Another burn mark on the surface of Bradford's mind. He'd seen the worst humanity had to offer, but he'd never found a way to tell anyone except Jennifer what he'd faced on the job. How could he? They wouldn't have understood.

This was the era of PTSD, critical incident debriefings, getting in touch with one's inner self. Bradford decided not to hop on that bus. He was fully aware that the suppression of feelings and thoughts was a ticking time bomb, but that would have to wait until he chose to face that demon. On his terms. Maybe after he retired. Probably too late to fix what was slowly eating him up.

Now, he was alone. But the job wasn't getting any easier.

He sighed and took a swig of cold coffee. The line was still on hold.

Near his feet, Deja gave a little whimper as she chased something in her dreams. Her soft black lips kept quivering, going from a pout to a smile as she ran and ran and ran.

Just then, Deja awoke and looked at him alertly, and a moment later a voice came on the line.

How does she do that? Bradford wondered as the secretary's voice filled his ear.

"Agent Bradford? Thank you for holding. You are on the line with Judge Beaumont."

Bradford snapped his fingers and got Detective Stevens's attention. Both investigators huddled around the office phone. Bradford hit the speaker button and eased the receiver gently back in the cradle.

"What can I do for you, Officers?" the judge asked. "I understand you are seeking an emergency telephonic search warrant for the residence of a murder suspect? Before you start, let me ask you, what is the emergency that this matter could not be discussed with the District Attorney and brought before me on a written affidavit in the morning?"

"Your Honor, Detective James Stevens here. Sir, we feel that the individual who resides in the house, and has not currently been named a suspect, may dispose of certain evidence if and when he is considered a suspect, which could be at any time."

"Ok, ok. I see. Do you gentlemen solemnly swear to tell the truth, so help you God?"

Both investigators responded in unison, "We do."

"Go ahead, tell me what you have."

"Your Honor, this is Special Agent Canine Handler Thomas Bradford with the Bureau of Alcohol, Tobacco,

Firearms, and Explosives, Philadelphia Field Office. I'm assisting the Newport Police Department in the shooting death investigation of Officer—"

The judge interrupted, "Agent, we can skip the case background, I'm fully aware of what you guys have got going on there. And I'm also aware that the husband let you search his house earlier today. Just tell me what you're looking for and what probable cause you have to believe the murder weapon is in that residence."

Bradford liked this judge. He was a cut-to-the-chase type of agent, so he jumped right in. "Your Honor, the officers this morning conducted a very basic initial search. Since that time, we have discovered some additional information from Mr. Donahue, and we also obtained some initial forensic results. Regarding our latest interview that occurred a few hours ago, Donahue left out some key information when the police first spoke to him, namely that he had practiced shooting the day before the murder. And the second piece of information we just received is a surveillance video. It shows a vehicle that could be Mr. Donahue's driving from the direction of the murder scene toward the direction of his residence following the murder. Based on that information, and my nineteen years of experience conducting firearms cases, I believe that located inside 9437 Old Mill Road in Newport, Delaware, is certain evidence including firearms and ammunition used in the homicide of Officer Ellen Donahue."

There was silence on the line. Bradford was just about to

say, "Hello?" when Judge Beaumont spoke.

"I have a couple of questions. So he hid that fact that he was practicing his shooting from you?"

Bradford looked at Stevens for a response. "Well, sir, I wouldn't say he hid it. He just left it out."

"I see. And what kind of vehicle does Mr. Donahue own?"

"Your Honor, Agent Bradford again. He owns two—a 2014 white Chevy pickup and a blue 2020 Kia Optima."

"Which one is on the video?"

"We believe it could be the pickup."

"You believe? Is it the same make and model at least?"

"We can't tell from the video. It's very fuzzy,"

"Guys, can I talk to you off the record? I know what you're trying to do, and I respect it. You want to do everything humanly possible to arrest the person who did this to your officer. I'd give you this warrant in a New York minute, but there's just not enough probable cause here to stand up to a suppression hearing. If you were to find anything, perhaps the key piece of evidence, you'd lose its admissibility in court—and most likely the entire case. I'm going to deny your request. Connect a few more dots and come back to me. Good luck, gentlemen."

And with that, he was gone.

Bradford sighed and sat back in his chair, scrubbing his face. Deja was watching him closely.

"So what now?"

Detective Stevens's face was grim. His beard seemed

even grayer than before, but his eyes were steely and focused.

"I think it's time we call Mr. Donahue in for another chat."

SHERRY

5:09 p.m.
Eagle Pass Border Crossing
Eagle Pass, TX
October 2019

THE SUN WAS starting to sink in the sky as Sherry Fry made her way along the never-ending line of cars. She and Dolly were doing another sweep of the line after another long day on the job. Her feet were sore, and she was hungry, but she had three more hours ahead of her, so she sucked it up and focused on the task at hand. She knew all too well that if she was off her game, Dolly would be too.

"One-four, command," came the voice of her CO, Jimmy Gonzalez, over the radio. "How we looking out there, Fry?"

"More of the same," she replied, keying the mic on her shoulder. "Mostly Mexican nationals. A few college kids. Retirees crossing to get meds. Dolly hasn't hit on anything."

She knew it was good news, but at the same time, she couldn't help shake the feeling that they were missing something. Quiet was good—but too quiet always made her feel uneasy.

"Keep it up, one-four. We keep hearing chatter from the intel center in El Paso. EPIC says our Mexican counterparts just found two more policemen shot dead in an alley, not a mile from the bridge. The Zetas are making a big push, and the *Federales* want us to step it up on our side. Nothing gets across."

"Roger that, command."

Dolly looked up at the sound of the radio voice, but then went back to her work, tail wagging as if this was the best game ever.

I could use some of that enthusiasm right about now, she thought, then immediately chided herself. *Come on, Sherry, this is no time for a pity party. You can unwind when you get home. But right now, you gotta stay sharp.*

Sherry picked up the pace, moving along the line of cars waiting to cross back into Mexico. The afternoon traffic was always the heaviest this side of the border.

She walked Dolly around a few family vehicles, and then circled a large semi-trailer twice as the driver looked on nervously.

Nothing to worry about if you have nothing to hide, Sherry always said.

She was just about to head back to the main portal building to get Dolly a drink when she noticed the dog stick her snout in the air. Dolly's eyes narrowed, and the flaps on the sides of her wet nose started to work overtime. She was detecting something.

"You got something, girl?" Sherry asked, suddenly alert. "What is it?"

The smell had caught Dolly's attention, but not enough to move her in a direction.

Sherry looked back to the border crossing office. Beside the long line of waiting cars, the American flag was flapping in the wind, pointing toward Mexico. The wind was coming from the north. That meant the odor was coming from further back in the line of cars waiting to cross the border.

Sherry peered through her sunglasses and scanned the line. She had searched most of them, but many more cars had arrived at the end of the line in the last fifteen minutes.

"Come on, girl. Seek."

Dolly lowered her head and together they walked back up the one-hundred-degree pavement, which broke out into four lanes as the cars approached the border.

Dolly set her nose to the first car. Not interested. She completely blew past the next three.

She worked methodically, moving back and forth between the lanes as Sherry peered into windshields and windows as they went.

"Command, this is unit one-four," she said into her shoulder mic. "Send someone down here, will you? The dog is into odor."

"Copy that, one-four," replied Gonzalez. "Sending two officers your way."

Dolly pulled forward, zeroing on a car two lanes over. She slowed down her sniffing, working over the entire minivan. Sherry looked into the window as Dolly moved to the rear wheel wells. A young Hispanic woman sat upright with both hands on the steering wheel, trying hard to not look at the *policia* outside her window. Sherry caught her own reflection—dark sunglasses, hair pulled tight into a bun, military tac vest.

I'd be scared too, Sherry thought, but Dolly had already moved on.

Next, they approached a blue Dodge pick-up truck. Dolly again worked slowly and intensely, starting with the front bumper.

The windows on the truck were down, and Sherry heard Kenny Chesney on the radio. She looked in the cab. The driver was wearing a straw cowboy hat and the passenger appeared to be his teenage son. They both looked at her as she passed the window.

"Afternoon, ma'am," the driver said in a thick Texas accent.

Dolly tugged hard on the leash, working along the running board of the truck. She made for the rear wheels.

Sherry glanced over her shoulder. The driver was watching her in the side mirror. Further down the approachway, she could see two green-uniformed officers making their way to her position, still two hundred feet away.

"Good girl," Fry muttered. "Seeeeeek."

Dolly worked past the rear wheel, turned the corner, sniffed the rear bumper, then promptly sat.

Sherry quickly stepped out of the view of the side mirror. She bent down and praised Dolly quietly, giving her a handful of kibble from her side pouch. Then she stood and keyed her radio.

"Command, we got a hit here." Then in the next breath, she placed her hand on her pistol, stepped out to the rear corner of the truck, and said, "Sir, shut off the engine and step out of the vehicle."

She could see the driver's eyes in the mirror. He glanced around quickly, as if looking for an escape, a sliver of space to run, but there were cars on all sides.

The two other officers were hurrying down the approachway.

"Now, sir. Shut off the engine and step out of your vehicle."

She could see the driver tightening his grip on the steering wheel. Next to him, the teenager was whipping his head around, looking terrified.

Don't do anything stupid . . .

Sherry unclipped the strap on her holster and slid her hand around the black polymer grips of the pistol.

The family in the Rav-4 next to her started to panic, pointing and talking loudly inside their car.

The man with the cowboy hat opened the door.

Sherry bent her knees, expecting him to run, but then the engine died and his two hands came out.

"It's ok, it's ok," he said as he climbed out of the cab. He raised his hands as Sherry moved in to pat him down. "This is all just misunderstanding. I raise hounds, bring 'em all around the county. Your dog probably just smelled 'em is all."

The two other officers arrived just as the teen stepped out, pale as a sheet.

Sherry kicked apart the feet of the cowboy hat man and searched him as Dolly looked on happily.

"Sir, you clearly don't know my dog."

FIFTEEN MINUTES LATER, the officers had taken the truck into the emergency lane and brought it to the inspection canopy. Several ICE agents were inspecting the vehicle under the watchful eye of Fry and Dolly and Jimmy Gonzalez. One of them had a long screwdriver and was working on the rear bumper. The driver and his son were sitting in handcuffs on a curb twenty feet away, guarded by two CBP officers.

"Let's see what you've got," Gonzalez said to her as the ICE agents freed the bumper and pulled it away. Dolly's nose was in overdrive even as she sat patiently next to Sherry.

The ICE agent peered into the open frame with a flashlight, then reached under with a gloved hand.

"Aha, good job Dolly!"

A moment later, he pulled an AR-15 rifle from under the chassis. He reached back and pulled out a second.

Dolly's tail was wagging, and Sherry reached down to pet her head.

Next to her, Gonzalez looked proud, but he was in no mood to celebrate.

"You did good today, Fry. Across the bridge, these rifles could sell for ten times what these guys paid at Walmart." He shook his head. "The Zetas have been buying up all the guns they can find. Doesn't look like this war is going to cool off any time soon."

Sherry knew her CO was right. They'd prevented these two guns from crossing the border, but how many more were slipping through their fingers? How much more bloodshed would there be? Schoolchildren caught in the crossfire. Restaurant owners shoved into refrigerators and executed for not paying protection money. Policemen beheaded and left in the street. Innocent people, all of them. Sherry wondered how many more had to die before this all came to an end.

Mexico was burning, and all they could do was watch from the other side of the river.

CAMERON

4:52 a.m.
Forward Operating Base (FOB) Davidson
Nangarhar Province, Afghanistan
October 2019

THE HEADLIGHTS ILLUMINATED the front gate of the forward operating base. Engines idled in the early morning darkness, filling the air with diesel exhaust and kicking up dust that drifted in front of the high-intensity beams. Dark figures were finalizing comms checks and climbing into their respective rigs.

There were three Cougar MRAPs all in a line, with their enormous wheels and small impact-proof windows. Each truck was reinforced with thick steel plates on the sides and undercarriages, configured like the "V" hull of a boat designed to deflect outward the blast from mines and other IEDs that they might encounter on the dangerous roads outside the relative safety of FOB Davidson. The MRAPs were flanked by two up-armored M-1114 High Mobility Multi-Wheeled Vehicles—known to the military as HMMWVs and the civilian world as Humvees. The one in front was the command vehicle with the Major, and the one in the rear of the convoy was crewed by First Sergeant Brian Kelliher and his guys from 3rd squad.

Cameron and Dover and EOD Sergeant Delgado were in the EOD MRAP in the middle of the convoy. Even though it was a Cougar like the others, the EOD squad called it the JERRV, or the Joint EOD Rapid Response Vehicle. Inside were a mix of six Army EOD team members and four CIA specialists, all trained in ordnance seek-and-destroy. The 47th Ordnance Company was a tight-knit group out of Fort Bragg, and it showed. They ate, slept, trained, and partied in the EOD hut. It reminded Cameron of the clubhouse he built with his buddies when he was ten, when they spent the whole summer hanging out in their fort. EOD depended on each other for survival more than any other unit—and now, Cameron had joined the club. As the K9 unit on the team, the "seek" element of their mission fell to him and Dover. Both the Army and CIA had a few other K9 units deployed in-country, but none of them had the training in explosives and forensics that he had. All those months spent sweating under Instructor Adams's watchful eyes had come down to this.

At 0455, Major McNamara's voice came through the radio, giving the signal to move out. The two gates with their heavy chain-link and razorwire swung open, and the five vehicles slowly rolled out into the darkness, twisting their way through the serpentine concrete barriers that slowed the approach of any vehicle entering or exiting the base. Once they were clear of the gates, the sounds of rifle chambers being cycled bounced off the metal walls of the rig's interior. Everyone was now clear to lock and load as the driver picked up speed and drove into the Kunar River Valley.

Cameron sat in the back, getting jostled as the JERRV's massive wheels navigated the rutted roads. Dover was sitting on the floor next to him, alert and patient. The vision-preserving LEDs illuminated the interior, turning all the soldiers into red versions of themselves as they sat with their rifles.

The radio crackled with intermittent chatter as the convoy passed dry fields toward their destination, twenty-three klicks to the northwest. On top of each vehicle in the convoy, the turret gunners scanned the darkness with night-vision goggles. Not a soul to be seen, but everyone knew they were out there. You can't be covert when five military vehicles thundered down these underdeveloped roads. Someone, somewhere, was watching.

Cameron traced the edges of his cigarette pack through the stiff fabric of this tactical vest. His habit was getting worse, and he knew it.

There was no conversation in the back of the JERRV. Each of the specialists on the EOD team was focused on the task at hand. Even Dover looked serious, as if he knew this was more than just a game.

Cameron was certain the same was going on in the other vehicles. The Army entry team had done this before—they were specially trained in tactical entries, and their expertise went far beyond the training of SWAT teams back in the states. The remaining two Army squads would be providing perimeter security so the EOD team could get to work.

Cameron was always amazed at the amount of responsibility put on these soldiers, both male and female, many of whom were barely into their twenties.

About twenty minutes into the drive, Delgado turned around from the track commander's seat in the front and reached back to give Dover a scratch behind the ears, which made the dog smile. It gave Cameron a sense of pride to see Dover so in his element. This dog was a soldier, ready for whatever could be thrown at them.

Like dog, like handler.

But even so, Cameron's stomach got tighter as they trundled further and further away from base. This was their mission, what they had been trained for—but he'd never forgive himself if something happened to Dover.

TWENTY-FIVE MINUTES later, the column climbed over a low rise and then dipped down into the small valley north of Kuz Kunar. The staticky voice of Major McNamara came over the radio.

"Two klicks out. Target location should be at our two o'clock. Top turrets, let us know if you see anything. Repeat, anything."

"First squad copy"

"Deuce copy"

"Three is roger"

The soldiers and CIA specialists that made up the EOD team started to prep their gear. Dover watched as one of the EOD techs reached down next to his nose and flipped the switch on the small tracked robot on the floor. Once he did, the actuator arm moved into position. This surprised the dog, who stared at it like it was a creature from another world.

In the shadowy distance, the farmhouse began to take shape. The sky in the east was just barely starting to lighten, and the narrow valley was illuminated in the predawn light.

The five-vehicle convoy then broke off the main road and thundered down the dusty path that led to the farmhouse. The two HMMWVs each took a position on the southeast and southwest corners of the compound. There would be no crossfire accidents on this mission. The MRAPs came to a quick halt, strategically parking a hundred feet from the cluster of earthen and timber structures.

The farm seemed quiet. It was still half an hour before dawn, so those inside might have been still asleep. Except for the hum of the diesel engines and the faint crackle from the radio in the cab, there was little sound. All the operators wore headsets, and they came to life.

"Bravo one turret has nothing. No movement in the house."

"Bravo two, no movement to south and west."

"Bravo three has clear visual to the east. All clear."

"EOD gunner advises our six is clear."

"Bravo leader to cover teams, you're clear to go."

"Cover one roger."

"Cover two roger."

"Bravo leader to entry, you're clear to go."

"Entry is moving."

With clockwork precision, the rear hatches opened and two squads of soldiers spilled out of the MRAPs. They moved quickly but smoothly, M4A rifles planted firmly in their shoulders, cheeks pressed against the buttstock, trigger fingers alongside the frame. They fanned out and secured the perimeter before the third squad, the designated entry team, staged outside the mud wall leading up to the house.

Leaving Dover inside the safety of the armored vehicle with a strong command to stay, Cameron moved to a position of cover behind the open rear door of the JERRV. He drew his sidearm as the Army squads approached the front door. Dover was lying on the floor, watching intently as the action unfolded. As members of the EOD team, their orders were to hang back until the farmhouse was secure and all hostiles had been neutralized or taken into custody.

A squad of soldiers reached the front doors to the farmhouse, their night vision goggles now flipped upward against their Kevlar helmets since the dawn was upon them and the sky was lightening by the minute. One of the soldiers kicked down the rickety wooden door with one motion, and the other soldiers fanned out inside, weapons at the ready.

From his time as a Marine in Iraq, Cameron knew exactly what was unfolding inside. They would clear the house room by room, moving methodically like a choreographed play. There would be no need to verbalize commands. Every finger point and hand gesture spoke loudly as the team moved from room to room, always maintaining muzzle discipline, always aware of where every team member was should the shooting start. They would take prisoners, but if they found anyone armed inside, there would be no time to ask questions. Was it legal, justifiable? It would all depend on who and what they found inside.

From inside the rig, Cameron heard Dover give a little whine as he inched closer to the open door, his nose working, taking in all the odors of this foreign location. He was smelling goats, and dried mud, and the spices from the meal cooked the night before.

"I know, boy," Cameron said, "I want to get in there too . . ."

Cameron glanced over to Delgado, who had taken cover with the other members of the EOD team behind the first squad's MRAP. Delgado's men were ready, and one of them was already suited up in full bomb gear just in case he was needed. The key was speed. Every minute they spent at the farmhouse was another minute for the Taliban to use their system of radios and cell phones to alert the local militia—if they weren't already here.

But at the moment, all was quiet.

Cameron turned to scan the area around them. He saw the command vehicle parked to his left; the turret gunner was watching the south and west, the other HMMWV was parked on the southeast but a distance from the property. This vantage point allowed that unit, led by Sergeant Kelliher, to see the back of the farmhouse and the dry fields beyond, including some rickety old animal pens that were no more than a few wooden slats standing in the dust. There was no denying that this position was highly exposed. The farmhouse sat at the bottom of a spur off the main valley, and there was high ground around them on three sides. A perfect location for an ambush.

Why did those shitheads have to bring the ordinance here? Cameron thought as he pulled his eyes away from the threatening hills and looked back to the house. *Let's just hope this works.*

Fifteen more seconds passed.

Cameron kept bracing for the staccato pops that meant the entry team faced a threat and someone had gotten shot.

But there was no gunfire.

Moments later, the squad leader came through on the radio. "Main building is secure."

Major McNamara replied from inside the command vehicle. "Roger that. Get the EOD team to start their search. I wanna get the fuck outta here before the whole damn tribe gets here."

Delgado gave the EOD team a signal. "Alright, let's move out. Canine team, up by me."

Cameron let out a short whistle and Dover bounded out the back of the vehicle. Cameron kept his gun drawn and reached down to grab the loose end of Dover's lead in the dust.

Sergeant Delgado waited at the opening in the mud wall. "I want you right by my side," he said to Cameron. "If your dog has interest in something, let me know and I will go with you. I am personally responsible for both of you, got it?"

Cameron responded with a quick affirmative. He was a seasoned vet and he hated being on Delgado's leash, but Delgado was in charge, and Cameron respected him too much to give him shit.

Inside, they found a disheveled interior that looked like it had been abandoned for some time. There were moldy pillows and dusty rugs piled in the corner of the main room, an old TV from the '80s, and garbage strewn everywhere. In the kitchen, a rusty washbasin overflowed with pots and discarded yellow palm oil containers. Straw and mouse droppings littered the floor.

Dover's nose was working like crazy as he took in all the scents. He sniffed along the walls and under the ramshackle cabinets.

"C'mon, boy. Seeeek."

Dover continued his sweep, with Cameron watching his every move and signal. He noted the way Dover lifted his paw as he focused in on a scent, the way his tail would straighten when he smelled something that caught his attention. It could have been the ammunition on all of the soldiers and EOD guys in the house, or the fact that even with all the acclimation training they did in Kabul and at the FOB, this place was just different. Dover had been trained to ignore those distractors, but that didn't mean he didn't smell them.

And so Cameron watched, trying to read the signals and

zero in on the scents that mattered.

"Shit, you guys gotta come see this."

It was one of the EOD techs. He was in the other room with another technician. Cameron and Delgado followed the voice, and Dover let out a low growl when they walked into the room.

In the center of the back room, there were several hooks suspended from the ceiling and patches of dried blood on the hardpacked floor.

"Christ," one of the techs mumbled.

"What happened here?" Cameron asked.

Boyega, one of the CIA specialists, replied, "Shit like this happens all the time. The Taliban come through villages like this and torture families who aren't on their side—or who won't pay them protection money. Then they'll take over the house and use it for a few days or weeks before they clear out. It's how they keep moving, always a step ahead."

"Well, we're gonna get these fuckers today," Delgado said, his eyes hard. "Come on, let's keep looking."

The EOD team moved on, continuing to sweep the farmhouse and then moving on to the outbuildings. Cameron ran Dover through every room, but even though the dog would often pause for an extended period of time, there was no definitive signal.

The sun was coming up over the horizon when Cameron spilled out into the courtyard. An EOD tech was sweeping the yard with a metal detector, which kept going off every two feet.

He pulled off his headphones and spoke to Delgado. "This is bullshit, Sarge. There're nuts, bolts, shell casings, all kinds of shit through here." He bent down and scooped up a handful of dirt and let it fall through his fingers. Two rusty nuts and an old lag bolt remained in his hand. "Every inch of this place is like this. All of our readings are shit."

Delgado looked pissed. He turned to Cameron. "What says the dog?"

"We walked through all the buildings. His behavior changed a bit, and he showed some interest here and there, but nothing definitive."

Delgado swore. "They probably wouldn't keep the cache in the main house anyway. Alright, we'll start searching around the perimeter." He looked toward the rising sun. "I'll go tell McNamara that we're gonna be here a while longer."

BACK AT FOB Davidson, Juszczyk stood in the comm tent next to a CIA electronic specialist.

Major McNamara's voice came intermittently through the radio.

"We haven't . . . found anything yet, sir. What . . . last signal . . . location."

Juszczyk was getting annoyed. "We got a strong signal there at 0800 hours yesterday, right in the middle of that house. It was intermittent at 0300 hours today, but still at that same location. No signal since 0400. The drone showed no one leaving that location prior to your arrival. Gotta still be there, Major. Have those guys check it good."

The major responded, "Sir, we checked the rafters . . .
looked for hidden . . . in all three buildings. EOD's out
with . . . metal detectors . . ." He paused, and static came over
the line. "The perimeter is secure but . . . exposed in this
location."

"Keep looking, Major," Juszczyk insisted. "It's gotta be
there."

JASON

10:29 a.m.
Public School 134
New York, NY
October 2019

THE CHILDREN ALL sat with rapt eyes as US Marshal Jason Hernandez gave his presentation, but they weren't looking at him. They all were focused solely on Disney, who sat there with her tongue hanging out of her mouth.

"So, like we talked about earlier," Jason was saying, speaking loudly and clearly to not lose their attention even further, "Disney here only gets to eat when she finds an explosive. So that means she's always working, all day, every day."

One of the little girls shot her hand in the air.

"Yes, Isabella?" the teacher asked.

"Does that mean Disney never sleeps?" the little girl demanded.

"No, Disney gets plenty of sleep," Jason explained patiently. "It just means that she has to work for her food, breakfast, lunch, and dinner."

Isabella clearly didn't think that was fair, so Jason hurried on.

"You know, Disney could probably use a snack right about now. Who wants to see her get to work?"

The third graders all shouted with excitement.

"Ms. Ruiz, would you do the honors?" Jason said to the teacher, a pretty young woman who couldn't have been older than twenty-four.

Jason gave a little sigh as he handed over Disney's lead to her. He didn't mind working kiddie duty—it was certainly better than sitting behind a desk—but this was not what he'd imagined a K9 detail would be. Sure, he'd been assigned to security details at various courtrooms around the city, and he and Disney had done an interesting sweep around a federal judge's house after a bomb threat, but it wasn't the gripping assignment he'd hoped it would be. Nothing brought him joy like seeing these children laugh, but this was not where he was meant to be. He was supposed to be out on the streets.

Once the teacher had led Disney outside, Jason produced a training aid from the sealed bag in his pocket. He held the red crinkly firecracker wrapper up for all the children to see.

"This paper once had firecrackers in it, but it's empty now." He whispered dramatically, "Do you all think that Disney will find it if we hide it real good?"

"Yes!" they all cried out at once.

"So where should we hide it?"

He was bombarded with fifty suggestions all at once, but he settled for hiding it in a box of crayons in one of the cubbies in back. Jason dramatically tip-toed away from the cubby hole and put his finger up to his lips.

"Shhhh, now nobody say anything. Ok, Ms. Ruiz, you and Disney can come back in."

The teacher came in, handed Jason the lead, and stepped back.

The children eagerly giggled, following Jason's long *seeeek* command as Disney put her nose in the air, taking in the easily detectable potassium perchlorate used in flash powder that now floated in the air. She effortlessly made her way to the back.

The children exploded with shrieks and giggles and applause as she put her nose right to the crayon box and assumed the sitting alert position.

Jason smiled. The sound of laughter made it all worth it. Maybe one day he would have kids of his own. He just needed to find the right woman first. He thought about giving Ms. Ruiz his number once the demo was over, but instead he checked his phone, wondering if Sherry Fry had replied to him.

There was no text, but a moment later, his phone rang in his hand. It was Bill Simmons.

"Yo Hernandez, wrap it up. We need you and the dog back here ASAP. We got a tip on a fugitive."

Jason wanted to shout for joy.

"It's about time," he said to his old partner. He got the address for the briefing location, then said, "I'll be there in twenty."

"With this traffic?" Simmons barked. "From Brooklyn?

Not a chance. We'll wait for you."

"I'll be there in twenty," he repeated, then he hung up and turned to the class. "Sorry, everyone. Looks like Disney and I have to go. Urgent police business."

The kids gave a loud "aww," and even Ms. Ruiz seemed particularly disappointed, but Jason just gave her a smile instead of his number. He had his heart set elsewhere.

He'd make sure to text Sherry again later tonight.

JASON ACCELERATED HIS canine vehicle down the FDR Drive as Simmons's voice came through the speakerphone.

"This guy is no joke," Simmons was saying. "Wanted for armed bank robbery, possession of a firearm by a convicted felon, and a whole laundry list of other fuck ups. He was initially charged by the state, made bond, now the feds have indicted him. Of course he was a no-show at his arraignment on Tuesday and hasn't been seen since, but we just got a tip that he's shacked up with a girlfriend."

Jason's hands were sweaty on the steering wheel. After weeks of mindless duty, this was finally his break to get in on the action. He loved fugitive work, but since being assigned a K9, it seemed like he was an afterthought to the apprehension unit. He was always called after the fact, following the route of a foot chase looking for the tossed gun or sweeping a vehicle before going into the seizure garage to make sure no guns were missed. He missed the hunt.

But as he sped up the FDR, he began to realize that it had been months since he'd seen any real action in the field. It was the kind of thing that could make a marshal lose his edge. And when a marshal in the field lost his edge, people had a tendency to get hurt.

"I'm assuming the dude will be armed?" Jason asked as he wove between traffic, the dashboard lights on his unmarked car flashing.

"I would be shocked if he wasn't. You and your partner should get a gun outta this."

Jason turned to look at Disney through the open sliding door between driver and canine compartments. He always left the door open because Disney loved to lay her head on the armrest while they drove. But now Disney was sitting at attention, looking past the windshield. She knew something big was up. Jason tapped the siren button a couple of times for a truck that was driving slow in the fast lane.

"The fugitive task force is meeting up the block from Yankee Stadium before we move to 1839 Riverside Terrace," Simmons said.

"We have time to catch a game?"

"Very funny. Get your ass down here. We don't have much time."

Jason finally was able to pull around the dump truck, and he sped as fast as he could.

Seven minutes later, he pulled into an empty parking lot in the shadow of the new stadium and met up with the task force that had already assembled. There were five agents getting into their black tactical vests.

Jason hopped out of the car with Disney as Simmons was handing out sheets of paper with the fugitive's picture along with his rap sheet and a photo of the townhouse.

"Ok, we have to move quick if we want to get this guy," Simmons instructed. Jason still wasn't used to taking orders from his old partner, but Simmons had recently gotten a big promotion and was loving every minute of his new role. "The info we got is pretty good that he's here. Schmalz and Oviedo, you two will do the initial approach at the front door. We just have the arrest warrant, so do your best at talking your way in there. But, as always, officer safety first. If you get anyone stalling you, running, hiding, pushing you out the door, get your asses in there immediately and notify your outside teams. Ok, Hernandez, you and the dog will cover the back yard. I'll watch the front and cover the north gangway. Gamboa will be in the alley watching the south gangway, and we will have uniformed officers on the cross-streets. We're gonna get this son of a bitch."

Simmons got on the radio and notified the marked squads to get into position, then he turned back to the fugitive team.

"Alright, let's move out."

Jason parked the USMS canine Explorer one block over and took Disney by the leash as they set out down the street. He loved the feeling of being out in the field again, but a nagging worry was forming in the back of his mind. He knew he was the best marshal in the office—but he hadn't been on a live arrest in over six months.

And now he had Disney to think about.

Come on, Jase, you got this, he told himself as the team headed down the street and moved into position. *Just don't fuck it up.*

BRADFORD

10:04 a.m.
Newport Police Department
Newport, DE
October 2019

PETER DONAHUE ONCE again found himself in the interrogation room of the Newport Police Department. He fidgeted at the table, looking up at the acoustic ceiling tiles and then into the one-way mirror—a futile attempt at watching whoever was watching him.

Bradford and Detective Stevens were in that observation room, indeed watching him as they went over their notes and their strategy when Detective Richards burst into the room. His big barrel chest stuck out from his jacket, and his face was livid.

"What the fuck is going on here, Stevens? I thought I told you to leave Mr. Donahue alone. Just what the hell do you think you're doing?"

Stevens didn't back down. He very calmly set his pen down on his notepad and turned to face the younger detective. Bradford stepped back, sipped his coffee, and watched the pissing match unfold.

"First off, keep your voice down and try to act professional. Peter Donahue is still a person of interest in this case," Stevens said directly. "And as a person of interest, we have every obligation to track down any potential leads."

"Leads? What leads?"

"Surveillance video came in last night, showing a white pickup heading westbound on Old Mill Road. I don't have to tell you that's heading from the 7-Eleven toward Donohue's house. The gunshot residue also came back positive. We know that when he gave you his statement, he happened to leave out the fact that he had been to a gun range two days prior. That's strange. Especially when we swabbed him. I had planned to fill you in on these developments but..."

Richards blew air through his nostrils. Deja perked up at the sound.

"But what? You tell me to act professional and you do this shit behind my back? Come on, give me a fucking break. The guy's grieving for his wife, he didn't know what we were swabbing him for. We don't need to keep dragging his ass down here. All you're going to do is make him lawyer up, which means we're going to get nothing out of him. Way to go, genius."

"These are the only leads we have," Stevens shot back. "And if we don't pursue them, we are guaranteed to get nothing."

Richards was about to respond but was interrupted by a bald man in the doorway. He was late fifties, wearing a white uniform shirt with his hat tucked under his arm. The gold stars on his collar identified him as the Chief of Police.

"Gentlemen."

"Sorry, sir," Richards said. "I was just informing Detective Stevens here that he is harassing Mr. Donahue needlessly at this point in the investigation."

Stevens was about to fire back, but Chief Michael Bukowski cut him off with a raised hand.

"Look, I know tensions are running high around here. We all want to get the son of a bitch who murdered Ellen. But let's not lose sight of what's important here. We need to bring justice for our officer. We have to all work together. Richards, I got briefed on this last night. I wanted to sit down with all you guys first thing. I should have known my detectives would be at it before the sun rose. And for that I am sorry."

"Sir, Agent Bradford and I have a new angle we want to try," Stevens explained.

"Well, then, let's get this right," the chief said firmly. He glanced through the one-way mirror at the twitchy form of Peter Donahue. "It looks like we've used up all of his patience. And from what you told me last night, we don't have much. So let's not screw this one up, ok?"

Chief Bukowski set his hat on his head and left the observation room, not shutting the door behind him.

Detective Richards's neck had gone red, but the chief's words were final.

"You're going to fuck up this case, Stevens," was all he said before he too stormed down the hall.

Once they were gone, Bradford handed Stevens a cup of coffee. "No pressure, right?"

PETER DONAHUE SAT upright on the uncomfortable chair, his arms resting on the cold metal table. He was here as a witness, plain and simple. Free to tell the interviewers to go to hell and walk out that door forever. But he knew people were watching. His family, friends, co-workers, the press, and the public. Like every other husband of a murdered or missing wife.

Donahue was dressed in blue jeans and a dark jacket. Unlike before, he wore boots instead of dress shoes. Clearly he had come straight from home rather than from work.

Bradford and Richards sat on the other side of the table, sipping their coffees and letting the silence fill the room. Deja was sitting beside Bradford, her nose working and her ears erect. She was curious about the person in the chair—much more curious than when she took in all of his various odors eleven hours ago. He smelled different. Shampoo, deodorant, laundry soap on his clothes. All the normal smells on people in the morning. But Deja remained curious.

It was Donahue who spoke first.

"Look, Bob, you know I respect you. I know all you guys are doing your job, but this is getting ridiculous. How many more times are you guys gonna call me down here? I called my lawyer this morning, and he told me not to come." He paused. "I want to find Ellen's killer, but the more time you waste with me is more time for the killer to get away."

"Right now, you are Ellen's voice," Stevens said directly. "She wants to tell us who did this to her. You knew her better than anyone. You knew what problems she was having. It really comes down to you."

"What do you mean it comes down to me?"

"You know more than anyone. It's up to you to let Ellen speak."

"But I don't know anything."

"You know Ellen. You know what was bothering her. You talked about her job. What else, Bob? What else was bothering her? Was it you?"

Stevens was all business, and Bradford knew it was intended to throw Donahue on the back foot right from the start.

"I already told you about all that."

"Well, tell us again."

Donahue sighed. "I don't know, it was about a week ago, I think. I called her to check up on her, see how she was doing."

"And what did you two talk about?"

"Just the usual stuff. I asked her about work, like I said. Seeing if she needed anything brought over to her mom's place."

"We got her phone. All the calls from you are incoming. She never called you, it's always you calling her. Did that bother her?"

Donahue stiffened. "Look, Ellen and I wanted to stay on

good terms. We didn't hate each other. Things just . . . didn't work out. For her, at least."

Stevens leaned forward. "What do you mean?"

"C'mon, Bob, you know I didn't want to split. Of course I called her. I wanted to make it work. She didn't."

Both investigators could see the rage. Deja was alert to it as well.

"I told her I wanted to work it out, but she wasn't having it. She said that she'd made her mind up."

"Made her mind about what?"

"About leaving."

"What made her make up her mind to leave?"

"Shit, I don't know. It just all the stress of work, you know. She would put in long hours on her shifts, and I'd work late most nights at the office. Some weeks we didn't even see each other until Saturday. And then, you know, it was always just catching up on all the stuff we didn't get to during the week. It was just a grind. In the end, I guess she just wanted something different."

"So there wasn't an affair or anything of that nature?"

Donahue suddenly frowned. "What?"

Stevens pressed on. "So you weren't having an affair? Seeing another woman? Was there any infidelity in your marriage?"

Clearly Detective Richards had not asked that line of questioning. Donohue's eyes narrowed. "How can you ask me that, Bob?"

"You're telling me that you never cheated on your wife? Or that she cheated on you? How would you feel if she had?"

Peter Donahue leaned forward and drove his finger onto the desk. "Ellen and I loved each other, alright?"

He was getting frazzled. Stevens had struck a nerve, and now Bradford stepped up to the plate.

"Did she ever talk to you about her coworkers?"

"What, like, here at the PD?"

"Did she ever talk about her friends? How much do you know about her social life?"

Donahue was starting to reel from the quick-fire questions. He glanced over into the mirror, then back at the investigators.

"I don't know, yeah, I guess we talked about it. She'd hit the bars sometimes with her friends. She had some high school girlfriends she saw from time to time. And there were the shift parties. You know, getting drinks with the officers after duty." He looked to Stevens for confirmation. "Hell, Bob, I saw you at some of those shift parties."

Stevens's face was unreadable. "Do you recognize this man?" He asked, reaching into his jacket pocket. He pulled out his phone and set it on the table in front of Donahue. It was open to Ellen's Facebook page. Stevens was her friend, and she had made a friends-only post of a selfie of her smiling with a man. There were trees behind them, and a glimpse of water. Their faces were close together, and they looked like two healthy thirty-somethings out for a hike. The chemistry between them was undeniable.

The caption read: "Happy."

Donahue gave no expression.

"Never seen him before."

"Were you and Ellen still friends on Facebook?" Bradford pressed.

"Well, yeah, I guess so. I defriended her right after the split because I was pissed, you know. But after a while it just seemed stupid, so I sent her a request." Donahue shifted his weight. Deja's eyes tracked him. "Why? What's this got to do with anything?"

"Will you tell me when this was posted?" Stevens asked, tapping the table next to the phone. Ellen still stared up at them, smiling and happy.

Donahue hesitated. "What? I don't understand." Stevens tapped again. "Look at the post and read to me when Ellen posted it."

Donahue didn't move at first. He looked from Stevens to Bradford then back to Stevens. He looked like an animal leery of a trap.

Finally he leaned forward and read. "She posted it on Monday night."

"What time?" Stevens insisted.

"9:32."

"Less than five hours before she was murdered," Stevens said, pocketing his phone. "That was her last post before she was killed on her lunch break. At the same 7-Eleven she always went to."

A loud silence filled the room. Next to Bradford's leg, he could feel Deja tensing. She was wanting to tell him something.

"Mr. Donahue," Bradford said after many seconds had passed. "Can you explain how there came to be a hole in the wall of your hallway?"

Donahue blinked. He certainly didn't seem to be expecting that.

"What? That, I—?"

"Did you punch the wall, Mr. Donahue? The wall above the hall table where you keep your phone charging. We saw that last night. I'm sure we can pull up a photo of it when your house was searched. That's not something I would expect from a banker who keeps such a tidy home. What made you angry enough to do that?"

Donahue was beginning to stammer. "Look, I don't know what you—"

"I'll tell you what I think," Bradford said, looking him square in the eyes. "I think you keep your phone on the table in the hallway, and two nights ago I think you saw this very post. I think you put your fist through the wall."

A nervous smile spilled from Donahue's mouth. "This is ridiculous. I don't have to listen to this shit anymore."

Donahue was just about to stand when Stevens pulled an enlarged photo from under his notepad.

"Do you recognize this vehicle?"

It was a grainy still from the surveillance camera at the high school. It showed a blurry white vehicle traveling down a dark road.

"I don't—"

Stevens insisted, "Is this your Chevy Silverado traveling down Old Mill Road at 2:30 yesterday morning?"

Donahue was getting more flustered by the second. He ran a shaky hand through his hair. "No, no. I never go that way."

Immediately, Bradford sensed an opportunity, and he pulled his own phone from his pocket. He opened his maps app and set the phone in front of Donahue.

"Show me the way you usually get home," he said urgently, trying to keep Donahue disoriented and reeling. Deja looked up at him, her eyes sharp and focused, nose taking in all of his odors.

"What?" Donohue asked, trying to come up with an answer to a question he was not expecting.

Bradford spoke loudly and clearly. "Show me."
In an instant, Bradford saw a yellow blur move from her sitting position by the wall toward Donahue. Deja buried her nose on Donohue's boots.

"Jesus, what the fuck is he doing!" Donahue shouted. He jumped back like an overloaded spring, knocking the chair over in the process. "Get that dog away from me!"

Deja sat calmly and looked at Bradford with a satisfied, expectant look in her eyes.

Bradford realized what he'd said, and he repeated the unintentional zeroing-in command. "Show me, girl."

Again Deja pushed her nose on the side of Donahue's left boot near the toe where the leather met the sole.

Bradford shared a glance with Stevens, and then he said to Donahue, "My partner here just hit on gun residue on your boots. Care to explain how it got there?"

The color was draining from Donohue's face.

"I—I told you already. I went to the gun range."

Stevens turned to his notes, moving slowly and methodically despite the tension in the room. "According to the statement that you gave us last night, you went to the gun range after work before you met up with your friends for pizza." He cocked his eye above his gray beard. "You mean to tell me you wore those boots to work?"

Donahue looked trapped, as if the sweet-faced yellow Lab by the table was a snarling Doberman.

"You were adamant that they have video of the range. It should show us what shoes you were wearing that day."

"I want to call my lawyer."

Bradford reached into his pocket and fed Deja a big handful of kibble. "Yes, Mr. Donahue. I think that's a good idea."

CAMERON

6:16 a.m.
Farmhouse near Kuz Kunar
Nangarhar Province, Afghanistan
October 2019

"WE'VE BEEN ALL over this place," one of the EOD technicians was saying, metal detector still in hand. "I'm telling you, there's nothing here."

Delgado spit in the dirt. They were gathered in the courtyard of the Afghani farmhouse as the sun kept rising above the horizon by the minute.

"Do another sweep of the outbuildings," Delgado ordered. "We can extend out the perimeter by fifty feet, see if we turn anything up."

The EOD tech seemed unenthusiastic. "There isn't anything past the perimeter except a tight sphincter." He cast his eyes around the farmhouse. The soldiers charged with security had taken up positions around the compound, but the tech cast a nervous glance at the foothills a half-mile away. "I could feel eyes on me from those mountains."

A soldier nearby heard the comment and leaned around the corner of the structure to get a better view of the hills.

"Look," Delgado insisted, "Juszczyk said the transmitter was active this morning. Something's gotta be here."

Major McNamara had his ear to the radio, but when he heard this, his head swung on a swivel. "Delgado, get your crew to hurry up. I don't give a fuck what the transmitter says. We don't come up with something in the next five minutes, we're saddling up and getting gone. We've been here way too long already."

Cameron watched the whole scene unfold. He was surprised that McNamara had left the command vehicle in the first place, but they had already been here for twenty-five minutes and everyone was getting antsy. Word spread quickly in this part of the world—their presence here wouldn't go unnoticed for long.

Next to him, Dover gave a low whine. They'd been all through the house and the courtyard and the perimeter, but Dover hadn't found anything concrete enough to give his sit signal.

"Ok, you heard the major," Delgado said, clearly pissed. "We do another pass. Fast as hell. But don't get complacent. Stay focused."

Dammit, Cameron thought. They were wasting their time talking here in the courtyard. Wasting their time sweeping over the same places Dover had already checked.

The EOD team spread out, and Cameron led Dover along the edge of the courtyard to the far fence line. He was fully aware that he had strayed from Delgado's watchful eye, but there was no point covering ground they had already covered. But Dover's behavior had changed when they had come through here the first time, and Cameron wanted to take another pass. Whatever the dog was smelling, it wasn't strong enough to make him sit, but it was enough to let the dog search a little farther.

"C'mon, buddy. Show me what you've got. Seeeek."

They worked their way along the low mud wall that separated the compound from the dry fields. The farmers had grown corn, but now the field was nothing but stubble from the harvested stalks, like a massive five o'clock shadow over the entire valley.

Cameron and Dover went through an opening in the wall, passing a nineteen-year-old soldier who was covering the perimeter—M4A held at the ready, watching the hills, only taking his eyes off his area of responsibility to suck down some water from a plastic bottle in his ACU pants pocket.

Dover's nose was again working overtime in this corner of the property.

"What do you have, boy? Show me. Show me."

The dog started to work faster, and before long, he started to pull the lead out into the wide-open field, past another soldier who was kneeling next to an old fence.

They were fifty feet beyond the mud wall, but instead of turning back into the compound, Cameron decided to say, *Fuck it*. They stepped past the last soldier and went out into the open field.

It would be impossible to search this entire field, and they only had a few minutes left before McNamara pulled the plug—and maybe less if Delgado figured out that they were not by his side as ordered—but Cameron's restlessness was getting the better of him. The thought crossed his mind to unleash Dover and let the dog work the whole field quickly, but no matter how impatient he was, he would not risk Dover's safety.

He knew the munitions had to be here. He believed the Agency's intel, but it was more than that. He didn't want to go back to base knowing there was a cache of explosives still out in the wild. Explosives that could be used against the base.

Explosives that could be packed in the back of a Nissan Atlas truck . . .

The familiar refrain of that terrible explosion played itself out in his mind again and again as he ran Dover through the field. They were moving fast, working along the dried-out cornstalks.

This is crazy, he told himself as they got further from the farmhouse. Dover might be on some other scent, or maybe he was just responding to Cameron's nervous energy. Cameron knew that he had an effect on his dog—but he just couldn't give up and pack it in. Not yet.

Then an ugly thought popped into Cameron's head. What if Dover is on the scent of a booby trap, or a mine? What if he had led them straight into the middle of a literal minefield? Cameron tried to shake his mind free of the image of Dover being blown thirty feet into the air.

No, it wasn't a minefield. There were fresh tire marks from when they harvested the corn, not more than a week old.

None of the stalks had been disturbed.

Cameron drew a deep breath and pressed on.

Keep it together, man.

After a minute, Dover took them further and further away from the farmhouse and the perimeter.

"C'mon, seek, Dover. Seeeeeek."

A few deep sniffs later, the dog took a hard turn and started to make his way to an old goat pen out on the edge of the field. It was a good two hundred feet from the farmhouse.

Just then a peal of radio chatter cut through the still morning air.

"Bravo-1 from Bravo-6. We got movement to the northeast, about two klicks out. Two, possibly three individuals midway up the foothills."

"Bravo-1, roger that. Any weapons?"

"Bravo-2 unable to tell, they are currently behind the hill."

Cameron looked to the foothills. Everything seemed quiet, but they were running out of time.

"What have you got?" Cameron said as they approached, but before they got there, he heard his name ring out.

"McNeil!"

He turned and saw Delgado sprinting across the field, his M4A slung across his shoulder.

"What the fuck are you doing out here, man? I fucking ordered you . . ." Delgado clattered to a halt. He was out of breath from his sprint across the field. "This area hasn't been secured. We've got incoming, so we're packing up."

"The dog's got something," Cameron said, but Delgado looked more pissed than usual.

"There's nothing out here but corn and goat shit. You don't go running off without me. McNamara didn't want anyone out past the perimeter."

"No," Cameron insisted, his face twisted with tension. "It's here."

Delgado paused. "What?"

Cameron felt a sharp tug on the leash, and they both looked down at Dover. The dog had gone stiff, nose glued to the ground. He was leaning against his lead, which he rarely did. His tail was still and low.

Cameron had seen this before back at Front Royal.

Dover was into odor.

Cameron abruptly took a knee next to Dover and spoke into the dog's ear. "Gotta find it, boy. Seek."

Then he unclipped Dover's leash, and with tail wagging and tongue hanging out, the dog made straight for the center of the goat pen.

"Come on, man," Delgado protested, "we don't—"

He trailed off as Dover entered the pen through the gate and sat down decisively, looking confidently at his partner.

"You've got to be shittin' me . . ." Delgado muttered as Cameron went forward, already reaching into his food pouch. Cameron sounded decidedly unmanly as he used his highest-pitch voice, full of pride and relief.

As Dover gulped down his handful of kibble, Cameron

turned to Delgado and said. "It's right here. It's buried right here."

"You sure?"

"Yes I'm sure. This dog is on it."

Delgado immediately got on the radio to McNamara and the other EOD techs.

As Dover ate through the second handful, Cameron couldn't help but think back to the motto painted on the wall in the Federal Training Center: *Trust Your Dog.*

SHERRY

10:12 p.m.
Highway 277
Ten miles southeast of Quemado, TX
October 2019

THE DARK DESERT sped past the headlights as Sherry accelerated down the empty stretch of highway. Her eyes were heavy after a long day of work, and she tried to focus on the white lines racing past on the highway. In the back of her canine vehicle, Dolly was sleeping soundly, her head curled up on her tail. Sherry had the rear AC blasting to help her cool off.

Sherry didn't mind the hour-long commute between Del Rio and her current assignment at the border crossing in Eagle Pass. She had been renting the tiny one-bedroom apartment in Del Rio for over a year. At first, she would only sleep there during her five days on, and then make the four-hour drive back to her home in San Antonio on her five days off. But as time went on, and as she and Darryl grew further and further apart, she had started to spend her days off there, too. She didn't like Del Rio, with its dusty streets and military-base vibe, but it was better than being swallowed by the silence of her home in San Antonio.

Sherry fought off a yawn and turned up the music. Dolly was so pooped she didn't even stir. These twelve-hour shifts were a killer.

As she drove, Sherry couldn't help but think about the two guns they pulled out from under the blue Dodge pickup this afternoon. Had they made it across the border, how many innocent civilians would have been gunned down? How many murders would the Zetas have committed, or the Gulf Cartel, or whoever else got their hands on the military-grade AR-15s with high-capacity magazines?

At the daily debrief earlier this evening, one of the ICE intelligence officers shared reports of a major spike in Zetas activity along the border the last few days. EPIC's chatter was essentially confirmed: there was a major offensive happening in the war between the Zetas and the Gulf Cartel, and the regional Mexican police were all wrapped up in it—turning a blind eye at best, or at worst, actively covering up their connection to both sides.

"We have to stay vigilant," Gonzalez said after the ICE agent gave his report. "These next days and weeks will be of the utmost importance. We cannot let any weapons make their way into Mexico, and we cannot let the violence spill over to this side of the border."

Sherry yawned again and rubbed her face. Thankfully there was no traffic on the highway, so she pushed the accelerator and hit eighty-five.

Just then her face was illuminated by her phone, which

sat in the clip-on holder on her dashboard vent.

She had gotten a text.

It was Darryl.

Look, Sher, I know you're fed up but plz don't give up on us

The bluntness of his text shocked her. Usually they beat around the bush, dancing around the things they'd rather not talk about, but tonight, Darryl went straight to the heart of it. He hadn't sent a text in over a week, and now he hit her with this? She wondered if he had been drinking.

Usually she wouldn't take the bait, but tonight, she was too tired to deflect. The anger started to rise in her throat, and she snatched the phone from its cradle.

I didn't give up. You did.

His reply came back moments later.

that's bullshit I was always there. I didn't leave I just had to work

Sherry blew air from her nostrils as her thumbs tapped out a response, holding the phone against the steering wheel. The bright screen drowned out the dark road ahead of her.

Who's bullshitting now? you could have taken a job in

SA, but no you went all over the fckn country so dont give me that I had to work crap

He answered immediately.

what did you want me to do? quit my job? stay home? what the fuck sher it was hard on me too you know

Sherry could have thrown the phone she was so mad.

hard for you??? you weren't there at the hospital. then as soon as we got home, you were around for like two days and then you were gone again. I was alone darryl I went through all that shit alone

The three bouncing dots appeared as he started to reply, but Sherry beat him to it. The white lines on the highway sped by.

Don't even bother Darryl. I'm done. I'm fucking done

The three bouncing dots stopped. Sherry tried to put her eyes back on the road, but she was shaking with rage.

A moment later, the dots reappeared, followed by Darryl's blue text box.

I'm sorry we lost the baby. I don't know how many times

I can tell you that

Suddenly there were taillights in front of her. She slammed on the brakes, her phone flying against the windshield and bouncing to the floor. Her seatbelt dug into her collarbone as her canine vehicle fishtailed on the highway. She cranked the wheel, trying to keep the car on the road as Dolly bounced around in the back.

"What the fuck!" she cried as she finally brought the car to a halt.

A massive dust cloud filled her headlights, and she could see a pair of red taillights speeding away.

Someone had pulled off a dirt road right in front of her, and now they were accelerating down the highway.

Sherry immediately knew what it was.

Runners.

This stretch of deserted highway was only two miles from the river, and whether they were running guns, people, or drugs, whoever was in that car was definitely up to no good.

The rage was still clouding her mind, and without hesitating, Sherry floored the accelerator and started after them. Dolly was getting her precarious balance in the back as the automatic transmission burned through the gears. The emergency LEDs on her car painted the desert in electric flashes of blue and red.

Sherry reached over and grabbed the radio mic from the shoulder of her tac vest, which she had tossed in the front passenger seat.

"This is unit thirty-six. I'm in pursuit of a black sedan heading westbound on 277. It just came out of the desert north of mile marker fifty-two. Requesting backup!"

Her voice came fast and shaky as she roared down the highway, gaining ground on the taillights ahead. Technically she was off duty, but she knew that as soon as she stepped in her take-home squad, she wouldn't be *really* off duty until she pulled into her driveway.

Other officers came on the radio.

"10-4, tango six-two responding."

"Nine-eight is also responding. Be advised I'm about fifteen minutes south of marker fifty-two."

The car ahead must have seen her emergency lights and knew they couldn't outrun her on the highway, because they suddenly slammed on the brakes and skidded onto another dirt road that bisected the highway. The tires sprayed dirt back across the roadway and kicked up a massive cloud of dust as they bounced into the dark desert.

"Suspects have left the highway at mile marker fifty-three!" Sherry called into the mic. "Heading northbound on the fire road."

Then came her CO's voice. Jimmy Gonzalez was still at work. "Three-six, keep eyes on them if you can, but do not attempt apprehension until back-up arrives. Do you copy, Fry? Follow and wait for back-up."

Sherry ignored him and cranked the wheel hard, tapping the brakes just enough to make the turn onto the fire road. A cloud of dust enveloped the canine vehicle as Dolly tried to keep her footing in the back. The emergency lights were blinding in the dust, so Sherry killed everything except her fog lamps.

She knew Gonzalez would be pissed, but it wasn't in her nature to sit on the sidelines. This was her arrest. She's done this before and she'd do it again. How could Gonzalez expect her *not* to engage after the speech he'd given earlier that day, warning them all about Zetas activity up and down the river? She may have been on K-9 duty, but she was a Border Agent first.

Her vehicle rocked and bounced as she sped up the dirt road that snaked through the desert. She looked back through the open cage door to check on Dolly. The glow from the dash lights reflected in her alert eyes. She was ready for whatever came next.

The dust cloud was thinning, and up ahead Sherry could see the taillights getting closer. Then the taillights suddenly bounced and went sideways, leaning at an angle. A moment later, that same dust cloud enveloped the canine vehicle.

They must have bottomed out in a ditch, she thought, making a split-second assessment. She knew that they would flee on foot.

Sure enough, as she pulled up, she hit the switch that turned on the floodlights in the light bar. She could make out three young men exiting the car. She instinctively keyed in on their hands. The first one pulled himself out the driver's door by the B pillar—nothing in his hands. The other two, she couldn't tell.

Then they sprinted into the desert, duffel bags over their shoulders.

Without hesitating, Sherry threw the car into park, grabbed her phone from the floor, swung on her tac vest, and hopped out of the vehicle.

Had she been in her right mind, she would have radioed in their descriptions and the direction they were heading. She would have waited for backup. She would have coordinated the responding units, maybe tried to reach the Kinney County Sheriff's Department on the local police radio band. She would have done anything other than charge into the night after them.

But she was not in her right mind. She was still enraged from her texts with Darryl, and in her powerlessness to fix her life, she fixated only on the runners in front of her.

And with that, she bolted after them, running into the dark desert. She had left her door open, and Dolly instinctively squeezed through the open kennel door into the driver's compartment and bounded out after her, determined to stay with her person.

In an instant, her partner was by her side. Sherry knew she should turn back. Dolly didn't belong out here on a pursuit, but she could see the runners just ahead, encumbered by their bags. If she pressed on, she could get them . . .

Fuck Darryl. Fuck everything else. She was a cop, and she had a duty to uphold.

As she ran, she could hear Jimmy Gonzalez's voice—not on the radio, but in her own conscience. *Don't do anything stupid. The most important thing is coming back alive.*

Sherry sprinted up a low hill, her boots churning rocks and dust. She grabbed her flashlight with one hand and secured the Velcro bands on the sides of her vest with the other.

The night was still hot, and the heat and adrenaline and the rage made the sweat pour down her face. Her hair clung to her cheeks as she ran. The three-quarter moon painted the desert white.

Dolly kept pace right beside her, eyes focused and tongue flapping from her mouth.

Sherry mounted the low rise and saw the three runners thirty yards ahead. They had slowed as they climbed over a low field fence.

She sped down the other side of the hill, trying to make up the ground between them. The rocks rolled beneath her feet as she wove between sagebrush. A few seconds later, she came to the fence and worked her way over the old, twisted wires. It snagged her pant leg, but she was over the hurdle and running in a matter of seconds.

Then she heard a noise that made her heart stop.

It was a high-pitched yelp, followed by a steady whine that pierced the night.

Dolly.

Sherry whipped around, fearing the worst—and having the worst confirmed. Dolly, her beloved dog, was lying in the dirt beside the fence, her yellow belly fur stained with blood.

Sherry dropped her flashlight and ran to her.

"Oh god, Dolly! What happened? Oh no!"

Sherry's hands were soaked in blood as she felt around Dolly's stomach. There was a long laceration that ran from Dolly's back leg diagonally across her belly, running nearly to her breastbone. In the darkness, Sherry could see a clump of bloody fur on one of the spurs of the lowest fence wire. She hadn't known it was barbed wire when she had climbed over—Dolly must have jumped through the lower opening with exposed barbs at full speed, trying to keep up with her.

A sinking feeling overtook Sherry Fry. This was all her fault.

The dog whined and howled and tried to escape as Sherry pressed the wound closed. Sherry could feel the warm, smooth intestinal tract protruding from the wound. For a moment, she was sure Dolly would bite her, but Sherry put her other hand on her head and spoke calmly in her ear.

"You're ok. You're ok. Just hang on."

Sherry reached up to her radio and called it in, her voice choked with grief.

"We have an officer injured! I'm staying to provide aid. Suspects heading north-northwest on foot!"

Sherry watched for a moment as the runners fled into the night, but all her rage and her desire to catch them had melted out of her, pooling on the sand like Dolly's blood.

A voice came over the radio.

"Unit six-two, I'm at your vehicle. What is your location?"

Sherry weakly pressed the button on her radio. Tears were blinding her eyes.

"Three-six, I'm two hundred yards northwest. Grab the K9 first-aid kit from the back."

She kept pressing on Dolly's stomach. The blood was thick against her fingers.

"Oh God, please help her," Sherry prayed quietly, wiping tears from her eyes and spreading blood on her cheeks. "Please don't take Dolly from me. Please help her."

Dolly was still whining loudly when a flashlight beam appeared at the top of the hill. Officer Willard came racing down the hill, medkit in hand.

"Three runners!" she cried, pointing with red fingers. "They're headed that way!"

Willard took one look at all the blood.

"I'll stay with her," Sherry insisted. "Go!"

The border officer nodded and sprinted off into the darkness, leaving Sherry and Dolly alone.

The blood on Sherry's hands made the zipper slip through her fingers as she opened the medkit. Dolly's whining turned to sharp cries as Sherry brought out the medical stapler and worked her way along the gaping wound. She pressed the spilled intestines back inside the cavity with her hands.

"It's okay girl," she choked. The sensation of stapling raw skin was unbearable. "It's okay."

And then it was done, and Dolly lay panting in the dirt.

Sherry lay next to her dog and held her in the hot desert night.

"Hang on, girl. I'm with you. I'm not going anywhere."

She held Dolly's abdomen and waited. The night had gone incredibly quiet. It was the loudest silence Sherry had ever heard, broken only by Dolly's faint panting.

Sherry stared up at the stars, holding Dolly close to her, and before she knew it, she was crying all over again.

"I'm so sorry, sweetheart," she said, pressing her face into Dolly's fur. All the years of heartbreak and frustration suddenly came pouring out of her. "I'm so sorry for all of it. Look at what a mess I've made of everything."

Dolly gave a low whine and watched her person from the corner of her eye.

Sherry held her tight. She had only felt this powerless once before in her life, lying in a hospital bed when the OB-GYN delivered the news that shattered her heart and devastated her marriage. She wanted to cry out at the top of her lungs—why had no one told her that life could be so unfair?

All she could do was hold onto her beloved dog and pray.

"I'm so sorry. I'm so sorry."

Dolly whined again, and Sherry could see her eyes starting to glaze over.

"Oh, baby, please! Please hang on! I won't ever let you down again. You just keep hanging on."

She could see more lights gathering in the distance, more

officers arriving on scene. Flashlights appeared on the hill, running toward them.

Then her phone buzzed in her pocket. She swiped the screen and smeared it with blood.

I'm not going to quit on us Sher. I know I dont say it enough, but I love you. I wont ever stop loving you

The three bouncing dots appeared next to Darryl's name.

I'll be there when you get home. We can work it out . . . Just promise me you wont run away this time.

JASON

12:03 p.m.
Riverside Terrace, The Bronx
New York, NY
October 2019

US MARSHAL JASON Hernandez ducked low as he cut through a cramped alley behind an old rowhouse in the Bronx. Disney diligently followed by his side, jumping through a hole in the fence that Jason opened for her. Discarded children's toys littered the yard, faded and cracked as if they'd had seen too many summers and too many winters.

Disney was focused on their destination, and she didn't give the toys a passing sniff as she trotted alongside Jason, moving swiftly and silently through the stranger's yard. Jason's eyes kept shifting from where he was going to where Disney was going—looking for broken glass, exposed nails, dropped syringes, anything that might harm her. On top of that, he had to be alert for any possible threats. This was gang territory, and although he wore a black tactical vest with US MARSHAL emblazoned across the back and POLICE across the front, it was not a guarantee that someone wouldn't mistake the sneaking people as rival gang members, or possibly even a burglar.

They hopped a low retaining wall covered with graffiti and entered the yard behind the suspect's rowhouse.

"Lay down and stay," Jason said firmly to Disney, using the voice he used whenever he was issuing an order and not playing with her. Disney knew this serious tone.

Disney obediently sat down behind a rusted barbecue, her eyes alert and concerned, her nose working the air. She cocked her head to the side, as if asking Jason a question.

"Don't worry, girl. We got this."

He said it just as much for himself as for her.

It had been months since Jason had drawn his weapon in earnest, and he set his sweaty hand on the grip of his Sig Sauer pistol.

Jason moved across the yard, ducking low and watching the windows and the back porch. He knew that Marshals Schmalz, Oviedo, and Simmons were in position in the front of the house. He knew Gamboa had cover down the alley. Although he couldn't see them, he knew where they would be. And just like when he played college baseball, and there were runners on base, he saw in his mind what he would do if "the ball" came to him. Always mindful of crossfire situations, he knew that if the suspect came down the gangway, he would not chase—instead he would corral him so that he ran into Gamboa. If he came out the back door, he was all his. If he was armed, a whole new set of rules would come into play. He ran each one through his head. And then there was his four-legged partner . . . another set of possibilities.

He gave one last look at Disney before he quietly climbed the steps to the back porch. They were rickety, the wood rotting.

The back door to the house was open. Standing off to the side, using the door frame as cover, Jason peered inside through the screen door. Further inside the house, he could see movement. Someone was in the living room, and they were moving quickly.

He whipped his head away, pressing his back to the brick wall beside the door. He gave another look at Disney. She hadn't moved, still watching vigilantly beneath the rusty barbecue.

He waited for an update through his earpiece from the marshals entering through the front door. There was nothing but silence. He waited for ten seconds before he reached up to key the transmit button on the collar of his tactical carrier.

Just then, Jason heard the telltale sounds of a door being thrown open, followed by shouts of "US Marshals!" ringing through the house.

The chatter finally erupted in Jason's earpiece, and he heard Oviedo ordering him to get in there. He swung around and opened the screen door, gun at the ready. He stepped into the kitchen as three marshals detained a young black woman in the living room.

She wore a large sweatshirt that covered her arms, and she quickly lay on the ground and put her hands behind her head. It was as if she had spent more than enough time around law enforcement.

"He's not here!" she shouted into the dirty carpet. "I'm telling you, he's not here!"

Schmalz proceeded to pat her down while Oviedo started to sweep the house.

Jason stepped into the living room, gun drawn.

"Look, we didn't do nothin', alright?" the woman was saying as Schmalz helped her to her feet. "You all can't just come in here like this! We have rights!"

Schmalz gave a motion with his head, telling Jason to take her outside.

"Ma'am, you're not under arrest. We just need to check the home for a wanted individual," Jason said, holstering his gun. He gently but firmly took her arm and led her back into the kitchen.

"Man, this is fucked up! You cops can't just come in here! This is our home. Let us have some fuckin' dignity!

Her eyes were full of rage. Jason had seen that look before. He knew this woman had probably had bad experiences with police in the past—maybe she'd even done time.

Jason tried to reassure her. "Don't worry, ma'am. If he's not here, we'll be on our way."

The woman didn't resist, but she didn't look happy about being led outside. She kept looking anxiously back into the house.

Based on the briefing info, Jason wondered if she was the suspect's girlfriend, and at what length she would go to protect him. He had been on enough of these ops in his career to know about bad info from someone who heard something from someone about the location of a fugitive. If this was the case, there surely would be formal complaints filed and lawyers hired. And of course, an IA investigation going over every single action taken by each marshal this day.

Once they were out on the porch, the woman started to pace nervously, chewing on her fingernails and peering back into the house whenever she passed by the screen door.

She was starting to make Jason nervous, too. He decided to go into interview mode.

"Hey, what's your name? I'm Marshal Hernandez."

At first it didn't seem like she heard. She kept pacing and glancing around, chewing on her nails.

Something is definitely not right here, Jason told himself.

UPSTAIRS IN THE house, Marshals Schmalz and Oviedo had been joined by Simmons in their sweep of the interior of the residence. The place was filthy. One of the bedrooms looked half-livable, but the other was trashed. In a third bedroom, they found an elderly woman sitting up in bed, a nervous young woman sitting beside her and clutching her hand. They both looked terrified.

"If you lookin' for Tariq, he ain't here," the young woman said. She had a round face and kind eyes, but the marshals could tell that she was lying. Or at least not telling the entire truth.

"Baby," the old woman breathed, "what's going on? Who are these men?"

"Don't worry, mama," the young woman said, tears in her eyes. "It's the police, they're just here to harass us. They'll be gone soon."

The two marshals moved through the rooms, guns and flashlights drawn. They searched in closets, bathrooms, under the bed frames. Finally they pulled down the retractable stairs to the attic space. Before climbing up, Schmalz pulled out a small mirror on a retractable handle to surveil the attic before taking the final steps up and peering in with his flashlight. The many cobwebs told him no one had been up there for a while.

Their earpieces chattered with a report from Gamboa that the crawlspace under the house was clear.

"Dammit," Oviedo said to Schmalz as he climbed back down. "He's not here."

"I'll call it in," Simmons said, about to get on his radio. Then he noticed the dresser at the end of the hall. It was pressed up against the far wall, between the door to the bathroom and the old lady's bedroom. It was crooked. One corner had been pulled a few inches away from the wall.

"Did you check that dresser?"

Schmalz shook his head.

Simmons drew his gun and approached the dresser. He and Oviedo worked to swing it out of the way, revealing a rough hole that had been knocked into the adjacent townhouse.

"Son of a bitch," Oviedo muttered as he rushed into the hole that led into the abandoned neighboring duplex.

JASON STOOD ON the back porch, trying to get the young woman to calm down, but nothing would get her to stand still.

"You alright, ma'am?" Jason pressed. "You seem nervous."

"There's cops all up in my house," she spat. "Course I'm fucking nervous."

"Fair enough," Jason replied. But something told him there was more to it than that. "So you do know the guy we're after? Tariq Simpson."

She snorted. "Ya, I know him, but I ain't got nothin' to do with him. He's a piece of shit as far as I'm concerned. You can get that motherfucker off the street and lock him up for all I care. But he ain't been here for days, so you should all just leave. My mama's sick in bed and y'all are scaring her to death."

Jason made a mental note. *No love lost there. Maybe she'll help us locate him, or even set him up.*

Then she suddenly paused. She had been looking around the yard, and her eyes fell on Disney, who was still waiting alertly under the barbecue.

Jason may have been imagining it, but he could have sworn a look of recognition crossed her face.

"You like dogs?"

To his surprise, the woman stopped pacing and gave him

a look that spoke volumes.

"Yea, you could say that."

Jason thought he'd try her again.

"So what's your name?"

"I'm Wanda," she said a moment later, still looking at the yellow Labrador retriever waiting diligently beneath the barbecue. "Shawanda Jackson."

Then suddenly, her face changed. In an instant, it contorted into a look of pure fright. She screamed out:

"Tariq, NO!"

Jason heard her just as he spun around to see a tall black man charging across the porch from the neighboring duplex. Jason reached for his gun, but he hardly had time to react before Tariq Simpson bore down on him with a tire iron.

But Tariq's swing didn't make contact.

Shawanda Jackson had sprung forward, pushing Jason out of the way as the tire iron came down with force. The blow landed just above Shawanda's right ear, and she crumpled to the ground in a heap.

It all happened in an instant, and an instant later, Jason had gotten his bearings and tackled Tariq to the ground before he could raise the tire iron for a second blow. The big man started to put up a fight, but moments later Gamboa emerged from under the house and Oviedo came barreling out of the neighboring duplex. Together the three marshals wrestled him to the ground.

As Jason cuffed the fugitive, Disney ran up and put her wet nose on Shawanda's arm. Then she gently licked her face as Shawanda lay on the porch, a pool of blood forming next to her head.

CAMERON

6:22 a.m.
Farmhouse near Kuz Kunar
Nangarhar Province, Afghanistan
October 2019

THE EOD TEAM had sprinted across the field from the courtyard and outbuildings, and now they were carefully digging through the dirt in the center of the pen. Three more of McNamara's soldiers were re-positioning to provide cover while EOD worked. Kelliher's HMMWV had driven to the far side of the pen to cover their new location.

"Careful now," Delgado ordered. "Keep an eye out for trips."

The techs kept digging, stopping at times to get down on their knees and move dirt by hand. At one point, a tech ordered a stop when a black wire was exposed. The team didn't panic, but the tech who first noticed it carefully moved away the dusty soil and saw that it was a piece of black tubing, perhaps from an old water hose or vehicle part. They kept digging, working their folding shovels at shallow angles to keep from hitting any ordnance or booby traps that might be buried. The Taliban was good at rigging things to explode—they had even stuffed IEDs in goat or cow carcasses by the roadside. Nothing could be trusted.

Cameron stood beside Delgado as the techs worked. Dover was watching the digging with great interest, but Cameron also kept his eyes on the hills. The techs were working quickly, but it had been half an hour since they'd arrived at the farmhouse. Far too long.

"Sir," one of the techs said, standing up from the shallow hole.

Delgado and Cameron leaned over the rickety wooden fence of the pen. The techs had uncovered a tarp about a foot below the soil line.

"Clear that out of there," Delgado ordered.

Cameron hopped the fence and helped the three techs uncover the edge of the tarp and pull it away. Sand and dirt rolled down the sides, revealing a base of wooden planks.

The closest EOD tech, a young Asian-American about twenty-six years old, whipped out a penlight and closely inspected between the planks, looking for anything out of the ordinary. He gave a thumbs up.

"Careful now," Delgado said as Cameron and the techs started to remove the planks.

Just then, Sergeant Kelliher in the HMMWV to the right of the EOD techs broke in on the radio.

"Bravo 1 from Bravo-3 team leader, sir, we definitely have at least seven armed with rifles about two hundred yards to the right of that last sighting. They are currently moving to the north along some type of path in the hills."

A shot of tension raced through the team. They all looked

up at the foothills as the three soldiers from Kelliher's squad readied their M4As and knelt in the dirt.

Cameron knew this was not good. It sounded like they were being flanked. Even though they were a kilometer away, that was way too close, even for an AK. They were running out of time.

Cameron saw the two turrets from the HMMWVs cover that area while the MRAPs kept their guns pointed in the other directions, expecting anything from everywhere.

Delgado spoke, his voice clipped and fast. "We've got to open this up, guys."

Cameron had reattached Dover's lead and knelt in the dirt next to him, his sidearm drawn. They had no cover out in the field, just the rickety goat pen that was made of little more than twigs. This was probably the worst place to be if the shooting started, but nobody working in that pit was going anywhere.

The radio traffic continued at an ominous clip.

"Bravo-3, I've got more movement in the foothills. Northeast of our location."

McNamara's voice cut through urgently. "Task Force Team Leader to Bravo-3, what have you got out there?"

"Bravo-3, I can't tell sir. I counted seven combatants, but I just can't get a clear line of sight. They are moving through the underbrush."

There was more static and crosstalk as the squads around the farmhouse moved into defensive positions, then McNamara's voice came through again.

"Task Force Team Leader to EOD-1, report. What's your status out there?"

"We've located a buried pit, sir," Delgado answered, speaking into the radio on his shoulder. "Determining what we got, stand by one. But it looks like we got it."

"How much time do you need?"

"We'll need about ten to set up a countercharge."

"You've got three. Hurry the fuck up and get out of there before you draw any contact. Start sending back all unnecessary personnel. I'll start pulling back some of the perimeter security."

"Roger that."

The EOD techs were working faster now. Once they had checked for tripwires, they found the edges of the planks and started to pull them up one by one.

Cameron watched them intently as they worked. Dover could feel the tension, and his body had gone stiff. His nose worked furiously as the techs uncovered the pit. Inside were piles of Soviet artillery shells, boxes of Semtex explosives, grenades, mortars, and crates full of ammunition. One of those crates held a crapped-out CIA transmitter. No loss blowing that piece of shit up.

Everyone heard it at once.

The telltale whine of an incoming mortar round whizzing through the air.

A loud explosion ripped through the quiet valley. Everyone spun to see a huge dust cloud a hundred yards beyond the Major's command vehicle.

The two turrets on each of the HMMWVs opened up with their 20-millimeter cannons on the hills where Bravo-3 had called in the combatants.

This fire was answered by another motor round, striking just beyond the barn. The farmhouse was rocked on its foundations, and the soldiers around the perimeter started running for cover.

Sergeant Delgado shouted, "We gotta BIP this, right here, right now!"

One of the techs brought over a satchel charge and a reel of OD green shock tube. The shock tube was a special type of fuse used to set off the charge to destroy the ordnance, very stable even under adverse conditions.

Delgado and his techs began setting the satchel charge when a mortar round suddenly detonated a hundred feet from the pen, showering them with dirt and sending the soldiers and the EOD team diving for cover. Cameron threw himself over Dover, who had flattened himself to the ground.

"They're getting close!" one of the GIs shouted, opening fire with his M4A. In the distance, several Taliban militia had peeled off from the main attack and were headed in their direction. They opened fire with their AKs, the inaccurate small-arms fire creating puffs in the dust. A few rounds splintered the old rails of the goat pen.

"We gotta get the fuck outta here!" Delgado called out, ducking low as he attached the shock tube to the satchel.

One of the EOD techs was shouting into his headset

radio. "Send the JERRV for evac! We need cover out here—now!"

Cameron ducked low as a spray of bullets ripped over his head and tore away more twigs from the goat pen. The rounds from the GIs M4As were deafening as they returned fire, trying to slow the advance of the Taliban militia.

Another mortar struck on the other side of the pen. Their observer must have been directing the mortar crew to walk the rounds in on the GIs.

"Shit!" Delgado swore as he was knocked off his feet, dropping the reel of shock tube. One of the techs helped him back up and together they got the charge set.

A few seconds later, the roar of the JERRV's engine cut over the firefight as the large armored vehicle ran over the waist-high mud wall and sped into the field. The turret gunner laid down surpassing fire as the JERRV thudded to a halt between the goat pen and the militia.

"Everyone clear out!" Delgado shouted as the M-242 turret rained hot brass casings into the dirt. He turned to the sergeant of the fire team. "Get your men out of here! Have the JERRV fall back to the farmhouse. I'll set the charge and run back to the EOD truck once the area is clear."

Cameron couldn't believe his ears. "Yo, Del, you can't stay out here, man!"

Delgado ignored him. "Everyone in the truck. Now!"

Cameron knew there was no time to argue. He sprang to his feet, scooping Dover up in his arms as another mortar round landed nearby. He ducked low as he and the other techs ran for the JERRV.

Delgado got on the radio and notified Major McNamara. Once he saw that everyone was in the vehicles, he opened the flap on the satchel charge. Cameron watched from the JERRV as Delgado, on one knee, with stray rounds striking the ground all around him, carefully removed the detonator in its protective tube from the front pocket on his body armor. He connected it to the end of the shock tube and inserted it into one of the explosive blocks in the charge and laid it across the top of the ordnance cache. Then he started to unspool the shock tube as the JERRV peeled away from the goat pen, spraying dirt as its tires chewed up the field.

The Taliban militia had taken cover behind a low rock ledge as the turrets rained down on them.

As Delgado had ordered, the JERRV sped through the field, then came to a stop and drew up a defensive position by the farmhouse. The turret gunner maintained their suppressing fire as the GIs and EOD team disembarked once again. They took cover behind the JERRV and joined in the suppressing fire. Even Cameron took out his Beretta 9mm and fired toward the enemy. He knew it was useless, but all covering fire is good fire.

Cameron's heart was pounding as he watched Delgado unspool the olive-green tube as he made his way across the field. Delgado was moving as quickly as he could, but he had two-hundred-and-fifty feet to cover. It was like walking backward across a football field.

Delgado had made it two-thirds of the way when a mortar round exploded just behind him. The blast wave rocked the soldiers and EOD team and launched Sergeant Delgado high into the air. Dust sprayed into the EOD rig, whose back door was open in anticipation of Delgado climbing inside. He came down in a heap, crashing hard into the ground fifteen feet from the blast crater.

He wasn't moving.

Cameron's heart clenched in his throat. With total disregard for his safety, he dashed around the back of the JERRV, yelling "Dover, stay!" as he sprinted toward the motionless sergeant.

Dover, however, disregarded the order and instinctively followed without a moment's hesitation. Cameron never saw the dog running behind him.

As bullets struck the dirt, Cameron grabbed Delgado by the drag-handle on the back collar of his body armor and began to pull him toward the truck. With over thirty pounds of equipment on top of the sergeant's two-hundred-twenty pound frame, it was slow going. Two people so close together made an inviting target for the enemy . . .

But a moment later, Dover was there. The dog grabbed the edge of Delgado's Kevlar vest with his teeth. His back paws dug into the dirt as they dragged, leaving a smear of blood on the dirt. Delgado's left leg and right arm were mangled.

"Hang on, buddy!" Cameron said, struggling with his breath as more bullets flew all around them. The freshly risen sun shone brightly in his eyes. "We're gonna get you outta here."

By the time they got within fifty feet of the JERRV, another EOD tech raced out to help. Together, the three of them managed to get Delgado to the rig as bullets pinged off the armored sides of the massive vehicle.

The rest of the EOD team helped load Delgado into the floor of the truck, and Cameron and Dover climbed in after.

"Ok, we're in, let's get out of here!" one of the techs shouted into his radio, but to everyone's surprise, Delgado reached up and grabbed the tech's arm.

Delgado was semi-conscious, his face smeared with blood and dirt.

"Wait," he rasped, his voice cracked and broken. He pulled the EOD tech down and whispered something in his ear.

The tech nodded, then ordered the top turret gunner to open fire on the pit.

The gunner swung around his M-242 and unloaded into the freshly dug hole in the goat pen.

A few seconds later, the goat pen erupted into a column of fire. The blast rocked the MRAP and sent a bright red flash through the small, thick windows.

Cameron watched as the sergeant's eyes rolled back into his head and his consciousness slipped away, the weight from his tactical vest pushing the air from his lungs.

Then and there, Cameron knew his only friend wasn't going to make it, and his heart broke when Dover crawled over and licked Delgado's bloody, sweaty face.

BRADFORD

11:17 a.m.
6000 Block of Old Mill Road
Newport, DE
October 2019

BRADFORD DROVE THE K-9 Suburban up the gravel driveway and parked in front of Peter Donahue's house. There were several Newport PD cruisers parked by the mailbox. Officers had already stretched out yellow tape around the residence, wrapping it around the porch posts of the Cape Cod-style home. Bradford instinctively read the words printed on it. POLICE CRIME SCENE DO NOT ENTER. He hoped that it was in fact a crime scene, and not an investigative dead end.

Detective Stevens waited patiently on the front porch as Bradford led Deja up the steps. There were TV crews set up along the road, and worried neighbors who just a few days ago had brought food to the grieving husband of a slain police officer.

"My guys have done an initial walkthrough," Stevens said. "They took pre-search photos and secured all the rifles, ammunition, and one handgun from the bedroom. They're all on the table in the dining room, and that's everything he said was in the house. Do you want an ET for photographs in there with you?"

"That's up to you. People in the house won't distract the dog. She's got one thing on her mind, and that's to find what she's looking for. She just needs some room to work."

Stevens ran his hand through his hair. "Yeah, but what about the guns we already pulled out of there? Should we have secured them someplace else? They're not listed on the warrant, so we legally can't confiscate them. Please tell me we didn't screw up the dog."

Bradford cocked him a smile. "That's no problem. She's just going to look for the *hidden* guns."

Stevens made a confused face. "You mean to tell me she can tell the difference?"

"She sure can. She's been trained to ignore any distractors, and that includes explosives or firearms that are laying around in plain sight. She'll only go for the less obvious odors."

Stevens gave a low whistle and rubbed Deja between the ears. "You're pretty impressive, girl. We're counting on you."

"It's just another day at the office for her. She doesn't know how important this search is." But even as he said the words, he wasn't quite sure he believed them. Deja felt everything that traveled down leash—and Bradford was feeling the stress, much more than when he took that final certification test with Deja at Front Royal. He prayed Deja wasn't feeling the weight of this search, too.

Stevens straightened and looked him in the eyes. "Right, right. The dog is just a tool. I get it. You've got a heart of stone, Tom, but you can't tell me she's not special. I saw her taking in our words whenever we spoke about Ellen. She would have loved Deja." He reached out and put his hand on Bradford's shoulder. "You two do this for her, alright?"

Bradford felt a sudden tightness in his throat. He couldn't help but think of losing a loved one himself. His mother, and, of course, Jennifer. The only two people he really ever loved. He could never see himself giving his heart to another human being. Maybe that's why . . .

He noticed Stevens waiting for a response.

"We'll get this guy," was all he said, and that was all Stevens needed to hear.

The detective stepped aside and said, "Lead the way."

Bradford and Deja slowly walked inside and immediately got to work. They started in the living room. Bradford kept Deja close as he did a quick walk-around of the room to ensure there was nothing dangerous for his dog, and also to let the canine get a feeling for the environment. When she appeared ready, he gave the command for Deja to start her search. She ran her nose over everything she was physically able to reach in the room, and for what she couldn't, she paused and took in the molecules from the air. Every piece of furniture, outlet covers, heater vents, curtains—everything got a thorough sniff. Bradford even directed Deja's nose into the punched-in hole in the drywall.

They covered every square inch before they moved on to the next room. This would be a highly detailed search. Detective Stevens and a few uniformed officers followed them, shuffling along quietly as if they were on a guided tour of a museum. Deja and Bradford were not distracted by the occasional click and flash from the ET's camera.

They worked one room after another. As they worked, Bradford kept seeing pictures of Ellen still in the house. Either they had it totally wrong and Peter Donahue was innocent, or the guy was a total monster—the kind that can sit across from you, look you in the eye, and explain how he's not a killer. After that, he sells you a life insurance policy.

Upstairs, Deja continued her search, working closets, chairs, bookcases, edges of mattresses, and box springs. She even sniffed the cracks between the floorboards, checking for hidden compartments. She sniffed the bathrooms, the toilets, and inside the vanity, way in the back up where the sink was mounted. When she came to an empty rifle case in one of the bedrooms, she started to sniff and react, but before she could give the alert signal, Bradford quickly praised her but instructed her to "move on." It was one of the training scenarios that Instructor Adams had them run many times.

After they cleared the entire upstairs, they made their way down to the basement, searching through stacks of old boxes and dusty furniture. Bradford could tell that most of it was Ellen's—those things she didn't take with her. There was a sadness to all of it, a feeling of emptiness and loss, as if Peter Donahue couldn't let go of his past.

It made Bradford think of Jennifer—and yes, Copper. All the life he'd left behind in Chicago. But he shook his head to clear it away. He had to keep his head in the game. Any mistakes on his part and he could miss Deja's minute signals, and the search warrant, the whole case, would be shot. They only had one chance to nail Donahue by finding that key piece of evidence, and this was it.

After working through the first area in the basement, Bradford unleashed Deja and lifted her up into a raised crawlspace that ran under the first floor of the backyard addition.

"Seeeek," he said, focusing on Deja and Deja alone. "Find it, girl. Find it."

Deja vanished out of sight in the darkened crawlspace. He listened intently, hearing her panting and her sharp inhalations as she worked. He could hear her nails clicking their way across the rocks and boards placed across the subfloor. It took a moment for Bradford to pull out his Surefire flashlight from his belt. Deja's eyes glowed green, and she appeared machine-like as she searched.

A minute later, she returned, dirtier than before. But no signal.

Bradford hoisted her down. Stevens was hovering behind him, a worried look on his face. Bradford could tell that he was nervous, that he wanted some type of solid alert a half an hour ago. His stress was contagious to everyone in the house. Bradford wanted to remind him and say, "It takes time," but there was no need to say anything. Either they would find the gun that killed Ellen, or it just wasn't there.

They made their way to the back of the basement, where

there was a small room walled off from the rest of the space. It was like a walk-in closet, completely empty except for some homemade wooden shelves that at one time held jars of canned preserves. A single light bulb illuminated the partitioned room, casting a harsh light on the cement foundation walls.

As soon as she entered, Deja's nose immediately kicked into overdrive. Bradford felt a charge race up the leash as Deja drastically increased her search speed. Bradford kept up giving her slack in the lead as she worked her way quickly along every inch of the space.

Stevens filled the doorway behind them, and three officers peered around him, trying to get a view of what was happening. The exposed lightbulb washed out the features of their faces.

"What is it?" Stevens asked. "What'd she find?"

Bradford didn't respond. He kept his focus solely on Deja.

"C'mon, girl," he encouraged her, sending it all back down the leash to his trusted partner. "Find it. Find it, girl."

Deja stood with her front paws on the cement wall, nails attempting to keep her in place but sliding downward. She was still sniffing high into the air. Bradford knew that she was drawing millions of molecules through her nose, parsing each one down into its component parts. She was smelling the soil and the family of mice living in one of the boxes, an old pickle jar that hadn't been there in years. She was smelling oil and fiberglass filaments and the cigarette butt that one of the construction workers had left behind when the house was built. She was smelling stagnant water and old cardboard and twelve different kinds of mold spores.

And she was smelling gunpowder.

She planted her butt on the ground and looked up at Bradford.

"Is that her signal?" Stevens asked, stepping to the room.

"Yes, it is."

But one of the uniform officers quickly spoke up and brought everyone's high expectations back to earth.

"We recovered a rifle in a case from here before you came in. It's the twelve-gauge up in the dining room."

Bradford asked, "Where was it?"

He pointed with the beam of his mag light to the corner of the room. "Down there on the floor, right in front of that shelf."

Bradford turned back to Deja. She was still sniffing like crazy, but her butt was firmly down on the floor. Her nose was still held high.

"She's hitting up high," Bradford said, reading her signals only the way he could. He checked the top shelf, but there was nothing there. He followed the point of Deja's snout up to the unfinished ceiling. He could see the bottoms of the boards from the floor above, nothing visible. "Show me!"

With the command, Deja leaped upward, her front paws stretched up on the third shelf. Her back paws left the ground and landed on the edge of the bottom shelf. She was doing her best to climb up the shelves like a ladder, but gravity took over and she landed back on the damp cement floor.

"Whatever it is, it's gotta be up between the floor joists. Take a look up there behind that insulation."

Stevens was already pulling latex gloves from his pocket. He turned over a bucket and used it as a step stool to reach the ceiling. The flash from the ET's camera filled the room. He began pulling aside insulation as the uniformed officer shone his flashlight on the spot. Thick wads of pink insulation sifted to the ground as Stevens worked.

And a moment later, the beam of the flashlight glistened off the barrels of two pistols jammed deep between the floor joists.

"I'll be goddamned," Stevens said. He turned to one of the uniformed officers. "Get Chief Bukowski down here right away."

Bradford looked down at Deja. She was looking up at him, her eyes full of pride and love. She had just brought justice into the world, but all she wanted from him was validation and affection. It didn't even look like she cared about the food reward on this very special find. She hadn't done it just for the rewards or for the praise. She had done it for him—and for Ellen.

In that moment, Bradford's heart cracked open, and he let out an unexpected laugh. There was a sudden space inside his chest, one that hadn't been there before—and Deja took her place inside him, right beside Copper and Jennifer.

She wasn't just another tool for the job. She was a remarkable, wonderful dog. *His* dog.

He bent down to praise her, but before he fed her like he always did whenever she made a positive ID, this time he hugged her instead. He wrapped his arms around her neck and, ignoring the many police officers who were swarming all around him, whispered into her warm fur.

"I love you, too."

SHERRY

6:42 p.m.
San Antonio, TX
October 2019

SHERRY UNLOCKED THE door and stepped inside. She dropped the keys in the same bowl that she always did, on the long table that ran under the mirror in the entryway. The jingling sound they made was intimately familiar. No matter where she set down her keys, they never made the same sound as they did when she set them down in that very bowl.

Fall had finally arrived, and the night was starting to get chilly. The cold air followed her inside the house as she opened the door wide.

Dolly slowly made her way through the door and stepped into the hallway. She stood gingerly, her head in a cone, her shaved abdomen wrapped tightly with bandages around the one-hundred-and-sixty-four stitches, but her eyes were alert and curious as she took in all the new smells of the house. It smelled just like Sherry, but also other smells that Dolly immediately started to memorize.

"Come on," Sherry said, setting down her suitcase but keeping her large tote slung around her shoulder. "I'm starving.

Sherry walked down the hall to the kitchen, and Dolly's nails clicked on the floor as she followed. The fridge was mostly empty. Not a surprise. Darryl said he hadn't been home in a week, and it had been a month since she had set foot in the house. She promptly placed an order for pizza delivery on her phone and then cracked a beer. At least Shiner Bock didn't go bad.

After she had taken a few sips, she pulled a ziplock of some kibble and a sealed smelling tin of ammonium nitrate out of her tote. She had been placed on paid administrative leave for eight weeks—to tend to Dolly but also as a pseudo-punishment for disobeying a direct order and endangering both of their lives—but even while on the disabled list, Dolly couldn't miss a day of training, not if she ever wanted to get back out in the field again. So even in her ungainly cone, Dolly had to find explosives in order to eat.

Sherry smiled softly as she hid the tin in the living room under the coffee table, then told Dolly to "seek." Dolly waddled slowly right to it, and Sherry's heart melted even more. The proverbial two-foot putt. Dolly looked so vulnerable like this, and Sherry was glad that she could have a safe home instead of a clinic or kennel to recuperate in.

To her utmost surprise, Sherry Fry was glad to be home.

After Dolly ate, the pizza arrived, and Sherry ate a few slices and worked through a second beer. Inevitably, she pulled out her phone.

There were no texts from Darryl. They had spoken earlier that evening, just before she arrived in San Antonio. He was finishing up his assignment in Salt Lake City, and then he would be coming home. Indefinitely. He said he would try to get reassigned to the San Antonio office, but if he couldn't, he even floated the idea of leaving the Federal Protective Service and finding another agency. Or even leaving law enforcement altogether.

Sherry was thrilled and terrified to think about what it meant. All she knew was that they could only take it one day at a time. Taking care of Dolly was the most important thing right now. Everything else would follow.

She turned on her phone and saw a text from Jason.

How's our baby girl? Tell Dolly that Disney is sending her lots of kisses.

Sherry smiled. Jason had one of the kindest hearts of any man she'd ever met. In a different life, maybe it could have worked. But she was glad she never attempted to find out. Right now, she had a life to live—and who knew what life would bring?

All Sherry knew was that she wanted to give her and Darryl one more shot. They had been together for eight years, and they needed to spend some real, honest time together before they made any big decisions.

She didn't know how she'd break the news to Jason, but

she decided that tonight was not the night. Tonight, she just wanted to eat her pizza and enjoy her first night home with her lovely, brave, incredible dog.

Sherry Fry smiled as she clicked off her phone, dropped to her knee, and let Dolly smother her with kisses, cone and all.

SHAWANDA

12:03 p.m.
Bronx Lebanon Hospital
New York, NY
October 2019

SHAWANDA JACKSON OPENED her eyes. Her mouth was dry, and there was something beeping in her ears. The room around her was sterile and white. She looked around in a daze, but the pain in her head made her groan. She reached up. Her forehead was wrapped in gauze. It felt like someone had cracked her with a tire iron.

It took a moment for her to remember that was exactly what had happened.

She leaned back on the thin pillows and groaned again.

"Tariq," she murmured. "That motherfucker."

Then she suddenly realized that she wasn't alone in the room. There was a man standing in the doorway, looking at her. Her vision was blurred and she couldn't tell who it was. Was it Tariq?

She tried to cry out, but her dry mouth and her raging headache made it only come out as a squeak.

The man in the doorway put his hands out.

"Whoa, take it easy. It's alright. You're in the hospital. You're safe here."

It took a moment for the startle reflex in Shawanda to settle down, and when it did, she realized that she recognized the man from before. He was the Latino cop who had been talking to her on the back porch. Right before Tariq struck.

And sure enough, there was a sweet-eyed yellow Labrador retriever standing by his side.

"Is that . . .?" Shawanda asked, rubbing her eyes.

"This is Disney," the cop said. Then he smiled. "Do you want to say hi?"

Shawanda fought back a sudden wave of tears. After everything that had happened, after all the bullshit and everything she'd lost, she couldn't believe that one of her dogs had come back into her life.

"Of course I do," she said, hauling herself upright in bed, ignoring the worst headache she had ever had in her life. "Come here, girl. Come."

Disney immediately sprang into action, and the cop released her leash so that she could bound across the hospital room. She put her two front paws up on the edge of the bed and laid her head on Shawanda's knee, looking at her lovingly.

"That's my baby," Shawanda said, tears running down her cheeks as she rubbed Disney's ears. "Look at you. You got so big. You're all grown up now. Do you remember me? Do you, baby?"

Disney leaned forward and showered Shawanda with kisses.

"So you *do* remember me! I was there when you were

born. I held you in my in hand when you were just this big."

The cop took a step into the room. He stood behind the rolling tray that held Shawanda's uneaten dinner and melted ice chips.

"Once we got your ID from your sisters, I looked you up in our system. It says that you just got paroled from Bedford Hills, where you spent the last five years of your life. I also found out you had something to do with the Puppies Behind Bars program."

He smiled again. Shawanda wasn't used to cops smiling, but on this particular man, it seemed genuine. It was as if Shawanda could see his heart—and how much he loved Disney.

"And from the looks of it," he went on, "I'm guessing Disney was one of yours?"

"Yeah," Shawanda said, sniffling and running her hand across her nose. "She was one of mine. I raised her. One of the best."

She gave Disney a few more rubs, then the realization hit her.

This cop wasn't here just to make nice or give her the whole "small world, what are the odds" speech. She was an accessory to assault on a police officer. She was in violation of her parole by even being in the same house as Tariq.

This man was here to send her back to prison.

Shawanda immediately went on the defensive. "Look, I didn't do nothing. I didn't do anything wrong. And neither did my family. Where are my sisters? Where's my grandma?"

The cop must have read the expression on her face, because he put his hands out again. "Hey, look, don't worry. Everything's fine. Your family is safe. They're all still at home. We arrested Mr. Simpson, but no other charges are going to be brought. You don't have to worry about any of that."

At first, she couldn't believe her ears. Cops were always looking to bust whoever they could find. She'd never been given a break in her life—so why now?

She eyed him suspiciously. "You mean, you ain't gonna arrest me?"

He laughed. "Arrest you? God no. If it were up to me, you'd get a medal. Simpson tried to kill me and almost killed you. He opened up your skull pretty good, and that was just with a glancing blow." He puffed out his cheeks. "You saved my life, Ms. Jackson. I'm here to thank you."

Shawanda didn't know what to say. She looked down and stroked the velvet on Disney's ears. The dog beamed at her.

A long silence filled the room, broken only by the beeps from the monitor and the rhythmic thumps of Disney's tail knocking against the bedrail.

"So, I gotta ask," the cop finally said. "Why'd you do it? Why'd you stop him when you could've just let him take me out?"

Shawanda looked the cop up and down. He seemed uncomfortable, as if he was the kind of guy who worked hard to get what he wanted, but deep down, didn't expect things to go his way in life. It made Shawanda sad to think about—because that had been her life, too. He'd ended up a cop and she'd ended up a convict, but she guessed that was just how things worked sometimes. One choice here, another choice there. The small things that seem so trivial in the moment, but that ultimately put you on the path you can never see coming. Maybe if things had been different, she would have grown up to be a cop. Or a lawyer. Or a business owner. Who knew what kind of potential Shawanda Jackson had locked up inside of her.

But one thing she knew for certain was that if she let Tariq kill a cop in cold blood right before her eyes, the lock on that potential would be sealed shut forever.

She hadn't wanted this life, she hadn't wanted to make the choices she'd made. She had made so many mistakes, and she was full of regrets—but when she saw that tire iron rise up in the air, there was only one choice she could make.

The cop was waiting for her to answer, but she just kept rubbing Disney's ears.

"You know," she said quietly, "someone said something to me once. And it's stuck with me all this time."

Disney's tail slowed as she nuzzled her head deeper.

"They said, 'We need these dogs just as much as they need us.' You think that's true?"

The cop hooked his thumbs in his pockets and leaned back. Whatever sadness he seemed to feel was gone.

"You know," he said, "I think you might just be right."

For the first time in what felt like years, Shawanda smiled.

So many things had been taken from her, but in that moment, Shawanda Jackson knew some things lasted forever. She had a family that needed her. She had all the dogs that she'd brought into this world. She had given love, and was loved in return.

Maybe it wasn't too late for her after all.

CAMERON

One year later . . .

CAMERON STOOD ON the sidewalk, looking up at the cute house on a quiet street in a nice part of Columbus, Ohio. It had rosebushes in front, and a sweet little garden along the side of the house, turned down for the winter. There were toys stacked neatly along the path that led to the backyard, and since it was November, there were big orange cardboard leaves and paper turkeys shaped liked hands tacked to the front door. It looked like the sort of house you'd see on a Thanksgiving card, and Cameron was struck by the love that the family had put into the place.

Ken Delgado had never talked much about his family, but clearly they had been a big part of his life. Cameron wondered how his wife and kids even had the heart to decorate after everything that had happened—after they had lost so much.

Cameron went to reach for his smokes, but as soon as he took hold of the pack, it felt strange in his hand. Like it would somehow disrespect the family that he had come all this way to visit.

Without a second thought, he tossed them back inside the car.

Dover was waiting patiently in the back, and he hopped out when Cameron popped the rear hatch. He seemed to sense the gravity of the moment, and he looked at Cameron with heavy eyes.

"I know, pal. I don't want to go up there either, but we gotta do this. We owe it to Ken."

Cameron didn't bother to leash him as they walked up the path to the front porch. Each step felt heavier than the last, and by the time he reached the front steps, Cameron could hardly move. This was so much harder than he ever could have imagined.

The little paper turkeys were even cuter up close, and Cameron took a moment to draw a trembling breath.

Finally he mustered the courage to ring the doorbell, and it was answered by a pretty ten-year-old girl.

"Hi, I'm Cameron. You must be Lacey."

The girl rolled her eyes.

"I'm Daphne," she said as she stormed back into the house, clearly upset at the misidentification.

Cameron awkwardly cleared his throat, but then a man on crutches appeared in the doorway.

"Twins, am I right?" he said with a smirk.

"Hey, Sarge," Cameron said, grateful to see his old buddy up and walking around. Dover's tail eagerly beat the front porch. "You're looking good."

"And you're full of shit," Ken Delgado replied. "Come on in, no use freezing your ass off."

With that, Cameron was welcomed into the Delgados'

home. Alma Delgado greeted him with a big hug as the two girls looked on curiously, fascinated by Dover.

"Welcome, welcome," she said, touching Cameron's cheeks. "Oh, you're even more handsome than Kenny told me."

Cameron made a few uncomfortable noises, but then Alma got serious and looked him in the eye.

"Thank you so much for what you did for my Kenny. He wouldn't be here if it weren't for you." Then she bent down and rubbed Dover's ears. "And you too, my brave little one."

"Alright, let 'em be, Alma. The man hasn't even taken off his coat for Christ's sake."

Alma laughed and disappeared into the kitchen, promising coffee and food. Meanwhile, Delgado led Cameron into the living room, where there was a fire in the fireplace and a football game on TV.

Delgado sat heavily in his chair, letting out a sigh as he swung around his crutches. His right arm worked fine, but his left was still heavily scarred and looked like it gave him all sorts of trouble. He was wearing shorts, revealing a prosthetic limb from where his leg had been amputated below the knee. It had been over a year since that mortar round had dropped on him in Kuz Kunar, but Cameron could see how much pain he was still in.

They sat there in silence for a while, both unsure what to say next.

Delgado spoke first. "So you finish up your tour? You

back here stateside?"

Cameron nodded. "Yeah, I'm all done with my post at Davidson. I've been transferred to a new position in the Agency. I'm actually working down at Langley now, working on a counterintelligence team."

Delgado laughed. "What, you, an analyst? I'd pay good money to see Cam McNeil sitting behind a computer all day."

Cameron gave a small laugh. "Yeah, well, things change."

He wanted to tell Ken how everything had changed for him that day at the farmhouse, how all the fight had gone out of him as the mortars dropped all around them. He had spent so many years running from Yemen, but out there in that cornfield, he had realized that all he was doing was running toward an early grave. He'd let the ghosts of the people he'd failed dictate his life, and in the process, he had nearly become a ghost himself.

But somehow, when Dover came to his side and helped pull his best friend across the bloody dirt, everything changed.

In the deepest part of his heart, Cameron had always wished that he'd died back in Yemen—but as they dragged Delgado back to the JERRV as the bullets hit the dirt all around them, for the first time in years, Cameron had *wanted* to live. He wanted Delgado to live. And he wanted Dover to live, too.

After they got back to FOB Davidson after the firefight, he had watched Delgado get loaded onto the chopper to get flown to Bagram Airforce Base outside of Kabul, where he would then be medevaced to an Army hospital in Germany. He wasn't sure if he'd ever see his friend again, but as soon as the helicopter disappeared over the mountains, he went straight to Juszczyk and requested a transfer. It had taken eight months to finally go through, but then he was home.

And it had taken four months to finally get the paperwork sorted and make the call to Delgado.

"So to what do we owe this visit?" Delgado asked as Alma brought coffee and arepas into the living room. Lacey and Daphne joined her, and the girls continued their fascination with Dover.

"It alright?" Delgado asked as the girls inched closer to the dog.

Cameron cracked a smile.

"He's all theirs."

The girls giggled as they set upon Dover, petting him and stroking his ears. He rolled on his back and soaked it in.

"From your call," Delgado went on, "you made it sound like something was up. Don't get me wrong, you could've dropped by for dinner any day of the week, but what brought you all the way out to Ohio?"

Cameron cleared his throat. He'd rehearsed this moment for months, but now that it was here, his words failed him.

"Well, uh, like I said, I've been transferred to a new role in the Agency, so I'm no longer on the K9 unit. When this happens, they usually reassign the dogs to a new handler, but in this case, I went to the director and put in a special request."

Delgado put down his coffee slowly, and Alma grabbed his hand. The two girls perked up.

Cameron sat up in his chair. "On behalf of the United States Government, in appreciation for your service to our country and the sacrifices you made, and the pain you have endured, I would like to present to you Explosives Detection Canine Dover, who now has a new position: Support Canine Dover. May he always be there to support you and your family."

The girls' eyes widened and their mouths hung open. "Daddy, is he giving us Dover?"

Delgado was speechless. Tears were building Alma's eyes.

"Cam, man, I—" Delgado wiped a tear of his own. "I don't know what to say."

Cameron put out a hand to his old friend. "Look, you're the only other person who loves this dog as much as me. After what you and Dover went through out there, I can't imagine a better home for him. I don't want him going to another handler in the Agency—and I sure as hell don't want him going back into a warzone again." Cameron drew a breath. His voice was starting to crack. "I know you'll take care of him."

Delgado watched as the two girls hugged Dover and showered him with kisses. The house felt even more like a home.

"You sure about this?"

"I wouldn't have it any other way." Cameron's eyes got misty as he looked at his faithful partner, rolling around on the floor with Lacey and Daphne. "And it looks like Dover is happy about it, too."

BRADFORD

Meanwhile . . .

THOMAS BRADFORD WALKED along the steps of the Philadelphia Museum of Art, watching as the crowd gathered around the many booths set up near the starting line. The marathon wasn't set to start for another forty minutes, but thousands of runners and spectators had already gathered in the bright and cold November morning. There was a thrill of excitement in the air.

Explosive Detection Canine Deja walked faithfully by his side, her tail wagging as she worked through the crowd, sniffing the ground and the occasional backpack, but mostly just enjoying the crowd.

Bradford was content. He had just finished his second cup of coffee, and he found himself relishing the buzz before the big race. He had taken up running earlier that year, part of his plan to get healthy and take better care of himself. He was just a few months shy of fifty, but he had no plans to slow down. Life had thrown some unexpected twists his way, but for the first time in a long time, Bradford felt like he was himself again.

And Deja had played a big part in that.

He reached down and scratched her ears as they worked through the crowd, making their way toward the runners' corrals that stretched along Benjamin Franklin Parkway.

Along the way he spotted a Pennsylvania State Police Bomb Detection Canine team. He recognized the trooper, Randall Dockens, and his dog Max, a big ferocious-looking Belgian Malinois.

He and Dockens chatted for a bit and walked the crowd, and as always, people wanted to come up and pet Deja and take selfies. Bradford was patient and smiled for the pictures, but politely told everyone that Deja was working right now and shouldn't be petted. Max, with his sharp teeth and angular face, didn't get as much attention as the floppy-eared Lab.

After a bit, Bradford and Dockens parted ways, and Bradford started thinking about his vacation coming up in a few days. He and Deja were going to take a trip back to Wisconsin, where he would show her the cabin that he loved so much. If the weather cooperated, they might even get some hunting in. He knew that Deja wouldn't know the difference between a grouse and a golf ball; he just wanted to walk the woods with his dog. He hadn't gone out since Copper had died, but he knew it was time.

They continued to make their way down Benjamin Franklin Parkway, and Bradford was feeling grateful that he had an easy assignment before the Thanksgiving holiday.

He paused to survey the elite runners in the first corral

when he felt something tug on the leash. He looked down to find Deja staring intently at a nearby trashcan. Her butt was firmly planted on the ground.

THE END

AUTHORS' NOTE

Readers knowledgeable in police and military tactics will note several instances in this novel where alternate courses of action were used that may be in conflict with current procedures. These portrayals were used by the authors to increase drama and add to the story.

The Puppies Behind Bars program is a successful organization that helps incarcerated individuals, the dogs they raise, and the agencies that ultimately receive them. PBB acquires puppies from registered breeders after they are weaned from their mother, so no puppies are actually born behind bars. Each puppy is thoroughly checked for health then transferred to the various correctional institutions. You can learn more at www.puppiesbehindbars.com.

The National Canine Division and canine handlers use actual high explosives when conducting training exercises. The use of these training aids is governed by strict rules and regulations regarding their secured storage and control at all times.

The love and care the pups received from the inmates in this story is real, as evidenced from a letter authored by an inmate puppy raiser and placed in Deja's file when transferred to the NCD. This letter will follow this note.

Post-traumatic stress disorder is a very real and very serious disease that afflicts thousands of servicemen and servicewomen. The liberties we took in this book were entirely for dramatic purposes, and at no time did we wish to diminish or distract from the real challenges of living with PTSD. For more information or to support PTSD research, please visit www.ptsd.va.gov.

The authors would like to acknowledge and express their sincere thanks to the many current and former members of the Department of Homeland Security, Bureau of ATF, USMS-Fugitive Task Force, and U.S. Army EOD-Task Force Troy for their input, suggestions, and stories that made this book possible. You are the real American heroes.

For more info, please visit
www.partspermillionbook.com

Wednesday, Dec. 17, 2008

Dear A.T.F. Dog Handler,

The name of this puppy is Deja, she will be 11-Months old Saturday, Dec. 20, 2008. Deja, was born January 20, 2008. She has very nice pleasant energy, good confidence, well mannered, and walks very well on lead. Sometimes she might get a little distracted by cats and squirrels (meaning she will watch them as she is walking by them). Deja has a mellow temperament. She is good with people of all age groups, including small children. Deja is a soft puppy in terms of physical corrections from training collars, harsh tones of voices, and she do not like playing with dogs that's overly assertive, or aggressive. Here is a list of all the commands Deja know :

1. Let's-go, 2. Sit, 3. Down, 4. Stay, 5. Free, 6. Settle,
7. Come, 8. Easy, 9. Here, 10. Leave-it, 11. Hup, 12. Stand,
13. Quiet, 14. Get-busy 15. Kennel...

Deja will be greatly missed, she is a very good girl, Please take care of her. Sincerely, Deja's Raiser

Made in the USA
Monee, IL
11 September 2021